THE
BOMBER
IN THE
BASEMENT

To Nerissa,
I hope you enjoy the book!

[signature]

April 5/25

THE BOMBER IN THE BASEMENT

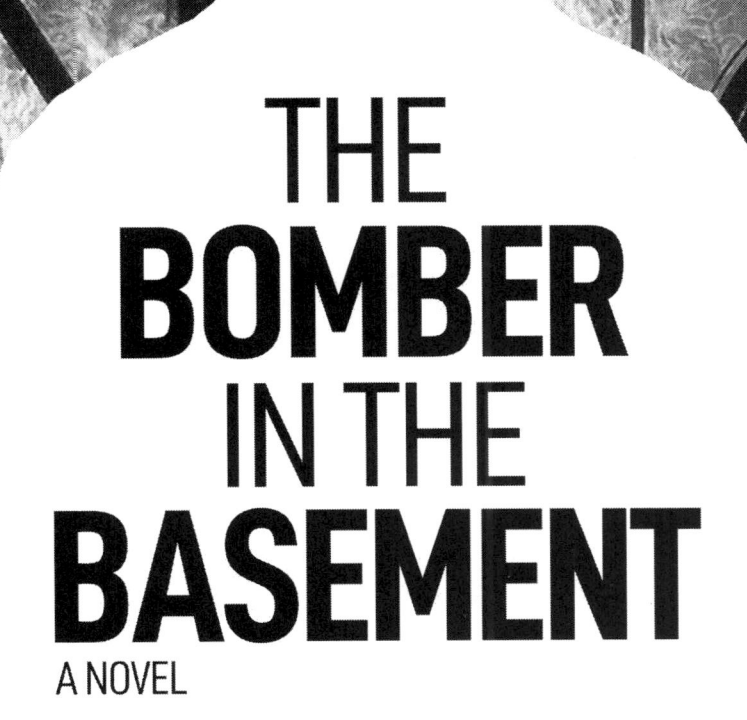

A NOVEL

COLLEEN ISHERWOOD

Copyright © 2025
by Colleen Isherwood
All rights reserved.

No part of this publication may be reproduced, distributed, or transmitted in any form or by any means, including photocopying, recording, or other electronic or mechanical methods, without the prior written permission of the copyright owner and publisher of this book, except in the case of brief quotations embodied in critical reviews and certain other non-commercial uses permitted by copyright law.

ISBN: 978-1-0691131-2-2 (Hardcover)
ISBN: 978-1-0691131-0-8 (Paperback)
ISBN: 978-1-0691131-1-5 (eBook)

This book is a work of fiction. Names, characters, businesses, institutions, agencies, places, events, and incidents are the products of the author's imagination. Any resemblance to actual persons, living or dead, or actual events is purely coincidental.

First edition February 2025

Publisher: Cami Communications
Cover & Interior Design: Adrian M. Gibson
Formatting: Adrian M. Gibson

This book is dedicated to my late father, Thomas McCavour, a fellow writer and my muse.

THE BOMBER IN THE BASEMENT

Preface	*The Explosion (June 1970)*
Chapter 1	*The New Lodger (Katie, November 1976)*
Chapter 2	*Growing Up (Barry, December 1976 & 1956-64)*
Chapter 3	*Dialogue & Friendship (Katie, December 1976)*
Chapter 4	*Vietnam (Barry, January 1977 & July 1966)*
Chapter 5	*Barry's New Job (Katie, December 1976)*
Chapter 6	*Mary-Anne (Barry 1964-66)*
Chapter 7	*Corporate Wife (Katie, December 1976)*
Chapter 8	*Dylan's Radicalization (Barry, 1966-1967)*
Chapter 9	*The Pub (Katie, January 1977)*
Chapter 10	*Early Explosions (Barry, 1967-69)*
Chapter 11	*A Cup of Coffee with Katie (Barry, January 1977)*
Chapter 12	*Preparing for the Big One (Barry, 1969-70)*
Chapter 13	*The Superintendent & the Haircut (Katie, February 1977)*
Chapter 14	*Draft Card (Barry, 1969)*
Chapter 15	*The Wind Buggy (Katie, March 1977)*
Chapter 16	*The Big One (Barry, June 1970)*
Chapter 17	*On the Run (Barry, June 1970)*
Chapter 18	*John is Gone (Katie, April 1977)*
Chapter 19	*The Fugitive (Barry, 1970 & April 1977)*

Chapter 20	*Power Trip (Katie, April 1977)*
Chapter 21	*Kensington Market & Mimico Creek (Barry, May 1977 & 1970)*
Chapter 22	*Panhandling & Early Days in Toronto (Barry, 1970-71)*
Chapter 23	*Sir John's Dinner (Katie, May 1977)*
Chapter 24	*Macramé, Cooking & a Green Thumb (Barry, May 1977)*
Chapter 25	*Out West (Barry, 1973-1975)*
Chapter 26	*He's a Rebel (Katie, June 1977)*
Chapter 27	*Communal Love & Quincy (Barry, June 1975-76)*
Chapter 28	*Katie & Her Dad (Katie, June 1977)*
Chapter 29	*Graduation Dinner & Bad News (Barry, June 1977)*
Chapter 30	*On the Run Again (Barry, June 1977)*
Chapter 31	*America's Most Wanted (Katie, June-August 1977)*
Chapter 32	*For Tom (Barry, September 1977)*
Epilogue	*(Katie, October 1982)*

PREFACE: THE EXPLOSION
(June 1970)

- - - - -

THE BUILDING WAS darker than the night, just a few lights left on for security purposes. One of them had already made the call warning of what would happen. The three of them huddled in the cooling California June evening, under an evergreen bush whose dried out needles scratched their skin. The soil beneath their feet was covered in needles that had dropped following another unusually dry spring. The only sounds were those of the highway in the distance.

Quiet, but not for long. The bombers' hearts were pounding; adrenaline was kicking in. A whole year of planning and a couple of false starts were tied up in this operation. It was almost time.

That building was evil, an instrument of war. The people who worked there were researching more efficient ways to kill innocents and to permanently scar the lives of those charged with defending the western world from communism.

They had checked the building carefully, timing the blast for four in the morning to make sure no one was inside. No need to perpetuate the killing—just a need to tell the world that the war was wrong!

They had planted the bomb—a crude but very large affair using a detonator, along with fuel oil and ammonium nitrate, not as easy to make as it sounds. But not beyond their capabilities, especially those of Allan, who had two degrees in chemistry.

Dylan's hand shook as they backed away and he pressed the button on the detonator. Then they all ducked, to shield themselves from the blast.

The explosion was more than they could have hoped for, filling the sky with light lapped by furious flames.

They called the police, as planned, and left to celebrate in an all-night diner two hours drive away from the blast.

It was there they found out that things had gone horribly wrong.

1: THE NEW LODGER
(Katie, November 1976)

- - - - -

MY PARENTS HELPED John and me buy the house in Toronto's Little India, with the idea that real estate is the best investment possible and now that John had a job with a major law firm, Kilbourne, Goodman and Blake, and I was working full time as an assistant editor at a little publishing company, we should get into the market.

They weren't terribly thrilled with the house we chose. It is a fixer upper for sure and the neighbourhood isn't the best. That's the negative side. On the positive side, Dad is Superintendent of Police for the area. There is also a basement apartment, so we can earn income that will help pay off the mortgage. And it's got character. My parents can't understand why I didn't want one of those new pink town homes in the subdivision behind the library, less than a mile from their place in Markland Woods, an upscale neighbourhood at the far west end of Toronto. Are you kidding! I would have to wait at an open-air bus stop out in the boonies, take a plodding bus that only comes once every half hour, through rain, sleet and hail to get to the subway, and then two subways to get to my job downtown. This way, I can just walk 20 minutes to the subway or take the Carlton streetcar, which comes quite frequently.

This house is pretty. Built in 1930, it looks a bit like those Currier and Ives Christmas cards showing old-fashioned houses with steeply peaked roofs, bay windows and big front porches. Our house has a brick front with aluminum siding on the sides and back. There's a back sunroom overlooking a long, narrow lot with a huge chestnut tree. The lot is something like 25 feet by 125, and it drops off at the back, so I don't know our back neighbours at all.

Best of all, from the back bedroom upstairs, which we use as our home office, you can see the CN Tower all lit up at night. I'm not sure why I'm so fond of that edifice, which just went up recently—maybe it's like an anchor, showing that I'm truly part of the city of Toronto.

The house next door is even prettier—the same shape as ours, but slightly larger than ours and finished in stone. That house was for sale at the same time ours was, but it had a big old octopus furnace in the basement that would cost a fortune to replace. So we opted for the aluminum siding and the house with the more modern furnace.

Good thing we had a small, compact furnace instead of one that took up the entire basement. The whole idea was that John, Quincy and I would live upstairs and we would have a tenant downstairs. Quincy is my dog, a big, lovable 100-pound mutt who is mostly German Shepherd, but also some other breed that has floppy ears. Those ears make his face look very friendly. One other advantage of my new house is that it is close to the Ashbridges Bay sewage treatment plant and beyond that, The Beach. The sewage treatment place is a great place for dogs to run (I'm not kidding). And The Beach is great too, except Quincy has to be on his leash when he is there.

The tenant. If it weren't for Quincy, we would never have entertained the idea. John works slave labour hours at the law firm and I am often on my own. But Quincy provides protection. As friendly as he is, he would have no trouble scaring off someone who was being mean to me.

The tenant selection process was daunting. I had in mind the perfect lodger, a young, Chinese woman attending University of

Toronto, with impeccable references. A very quiet person, who likes to keep to herself and would basically pay the rent and stay out of my hair. But before I found that person, I would have to talk to countless unsuitable candidates, I reasoned. That's why I was happy to have my dog as a bodyguard.

It isn't a bad basement apartment. You have to go in through the front door, down the hall and into the kitchen to reach the basement stairs, so it isn't ideal from a privacy point of view. We have fixed it up so that it has a panelled rec room that serves as combination bedroom, kitchen and living space. The bathroom is down the hall beyond the washing machine and dryer. The furnace is blocked off. There is even a queen size bed, since my queen size from home couldn't fit up the narrow stairs to our bedroom here, but could fit in the basement. It was kind of dark—could use a few more table lamps. And the ceiling is six foot four—no one taller than that need apply. The ad read, "Basement apartment for rent—$100 per month."

So far, I had very few calls.

When the phone rang, and a guy named Barry Burns said he would like to see the place, I was more receptive than I had been. To date, no quiet, female Chinese students had applied.

He looked okay, clean shaven with a young face, wispy hippie hair and a shy manner, meeting my eyes only now and then, as if he were uncomfortable with small talk. Quiet. Yes! And tall. That was problem number one. Would he fit in the basement?

I always talk too much when I'm nervous. "How tall are you? I mean, it's an older home and the basement isn't that high, but I think you'll fit." (That was my other point about the quiet, Chinese lodger. A short, quiet, Chinese girl would definitely fit.)

"But let's go downstairs and have a look."

Note to self: Shut up, Katie. Don't prattle on about stupid, inane things.

He followed me down the wooden steps (that needed painting) into the basement. Whew – it was close, but he fit.

Barry spent a few minutes looking around at the cheap panelled walls and ancient linoleum floors that I had dressed up with a rag rug. He sat on the bed, testing its firmness. He fingered the Formica table and chair set that I knew so well from my childhood.

"We used to have a set like this when I was a kid," he said.

"Early Mom and Dad," I said, describing the dining set's vintage. "I grew up with this one."

Thank goodness he didn't hit his head when we showed him the downstairs bathroom, which has a slightly raised floor.

"Tight fit, but it works," he said, bridging the three-inch space between his head and the ceiling with his hand. "You have no idea how hard it is to find a basement where I can stand up in Old Toronto."

And then he smiled. There was a gap between his top front teeth and the bottom ones overlapped. It was a winning, friendly smile. Quincy nuzzled him, obviously deciding he was one of the good guys. Not Chinese, not a woman. But quiet. One out of three ain't bad, I thought ruefully, especially when there was a shortage of people wanting my basement digs. Plus, Quincy is usually a good judge of character.

"So how long have you been in Toronto," I asked him upstairs, settled comfortably on the corduroy couch and chair John and I had bought from an office in my company's building. You can't rent to just anybody. You have to ask them a few questions.

"Off and on for about seven years," he said. He had a slow, languid way of talking that made me think of some of my old high school classmates when they were mellow on marijuana. But it was an engaging style of speech that put me right at ease.

Quincy had climbed up on the couch beside Barry and rested his big head on his knees. Quincy was not supposed to be on the couch.

"Do you like it here—Toronto I mean?" I asked.

"Sure, it's pretty good."

"Where are you living now?"

"With some friends—it's kind of like a commune. But my life is changing. I've got a full-time job and it's time to get a place of my own."

He sat there, nodding his head up and down as I processed this information.

"Where are you working?"

That smile again. "It's an okay gig. I'm working in a printing plant. Don't laugh, but I'm training to be a stripper," he said, grinning broadly as he gauged my reaction. "Um, it's not what you think—it's part of the print production process."

A sense of humour as well as a nice smile, quiet demeanour, and the Quincy seal of approval.

I adopted my best stern landlady voice and said, "Well, I was really hoping to have a quiet, female, Chinese student, but my phone isn't exactly ringing off the hook. You seem quiet, and you have a job, so I think things will work out. My husband and I live upstairs—he's a lawyer.

"The rent is $100 per month, due the first day of the month—no later. I have to come downstairs to do my laundry, but I'll try not to disturb you. Otherwise, your place is self-contained including the little fridge and hot-plate unit."

"Sounds good."

"You can move in at the beginning of next month, if that works for you."

"Sure."

He wasn't paying attention to me. He was fingering the

frayed electrical cord that led to my non-functioning living room table lamp.

"I can fix that," he said.

A sense of humour, a nice smile, quiet, Quincy-approved and a handyman. I think my new lodger and I will get along just fine.

"How old are you," I asked him as I showed him to my front door, which bore the wear and tear indicative of its fifty-year lifespan.

"Twenty-five," he said.

Two years older than me. I would have guessed younger.

2: GROWING UP
(Barry, December 1976 & 1956-64)

- - - - -

SO, I'VE FOUND a place. More space than I have had in a long time, though not much furniture. And a landlady who seems a bit ditzy but nice, and thankfully not my type. (That has caused problems in the past.)

She's tall and skinny and geeky looking and wears glasses. She has light brown hair pulled straight back from her rather high forehead with an elastic bauble of some kind and it hangs limp almost to her waist. She talks a lot. It's hard to understand her since she talks so fast, going on and on about how I'm not a Chinese student. What's that all about? And worried that I'd hit my head on the ceiling. That part was a valid concern. I'm 6 foot one—taller than most Old Toronto basements in houses I've looked at. I guess back in the '20s or '30s, when this place was built, people were a lot shorter.

She seems okay though. And since we will be living on separate floors, she shouldn't be chatting my ear off. I'm wondering what the husband is like. Lawyer, I hear.

- - -

MAN, BUT THAT Formica table at the rental place brought back memories of a time long ago when I was known as Scott Bronson! We had one just like it at our place in suburban Los Angeles, in the house where I grew up. It was gray, with little swirls on it. I liked to trace the patterns as I tuned in and out of family conversations. I remember family meals with Allan, Tom and me, plus Mom (Barbara) and Dad (Ron). Not quite the "Leave It To Beaver" family as seen on TV, but not unlike it either. We even had the Eddie Haskell character—Tom and Allan's friend, Dylan, who was handsome and super polite to my parents, but the more they got to know him, the less they encouraged the friendship.

Mom was a typical 1950s housewife, Dad was a mechanic and we lived on a little court in a modest house in Hermosa Beach, California. It was a rough and tumble house—only to be expected with three boys. I'm the youngest and tended to get the worst of those fights. On the other hand, the main rivalry was between Allan and Tom, and I could be protected if I sided with one against the other. It seems like I was sort of a pawn—each of them wanted me to be on their team. I got very good at reading those two and deciding how to please them.

I remember a time when all I wanted in life was to hang out with the three musketeers, Tom, Dylan and Allan. As a five-year old, I idolized them. Tom was 10 years old and Dylan and Allan were eight—age made such a difference at a time when I would proudly announce that I was five and three-quarters years old. They did such cool things—playing Cops and Robbers or Cowboys and Indians—shooting pretend guns and falling down dead. They paid no attention to the little kid making vroom-vroom noises as he pushed toy trucks around in a pile of dirt during that hot, dry summer.

Until one late summer day, when they found out how useful I could be.

I remember the day well, from the distant hum of the Interstate in the background to the rustle of leaves in the palm trees above me. Mid-August—the time of year when the games of summer became routine, when boredom started to seep in.

My Mom was watching Dylan, but not very closely. It was the '50s. We had a lot more freedom than kids do now. Dylan's Mom was playing bridge with her ritzy friends. Not many women worked in those days. And Dylan's Dad, a lawyer, was never around; he was always working. I think I may have met him once or twice, that's all.

On that particular day, Dylan's house was all locked up and the guys wanted to play with his father's bow and arrow set, which was in the rec room.

There was one possible way to get into the house—via the doggie door. It was a pass-through door built to let a long-dead dog go through into the house.

And it was small. Way too small for Dylan or Allan or Tom to fit through. But, given a shove, a skinny five and three-quarter-year old could fit. Dylan's eyes alighted on me, playing with my dinky toys in the sand.

"Can you do it?" he asked.

Of course, I could! I was delighted to be part of it. The arrows were in a wooden case, which was much too heavy for me to carry. I carefully opened the case and took the arrows out one by one and handed them through the doggie door. The longbow was a bit more difficult; I had to open the back door to pass that out, lock the door again and then get out via the doggie door. Getting out was a piece of cake—I was an agile little kid.

That afternoon was totally awesome. We went to a nearby field and shot arrows at the trees. Or at least the big guys did. Tom tried to help me, but I was too little to manage the adult-size bow. But they let me hang out with them. And that was bliss!

Was Dylan allowed to have his father's bow and arrow set? Definitely not, as he got in trouble later that evening when his Mom came home and found the case open, with no arrows in it. I didn't care. All I cared about was Dylan's praise when I emerged, triumphant, and the fact that Dylan let me wear his Davy Crockett coonskin hat. Luckily, his parents didn't think too much about how Dylan got that stuff out of the house!

Things didn't go quite as easily with my parents.

"You did what?" asked my mother when she had called for us and found us playing with the longbow set in the field. Dylan was abruptly sent home, and she confronted the three of us. I knew she was mad because her eyes had little creases between them and her mouth was set in a straight line. It almost looked like she was smiling, but I knew better.

"Dylan's parents let you play with a longbow? Wasn't it all locked up? Those things are dangerous."

"Scott, tell me the truth."

"It wasn't locked. It was just in a box in the rec room," I said. I had to fill the gap and say something. I couldn't stand silence when Mom was on the warpath.

"And you know this, how? I thought Dylan's parents gave you the set and that you had their permission to use it?"

There was no answer to that question, other than telling a big whopper of a lie. And Tom and Dylan were no help. They had learned that less talk is better when you're dealing with Mom.

"Did you sneak into the house?" Mom asked.

I couldn't help myself. I was just five—and I hadn't even truly earned the three-quarters part yet. I broke into tears and told her how the guys had helped me through the doggie door. Mom had that effect on me.

I got a lecture about responsibility, and how breaking and entering could lead to a life of crime, but I didn't get the wooden spoon or worse, Dad's belt. Allan was disgusted with me, and that took away a lot of the joy I'd felt at being part of their adventure. And we all got sent to our bedrooms without finishing dinner.

It wasn't until much later in life that I truly learned the benefits staying silent.

I cried and cried in my room, then became bored out of my mind with hardly any toys to play with, and a growling stomach. There was a quiet knock at my door. When I opened it, there was Tom. He had an O'Henry bar, which he held out to me. Tom was old enough to get an allowance that allowed him to go the store and buy stuff.

"You did great today," he whispered.

I sniffled and wiped my wet face with my hand. "But I ratted you guys out."

Tom wrapped his long arms around me and gave me a hug. "Mom can be pretty scary when she's mad. We all know that."

The chocolate bar was the best thing I had ever tasted. And I have held a special place in my heart for O'Henry bars ever since.

I'VE SEEN IT happen in some families of three kids where the oldest and the youngest get along well, and the middle kid, well, just doesn't fit in. That's the way it was at our house. Allan was a bit weird. Not in a bad way, just different from Tom and me. He liked sitting in his room reading books and tinkering with his chemistry set or his Meccano set, unless Mom pushed him outdoors, telling him to "skedaddle." Tom and I couldn't wait to get outdoors. He'd take me for rides on the handlebars of his bike. There was a huge hill separating our subdivision from the beach. I loved the rush of the wind as we zoomed down the hill—I wasn't sure whether it was terror or exhilaration I felt, but I always begged for more! Tom didn't get bored playing endless games of Hide and Seek, just to keep me happy. And best of all, he taught me to play guitar.

He was a good acoustic guitar player. At first, he played camp songs like "Camp Granada," "Down by the Bay" and "The Bear went over the Mountain." His voice was kind of raspy, like Bob Dylan's. Later on that Bob Dylan voice came in handy when he sang some of Dylan's songs like "Blowin' in the Wind" and "The Times They are A'Changin'," which came out in '63 and '64. I sang along in my high-pitched little boy voice at first and in an awkward, squawky voice as I got a bit older. Tom and I would laugh as I tried to hit the high notes that once came so easily. My voice later settled into one that could still sing some high notes and that complemented Tom's deep, raspy one.

Even when my little fingers had to stretch to reach the chords on his guitar, he would teach me modified chords that required only the first four strings.

- - -

THAT GUITAR WAS part of the campfires we had at Cubs and later Scouts. Tom was 16, old enough to be a junior leader by the time Allan and I were Scouts. We would go camping at a park in the mountains, about an hour and a half east of Hermosa Beach. Since Tom was a leader, we got to drive up the winding dirt road with him and one of the adult leaders, not our parents, which was very cool. Dylan was a Scout too, and he would come with us in the car. I doubt his social climbing parents had much interest in something as messy and primitive as Scout Camp.

But we loved it. There was a lake where we could swim, quite a different experience from swimming in the ocean. We did archery and slingshots, and I even learned how to fire a BB gun. Tom, Allan and Dylan got to use a real .22 rifle on the gun range. Sometimes we went for nature walks. The instructors were really into wilderness survival and taught us which plants we could eat, and how to build a lean-to in the forest. There were lots of hiking trails and a little creek with loads of tree frogs. I thought it was a piece of heaven.

AS WE GOT older, it soon became evident that when it came to brains, Allan had got the lion's share in our family. Allan was great at science, and if he had been born earlier, he might have been on that NASA team that got man onto the moon in '69. And Tom. He wasn't great at school, but man, Tom could talk! He would argue with Dad until he was blue in the face. Dad, who was quite knowledgeable, always liked to play devil's advocate. He'd argue that Hitler was a good guy, for example, just to get a rise out of the two older guys.

I didn't usually get too involved. I watched television, I read the sports section of the newspaper, and devoured the latest issue of LIFE magazine with all its pictures. I liked tinkering with stuff, and Dad encouraged me to do that. But I wasn't at all argumentative, and I wasn't all that interested in what was going on in the world. I didn't like my school much. I had a hard time sitting still. I was what my teachers would call "a daydreamer."

Schools were big on I.Q. testing back then. I got tested and apparently my I.Q. was well above average. There was just some link missing between being smart and being good at schoolwork.

But if the toilet was running, I was the one who fixed it—starting when I was 12 years old. I wasn't great at reading, but I could follow all those manuals with the little diagrams that showed how things were put together. If the vacuum cleaner broke, I would take it apart and figure out what was wrong.

Then Dad and I would go to the hardware store and root around to find the fiddly little part that would make it go again.

I figured I was headed for an apprenticeship while Allan would probably get scholarships and go to college. I didn't know what Tom would do—maybe go into sales or become a stand-up comic or a politician. Maybe he would open his own business, something cool like a restaurant or a record store. One thing for sure—he would be a good leader as well as a wonderful person.

As we became teenagers, and Dylan, Tom, Allan and I continued to hang out. I had my growth spurt very early, and I was as tall as they were. If you didn't look too closely at my babyish face, I could almost fit in. I don't know why they put up with me, but they did. And I couldn't think of any friends I'd rather have.

- - -

LOOKING BACK, MOM and Dad were decent parents. Dad and I had a shared interest in mechanical things, even before I was old enough to help him with repairs to the house or our cars. And Mom, well, you could tell Mom had always been cool. She wasn't wealthy or particularly gorgeous. (I had heard her called 'handsome' before, which seemed like a strange description for a woman.) But you just knew she had it all together. She wouldn't stand for any nonsense; she was rather strict. But every now and then a sharp and very funny sense of humour would pop out.

For example, Allan was always the kind of guy who lived by the rules and was very studious. One time, Mom called him, "L-7." When we asked her what she meant, she made a box with the thumb and pointer fingers of her hands. "It means 'square'," she said.

3: DIALOGUE & FRIENDSHIP
(Katie, December 1976)

- - - - -

JOHN WAS PLEASED that we had found a lodger. He tallied up the rent and figured out how quickly it could help fund the improvements we needed to make to the house—uncovering the vintage claw-foot tub that had been encased in sheets of fake pink panel board tile and getting rid of the pink shag carpet that smelled so bad in the bathroom, for example. Why did people do that? Our house had so many beautiful, old-fashioned features, like main floor walls panelled in real oak, not oak-look sheets of panelling. But it also had some horrible '60s features, such as fake brick on the dining room wall and that fake fuchsia-coloured tile surrounding the tub in the bathroom. The bedroom was enormous, with a wonderful, sloped roof and a bow window, but there were many levels of wallpaper between the top layer and the lath and plaster walls. I liked the yellow flowered wallpaper in the second bedroom—our office—but it was tearing in the corners where the walls of the house had settled, and it should likely be replaced. That was the room with the view of the CN Tower.

We don't have arranged marriages in Canada, but John and I had the closest thing to one. We grew up down the road from each other when my family moved to Markland Woods just as I started high school, our parents were friends, and from grade nine on we were the smartest kids in the class. Not cool at all, but we didn't really care about that. During high school, I would get the best marks in English, French and Latin, but I did well at Computer Science and Math too. I was editor of the school newspaper and the yearbook. John was better at History, Geography and Science, and he was on the debating team and the chess team. We were both in the choir. Our rivalry was intense, and to some extent it still is. He went to University of Toronto and got into Osgoode Hall law school. I thought about going to U of T for English but ended up going to Ryerson for Journalism. I had some girlfriends, like Allison who had moved to B.C., and John sometimes hung out with a group of guys who liked playing the board game, RISK, but in many ways, we were each other's best friends.

People say we are an odd-looking couple, as John is shortish and I'm so tall, maybe two or three inches taller than John. We both wear glasses.

By John's third year of university, we were more than rivals—we were in love. John had long, dark curly hair and coke-bottle eyeglasses. Like me, he wasn't particularly good looking—I doubted that either of us would ever grace the cover of a fashion magazine. It made sense to us to get married at the end of third year. That was more than two years ago.

John was already acting like a lawyer when he proposed in the dead of winter in front of Toronto's Osgoode Hall. He put on his pompous courtroom voice and said, "As a lawyer, I find you guilty of kidnapping my heart, distracting my thoughts, disrupting my sleep, and killing any interest in other girls. I hereby sentence you to a lifetime with me—if you'll have me, that is."

He was so cute! Of course, I said yes, and I laughed and danced with him around in front of the courthouse. He didn't quite join in the dancing, but he did smile and laugh too! Our wedding happened three months later, which was quick—in fact, some of our relatives erroneously thought it was a shotgun wedding and bought me baby stuff. But neither of us saw the point in spending a whole year planning for one day, especially when that year would make or break our careers.

As it turned out, I didn't have to worry about planning the wedding. My Mom did that for us, though every now and then something she wanted would rankle John and me, and we would put in our two cents worth. The wedding was held at Markland Woods Golf and Country Club in the west-end Toronto borough of Etobicoke, where my parents' friends and John's parents were members. I had my best friend Allison as maid of honour, and John had Ted, his good friend from high school debating club days, who was also working on becoming a lawyer. Neither of us had brothers or sisters. Despite that, it was a good-sized wedding with 125 people.

I'm not comfortable being on display, and I was happy when the celebrations were over and it was just John and me, honeymoon bound. We chose to honeymoon at a cottage up north in Huntsville for a week. The weather was a little cool, since it was Ontario in late May, but we explored the town, went for walks in Algonquin Park, and had a memorable meal at the fancy Deerhurst Resort. Both of us loved being up north in cottage country. John's encyclopaedic lawyer mind knew the names of birds, trees, plants and animals, and if he didn't know the name, he had a guidebook that did. We were both environmentalists before it was even cool. We had joined the Ontario Federation of Naturalists' "Mail a Can to John" campaign a few years ago. We worked hard to get Ontarians to mail in thousands of cans and bottles to Premier John Robarts so that he would enact legislation on disposable containers.

I thought the house would be another one of the things that really drew John and I together—we must have looked at 40 houses before we settled on this one. Our real estate agent didn't understand what we were looking for—he kept showing us semi-detached places and even apartment condos, when we told him up front that we wanted a detached home with a yard. We liked vintage—our first choice would have been a home even older that this one, a century old fixer-upper with gumwood panelling and leaded windows. And at first, we looked only in the west end of the city, until we realized that homes in the east end were about $10,000 cheaper.

We paid $44,000 for the house with $4,000 down, and mortgage payments at 10 per cent interest. At $400 per month in payments, we were making a dent in the debt. The basement apartment was a bonus.

We've been through so much together; we've come of age together. Lately though, I feel as though John is changing and I am staying the same. Some of the changes are good. Shortly after he started articling at the law firm, some of his work colleagues took him aside and told him he had to change his image if he wanted to succeed as a lawyer. John was initially royally pissed off; there's nothing worse than having people at work criticise you, especially about something as personal as appearance. But after a few days, he came around. Nothing was going to make him tall or slim, but I must confess that the changes made him much more attractive.

First, he ditched his heavy coke-bottle type glasses for contact lenses. This was not fun. There was huge learning curve trying to put the contacts in for prescribed lengths of time and keeping them safe in a saline solution when they weren't in. A few times, Quincy knocked over the eye solution with his big tail, and John was not pleased.

Then he got a haircut. I was less happy about this, as I really liked running my fingers through his longish dark curly hair. He had looked kind of like singer and songwriter Burton Cummings before, with perfect rocker hair. But I guess lawyers aren't supposed to look like Burton Cummings. His haircut was short enough that there were no more curls, but he did still look pretty good.

And then there were the clothes. I don't make that much at the publishing company, even though I'm an assistant editor at such a young age. (Publishing companies believe in giving you titles, not money!) I get my clothes at those bargain places on Bloor Street that pop up whenever a landlord has trouble getting a more high-end renter. I can get a skirt at places like that for under $10. I also like good sales. Once I even went to Holt Renfrew's 90 per cent off sale and got myself a long, tailored, winter coat at that posh store (total cost $40).

I was not prepared for the prices when we went to Frank Stollery's at Bloor and Yonge. Seven hundred dollars for a suit, $50 more for each dress shirt, $40 for a tie, and $150 for a second pair of pants. Yes, John was becoming a lawyer and had to look sharp, but this was ridiculous. The total with tax was close to $1,200, which was equal to three months of mortgage payments.

I got all huffy with the salesman and caused a bit of a scene as I argued with John in the store, but in the end we did get the suit and all the other stuff.

All of these changes make him look radically different from the man I married—but very sharp. More like TV lawyer Perry Mason than Burton Cummings now.

- - -

BARRY MOVED IN on the first of December, just as I was setting out the Christmas decorations and looking forward to a host of family and work celebrations. We had a little tree with a big root ball that we had obtained from a farm outside the city, driving up there in our 1970 Maverick that had a great engine but a rusty body. It was environmentally friendly to buy a live tree, and we could plant it in the front yard when Christmas was over.

Barry's furnishings were sparse at first. He used a grungy old blanket on the bed until I offered him some of our sheets and blankets. He refused, but a few days later I saw proper sheets and a comforter on the bed. "Salvation Army," he explained. I helped him move a slightly stained white couch down the steep steps to his place. "Can you believe it? I found this on the road. Someone was throwing it out." And then there was the table, painted bright neon green, which looked positively ug-lee! "I can refinish this," he said. "It's real wood underneath."

If I had to describe Barry's presence in the house in one word, I would say "easy." It was almost as though he made a habit of blending in, not creating waves. He was quiet to a fault—sometimes I found myself blathering trying to get more than a one-word answer from him. He didn't seem to understand small talk, and I was better at interviewing people than in making conversation.

But I had hoped for a quiet tenant, and that is what we got. I'm naturally nosey, and I wanted to know more about him, but his monosyllabic answers didn't reveal much. In addition to his job as a "stripper," he'd come and go, saying he was going for long walks or doing some odd jobs for people. I looked through the mail and didn't see that he was on any form of social assistance, though occasionally there was a package from the Toronto Board of Education, addressed to Mr. Douglas B. Burns, which piqued my interest. (Maybe Barry was his middle name?) And he didn't appear to have any family close by.

I ventured downstairs. "What are you doing for Christmas," I asked him.

"Not much," he replied, looking up from his relaxed perch on the slightly soiled couch, then turning back to the day-old front section of the Toronto Star. (We gave him our newspapers once we were finished reading them, usually the next day.)

"Will you be doing something with your family?"

"Naw, we don't keep in touch much."

Silence. I am not good with silence. I have the patience of a flea. I rushed to fill the void.

"Would you like to come with us to my parents' place on Christmas Day," I asked.

I hadn't even thought this through. Would my parents have an extra place at the table? Probably. But what would John think? Would he want to have our renter coming for dinner? John was kind of funny about things like that. More than once, I had got in trouble by asking guests over who weren't "acceptable"—and for John, that was a reasonably large category. Anyone with a sketchy background whose social status wasn't on a par with us or higher, or who didn't believe in environmental causes, for example. Did Barry fit his standards? Probably not.

Turned out, I didn't have to worry.

"No thanks," he said. "You go ahead and enjoy your family. I'm happy here on my own, just hanging out. Watching my TV."

He pointed to his latest acquisition, a wood-encased television set from the early part of the decade. He'd enlisted John and me to load it into the trunk of our car, where it stuck out a mile. It was a heavy piece of furniture, and hard to get down the narrow steps to Barry's apartment. John was not impressed. You'd think we were loading roadkill into the car, not an oak relic that was kind of pretty in an ornate, carved, old-fashioned way. At first the TV didn't work, but Barry fixed that. He borrowed a little lemon oil from me to polish things up, and voila—he had a decent television. And he was reusing found objects—very environmentally friendly.

    I didn't push things. It was probably best that Barry didn't come for Christmas. My parents would have been polite, but they could also be kind of judgmental.

4: VIETNAM
(Barry, January 1977 & July 1966)

SO, I AM settling in at my new place, though my landlady seems like a bit crazy sometimes. She's so obsessed with all this environmental stuff. There's a washing machine and dryer—small ones—right outside the door to my room, separated by a makeshift panel board wall. I thought I could just pop my clothes in the washer and the dryer, but I quickly learned it wasn't that simple.

I asked Katie if I could use the washer and dryer, just to be polite. I wasn't expecting the answer she gave me.

"No, no, no, no, no," she said to me. "We can do the laundry in the washing machine, but on a nice, sunny day like today we should dry the laundry outside on the clothesline."

"But won't it freeze?" I asked. After all, this was winter in Toronto, not a mild, sunny day in California. Mom used to put her laundry on the line all the time, but it made sense there.

"It does, but it dries too, and it smells so much fresher than laundry done in the dryer."

"What about rainy days or snowy days?" I asked.

"Then we use the drying racks," Katie said, pulling out what looked like a pile of sticks, unfolding it like an accordion.

Oooo-kay, I thought. Suddenly laundry became a whole lot more complicated.

"We're saving energy," Katie explained.

We had not had many dry, sunny days this winter. Toronto winters are usually damp and cold. So the drying racks were usually set up outside my room, and the whole place smelled of wet wool and dampness all the time.

That, and damp dog, when Quincy came downstairs to visit after some time outdoors.

I liked Quincy because he was a big, loving, friendly 100-pound bundle of affection. My landlady was big-hearted—she was trying her best to be friendly—but she was also a bit weird.

For example, when I first toured the house, there was gray, soapy water in my downstairs bathtub. I thought that was unusual and asked her why the water was there. She looked at me as though I was from Mars. She pointed to a bucket beside the tub. "We scoop out the water and use it to flush the toilet," she said. "Did you know that each time you flush, you waste four gallons of water?"

No, I did not know that.

- - -

BACK IN THE '60s, anyone my age or older who grew up in the States remembers the hammer that loomed over our heads. The draft. We'd all grown up playing Cops and Robbers, Cowboys and Indians or G.I. Joe. On television, we'd watch "McHale's Navy" and "Hogan's Heroes," but though we laughed a lot at those shows, we didn't necessarily want to go to war.

In contrast to those hilarious TV shows, were the images in LIFE and TIME magazines—a Vietnamese man with his eyes and mouth bandaged shut; prisoners being herded onto a boat; photos vivid with blood, suffering and humanity. Rumours began circulating about the effects of the napalm that was being used on Vietcong villages—sometimes murdering more civilians than Vietcong. We heard how the stuff would burn much longer and deeper than anything else—that napalm victims rarely survived.

Tom was the first of us to receive a draft notice and go to war in 1964. We all gathered in the living room before he left—Mom, Dad, Allan and I—to wish him well on his big adventure. Tom looked grown up with his new, army-issued haircut. He'd never had very long hair, just let it grow down around his ears a bit, but he sure looked different.

Mom gave Tom a big hug. "I've got to get my hugs in while I can," she said. "We're going to miss you so much. You take care of yourself." She was almost weepy—rare for Mom, who was usually so practical.

"So, how does it feel, getting ready to go to Vietnam?" I asked.

"Well, I've never been out of the States, so I'm pretty excited to be going halfway around the world," he said. "I've been reading about Vietnam in National Geographic. It looks like an exotic place, with jungles and rice fields.

"And I'm looking forward to being with a bunch of guys—you know me. I make friends easily. That part should be a lot of fun."

Mom looked at him with affection. "I'm sure you'll be the life of the party, the one cracking jokes, even though you're off to war," she said.

Allan looked up from reading Scientific American. He sometimes appeared to be giving his entire attention to reading, and then would pop up and act as though he was participating in the conversation all along.

"Don't think I'd like that part, the part about the bunch of guys," he said. "No privacy."

Dad just looked at him, puzzled. Allan always baffled Dad; he was so different from Tom and me.

"I was in the war, of course," said Dad. He'd been in World

War II, serving on a ship in the Pacific. "I got to go to a bunch of islands—Hawaii, Midway, the Philippines. It would be interesting to go back there and see how they've changed.

"And yes, you do have a special bond with your mates," he added. Dad still sent letters to a few of the guys he had met during the war.

"Everyone volunteered for that war. We all wanted to serve our country and stop the German and Japanese menace."

Tom nodded. "We'll do our bit. We'll stop the Vietcong."

I figured then that he was just being brave, and maybe humouring Dad, who was from a different era. Tom had seen those LIFE magazine articles. He knew that attitudes had changed since the 1940s, and that serving in Vietnam was not a clear-cut mission or a popular war.

Dad was onto one of his favourite subjects. "But you know, it took an atomic bomb to end that war. Two bombs actually," he added, referring to Hiroshima and Nagasaki. "It was the same in Europe—though I wasn't there myself. The Germans had no trouble bombing London—remember the Blitzkrieg? It wasn't until the Allies bombed Dresden in '45 that the tide started to turn. To end the war, we had to bring the bombs to them. It was only when the Allies brought the war to German soil, that they truly understood what was happening.

"We had to bring the bombs to them. It was only when the Allies brought the war to German soil, that they truly understood." Maybe it was because it was Tom's last night, but I recalled those words, and they made sense to me years later.

What I didn't know then was it was the last time all five members our family would be together as a happy, peaceful, well-adjusted group of people. It was the last time we truly felt comfortable together.

I WAS STILL a kid when Tom was called up, just 13 and not even close to being old enough to serve. Pretty soon, Allan and Dylan would be old enough—then they might be called up too. Allan probably wouldn't be—he was headed for college in a couple of years, likely studying chemistry on a scholarship. Dylan was a brainiac too—and the Hearst family was rich enough to keep sending him to college even if he didn't apply himself and flunked out. Dylan's family wasn't related to that William Randolph Hearst guy who had the big castle up the coast in San Simeon, but his house was bigger than ours and his parents had way more money than we did.

But Tom, like me, wasn't college material, and our family wasn't rich like the Hearst family. He had been eligible.

He sent us letters while he was away, but they didn't say much. They basically said he was fine and liked his platoon and asked for news about us. I couldn't help but wonder what kind of experiences Tom was really having in 'Nam. We love him to pieces, of course, and there was so much negative stuff coming out about the war. There were all these protests, where veterans were accused of killing babies. (That's bull of course—there's no way my chatty, party-loving brother would ever kill a baby.) There was all that stuff about the Mai Lei massacre, where soldiers killed mothers and babies while they were searching a village for Vietcong. But these were mostly ideas talked about by college guys, not working stiffs. Dylan and Allan might have some of those anti-war ideas, but not me.

At 15, I had already started working after school as a machinist. I liked the job just fine, but the guy who ran the place was a piece of work. In my sophomore year, I had started growing my hair a bit, and a few people told me it looked pretty good. The guy I worked for was always on my case to get it cut.

Long hair made me feel like a bit of a rebel—sort of like Bob Dylan or Mick Jagger.

We picked Tom up at the airport on a summer night in 1966. The last time we'd seen Tom, he'd been laughing and joking, despite his not-cool military haircut. He was sort of looking forward to an adventure. I remembered him jauntily waving good-bye as he boarded the military plane and went off to war.

The night he returned, Allan and I rode with Dylan in his bright red Mustang convertible, Mom and Dad in their car. Mom gave Tom an enormous, minute long hug. Dad shook hands—he was never much of a hugger, and guys didn't hug much back in those days. Allan was like Dad—he shook hands.

"Good to see you, man," said Dylan and I, giving him a playful shove.

Now, 24 months after he'd left, Tom looked different. Of course, he was different since he'd been fighting in the jungle for two years. It's hard to explain the differences. He looked older, skinnier. None of us Bronsons are meaty football-player types; we're tall and skinny, or tall, skinny, and geeky in Allan's case. But Tom was now much skinnier than Allan or me. Gaunt? Is that the word?

The other thing we noticed was that he didn't talk as much.

We picked him up at the airport, and as we walked through, we clamoured for news.

I thought Dylan's first question was kind of dumb.

"So, did you score some good drugs out there in the jungle?" He grinned and jostled Tom, and two years ago, Tom would have replied in kind.

This time, he just looked at Dylan—almost looked through him and ignored the question.

As we walked on, I noticed that Tom was getting some weird looks. He wasn't in uniform, but he was obviously a vet. Nobody in 1966 would wear their hair in a crew cut if they weren't in the forces. Those looks weren't necessarily friendly. Tom walked through the crowd without seeing them, his mind far away somewhere.

So much for a happy, welcoming homecoming.

I figured I'd ask some questions, just to keep Tom involved. "So what was it like over there? Tell us all about it," I said, not just to be polite but because I really wanted to know.

"I don't really want to talk about it," Tom said. Then, with a shadow of his old bravado, he said, "It's good to have the gang back together again. Let's go get wasted!"

The place to do that was in Dylan's recreation room. Their house was much bigger and nicer than ours—Dylan's family had so much money I was surprised they hadn't moved to something even classier in a better neighbourhood. The rec room was totally finished with a wet bar, and that bar was well stocked with beer, wine and spirits.

His Dad was a workaholic; his Mom was mainly interested in playing bridge and getting her beauty sleep. It seemed she was always either out or not feeling well, lying on her bed with weird beauty treatments like cucumbers on her eyes or an egg-white concoction on her face. It was supposed to make your eyes less baggy and your facial skin firmer or something. And maybe it worked; Dylan's mother looked younger and more stylish than the other Moms in the neighbourhood. Dylan's Dad, the one I had only met once or twice, believed that if the kids were going to try drinking etc., it was better if they could try doing this at home in a safe setting, under the watchful eyes of the parents. And then the parents didn't watch us.

So… bottom line, Dylan's rec room was the perfect place

for underage drinking. And we all agreed that 21 was a ridiculous drinking age limit when in some other states it was 18. That rationale didn't include the fact while Dylan and Allan were 18 and Tom was 20, I had another two to three years to go before I could reach the 18-year mark.

There was a plaid couch with wooden trim, and a matching plaid easy chair. The shag carpet was really comfy, so sometimes we just leaned against the furniture and stretched out on the floor. Dylan's family had a new stereo with a record player and a radio that got amazing reception. We had lots of records to choose from, and if we were too lazy to change the records, we could just set the dial to KHJ Boss Radio, which played all our favourites.

"Good to be home?" I asked Tom, who was trying to smile and act casual.

He nodded. "What have you guys been up to while I was away?"

"Beach, cars, girls, more beach, more cars, more girls," Dylan answered. "Even Scottie here has a girlfriend."

"Maaary-Aaanne," Allan said, drawing the name out to tease me.

"Mary-Anne Gillespie?" asked Tom. "Doesn't she have an older brother named Barry?" I nodded. Yes, she did.

Three beers in, he started to joke around with Allan, Dylan, and me. He acted something like the old Tom, but studiously avoided any talk about Vietnam.

Five beers in, his mood changed, and he became morose.

We walked home, Tom supported by Allan on one side and me on the other. I was glad he was home but wondered if our lives would ever be the same.

5: BARRY'S NEW JOB
(Katie, December 1976)

- - - - -

SO, BARRY LOST his job at the printing plant—layoffs he said, but I know he didn't like it very much. Crazy shifts, mean managers, and fellow workers who were very different from him. For example, I don't think anyone else had lived in a commune. We'd started chatting during the long hours when I was home, and he was home and John was at work. John was taking this lawyer articling business way too seriously. He was NEVER around, and it was driving me just a wee bit crazy.

So, I had the brilliant idea of killing two birds with one stone. The little publishing company I worked for needed someone to run the printer for our newsletters. And I needed the rent from a guy who had become more than just a tenant—maybe a bit of a friend.

Let me explain about our little publishing company, Rosedale Publications. They called it Rosedale because that's where it was located—right across from the Rosedale Subway stop in a modest four-storey building in one of Toronto's most wealthy neighbourhoods. The Rosedale area had lots of beautiful, traditional old homes, some of them with ravine settings. We were on the third floor of a building that was neither traditional nor beautiful. It was a little run down. There was a restaurant across the street called The Belair Café that served corned beef on rye, greasy hamburgers, watery soup, and milkshakes. It might not sound like much, but the price was right, and it was a favourite lunch spot for the 14 people who worked at R.P.

Yes, R.P. Everything has an acronym. For example, I work as

assistant editor on Environmental Control Operations (ECO) newsletter. That, I think, is a particularly good acronym, and I like writing about the environment. Energy Analysis and Research (EAR) is another of our publications. Another good acronym, implying that R.P. had its ear to the ground when it came to Energy news. We had other publications on subjects that included plastics, chemicals, and engineering. ECO, EAR and our other publications were all newsletters, ranging in size from four to eight pages, and in frequency from once a week to twice a month. We charged an arm and a leg for some of those publications—$350 per year. I couldn't understand it, when mainstream magazines like Chatelaine and TIME magazine cost a fraction of that. But apparently, people in the energy, environmental control, plastic, chemical and engineering fields want the quick digests of timely news that our newsletters provide.

To keep things timely, we had complete control over the typesetting, printing and mailing processes, doing all those things in house! I am pretty sure we had the only commercial printer in Rosedale. It was a big clunker of a thing that had defeated the two people who had run it in the year since the company bought it. It was temperamental, and we often heard f-words emanating from the printing area. When the second guy quit in disgust, I figured Barry might be able to help.

I thought Barry might enjoy the people I worked with, as everyone at R.P. considered themselves a bit quirky. It was something of a badge of honour. In fact, I played down the fact that I was respectably married and owned a home, just to fit in.

It was a bit of a weird demographic. The company was founded by a couple of engineers, Hugh and Gordon, who were also writers. That alone was somewhat unusual. Hugh was a typical engineer, a serious and talented writer who always had his head down, working on something, while Gordon was a combination of sales guy and technology geek, a person with optimism to spare, and an irrepressible sense of humour.

He was the one who recommended hiring Barry.

I couldn't help but overhear the interview. The building walls were not that thick.

"So, Barry, I heard you have worked at Lang and Harrison Printing out in the west end. Why did you leave them?" said Gordon in his engaging sales voice.

"Layoffs, sir. Lang and Harrison's main contract was the Eaton's catalogue and since that folded, they have been having some troubles and laying people off."

"And what did you do there?"

I could picture the glint in Barry's eye, the one he always had when asked this question.

"I was training to be a stripper."

Gordon had been around the printing and publishing industry for a long time. He knew there were at least two types of strippers in this world. But something in Barry's delivery caught his attention, and I think that's when they bonded.

Barry didn't talk about the mean boss, the shifts that completely screwed up his sleep patterns, or the totally incompatible co-workers. Instead, he talked about how his Dad had been a mechanic; how Barry himself had enjoyed tinkering with machines from a young age; how he had taken the technical stream in high school, but unfortunately hadn't been able to get to college or complete an apprenticeship.

"Is your Dad still around?"

"No, unfortunately neither of my parents are around," said Barry.

"I'm sorry to hear that," said Gordon, with real empathy. He was a decade older than Barry, and I'd heard he had lost his mother recently.

"So, where are you from?"

"Out west," he said. "But I've lived in Toronto for a while."

"Vancouver?" asked Gordon.

Barry must have nodded.

"Nice place," said Gordon. "You're kind of an anomaly. Most people your age are travelling to the west—oil industry and all that."

There was another pause.

"That printer is a bit of a beast. Do you think you'll be able to handle it?"

"I'll take a look, sir," Barry said. And then I heard no more through the wall because the two technical geeks had walked over to the printing room at the back of the office to introduce Barry to the temperamental beast.

As part of the hiring process, Barry also had to talk to Moira, the office manager, a plus-sized, genial woman in her thirties, who had a great sense of humour. I'd worked with Moira before, on a directory when I first started at R.P. Her office was beside mine, so I got to hear that conversation too.

The conversation seemed to go quite well. I smiled to myself. Barry was quiet, but he could turn up the charm when he wanted to. He wasn't bad looking when he did—he had a friendly smile.

"So, where are you from originally," she asked Barry. "Do I detect a little bit of an American accent?"

He hesitated a bit, and then he said. "I grew up out west, and we'd go to the States a lot. You know, for holidays or shopping."

I smiled to myself—I didn't think of scruffy old Barry in the Basement as much of a shopper.

But Moira seemed to take the comment in stride.

"Speaking of shopping," she said. "We have a bit of a dress code here—you might want to consider a haircut and some new clothes."

I could picture his face. He probably looked a bit rueful.

"Yeah," he said. "At my last job, I wore coveralls, so it didn't matter much. I'm flat broke right now, but when I get my first pay cheque, I'll get some new duds."

Moira cackled—that's the only way I can describe her laugh. "You do that," she said. "You get yourself some new duds."

Mission accomplished. I still had my renter and Barry had a job to pay the rent.

Whew!

6: MARY-ANNE
(Barry, 1964-66)

SO, I HAVE a new job at R.P. Nice little company. The people seem much friendlier than the guys at Lang and Harrison, most of whom had crew cuts, large bellies, sweated a lot, lived in the suburbs, and had many children, often not all with the same woman. Some of them rode motorcycles—and may have belonged to gangs. Rednecks, I'd call them.

I made the mistake of implying I came from Vancouver and did not get a great reaction.

"La la land, where they all smoke dope," said one guy, disdainfully.

"You go over those mountains and everyone's brain goes soft. All kinds of crazy ideas happening in that place."

Okay. Actually, I had never lived in Vancouver, but I took the insults to mean that these guys' beliefs would be the exact opposite of mine, and I stayed mum most of the time. I certainly never mentioned that I'd lived in a commune! But the point was, they didn't like me. Maybe it was my hair—at least four inches longer than anyone else's. Or maybe it was my age—at 25, I was a good ten years younger than the other guys at the plant.

My job as a stripper had involved arranging and joining film negatives as part of the process of preparing printing plates. It was important that I align each negative securely and use tape to secure it to a light-blocking paper or plastic mask. I got to use an eyepiece magnifier, while viewing my work on top of a light table to achieve exact positioning. Once secured, I'd remove the area of the mask through which light must pass using an Exacto knife.

I'd always been good with detail, and as my dad said back in the day, I had great hand-eye coordination. I liked the work just fine. What I didn't like was when one of my co-workers would pass by just as I'd painstakingly lined up the negatives perfectly, jostling my hand and moving the film out of place.

"Sorry," the guy would say, all the time grinning at his co-workers.

So yeah, I wasn't very upset when they laid me off.

The R.P. office is much closer to home, and even that monster of a printer seems tame compared to my work at Lang and Harrison. I like Gordon. He's cool. Hugh is kind of a mad professor type, who scurries down the hall on a mission or stares long and hard at his IBM Selectric typewriter. Every now and then he smiles, showing he too is a nice person.

IBM Selectrics are what all the editors and their assistants use these days. Once the editors have typed their stories, they pass them along to the typesetters. There is one Compugraphic photocomposition machine, and two typesetters. Linda, a pretty friend of Moira's, who has curly hippie hair, works during the day. Jenny, the quiet, Chinese girl of Katie's dreams, is the only person at R.P. who works the evening shift to make maximum use of the expensive Compugraphic machine. Linda and Jenny were also responsible for feeding the tape from the machine into a phototypesetter, and then pasting up galleys of text to create the final layout. Then, things come over to me for printing.

If I had downtime, I'd help them with the paste-up. It was a far easier job than being a stripper and employed many of the same skills. My work at R.P. can take place early in the morning, during the day or into the evening, depending how newsletter production is going. But no crazy night shifts like Lang and

Harrison.

I deal with both Jenny and Linda and like them both. Linda reminds me of my high school girlfriend, Mary-Anne. The hair is different, but they have the same sweet personalities.

Mary-Anne. She's the one who set the gold standard for any girl I've met since. I have always stuck to one type of girl—much shorter than I am with long dark hair and a wicked sense of humour.

- - -

I MET MARY-ANNE in my freshman year. We were both in the tech stream, the higher-ups having deemed that we were not university material. I was taking auto mechanics and she was taking hairdressing. As techies, we stuck together. Our high school life was not the All-American world of marching bands and football games, of Latin classes and advanced mathematics. We had courses in English, History, Geography, Science and Math, but they were all watered down versions of the A-stream courses. I never did the algebra and trigonometry courses Allan, Dylan and even Tom were taking, but I did learn how to work with mechanical distributors and spark plugs. I was never happier than when they put the old beater cars we worked on up on the hoist and I could explore the undersides.

Cars, cars cars! Cars were my life back then. I was driving when I was 14 years old. No permit at that stage. Dylan let me drive the brand-new Mustang convertible his parents bought him for his 16th birthday. The "pony car" was the hottest car around! Dylan had the new 1965 GT model, with a V8 engine and 225 horses. It was sporty looking, with racing stripes on the sides and brakes that stopped on a dime. It had bucket seats in the front (not so great for necking with girls), and a bench seat in the back.

California is the home of the Beach Boys, for goodness' sake. "Little Deuce Coup," "Fun, Fun, Fun," "Giddy-up, Giddy-up 409," and all that. The Beach Boys all had long hair like me and talked about driving fast sporty cars. We would crank up our music on the AM radio. Barreling down the road in the Mustang, top down, listening to the Beach Boys, was my definition of ecstasy in those days.

We didn't have a Mustang, as the Bronsons are not in the same snack bracket as the Hearsts, but Dad and I are working on an older car, a Chevrolet 409, just like the one in the Beach Boys song. We got a deal because ours had been in an accident, but we both enjoyed hanging out in the garage and looking for replacement parts. And it would be ready by the time I got my license, the minute I turned 16.

I soon developed a reputation for driving fast—Dylan encouraged me when he wasn't driving himself. We clocked the Mustang at 100 miles per hour on an open stretch of highway outside the city more than once.

But back to Mary-Anne. I knew she was the one, when I first met her with a gang of techies sneaking a smoke behind the school. That was the big game back then—sneaking smokes wherever possible, with guys in the washroom, or around the corner from the tech shop, with one person posted as lookout to see if any teachers were coming. I don't smoke much now—not regular ciggies or pot—but I did back then. My memories of Mary-Anne become clearest when I smell the stale but enticing smell of a habitual smoker, or the sweet scent of pot.

She smoked and she was a techie, but there were no hard edges to Mary-Anne. She had a distinctive laugh that was infectious, and she laughed a lot at our jokes, and her own jokes, even when they weren't really all that funny. Her face was sweet and gentle normally, but when she laughed, her whole face lit up. Hard to describe, but it happened all the time. Her laugh hinted at a bit of a wild side—which probably had the potential to bring her and me a lot of grief.

I remember what set me on the road to "going all the way."

Dylan had given me permission to drive Mary-Anne home in his car—wink wink. I thought I'd show off—I floored the Mustang so that it reached 100 miles per hour driving down a deserted stretch of highway. Until it wasn't deserted any more and there was a car coming our way. I braked and swerved—successfully. Man, the brakes on that car were good. My heart was beating quick and hard after that near miss—partly in pure fear, partly the high of a narrow escape, partly because I was underage and didn't have a license.

I parked down the street from her place.

"Are you okay?" I asked. Then I noticed that she was shaking uncontrollably.

"That. Scared. The hell out of me," she said, each word emphasized with a separate sentence.

I put my arms around her, pressing her close to stop the tremors. Gradually she calmed down. I don't know how you'd describe how I felt when she stopped the shakes. There was a sense of wellbeing, knowing I had the ability to calm someone down; a surge of affection because this girl meant so much to me. Perhaps a little guilt thrown in because it was my driving that had upset her so much.

When the tremors stopped, something else kicked in. I was still holding her close. Horny teenager that I was, my underwear and jeans were suddenly too tight, and I had no desire to control the feelings that were coursing through me. She felt it too—when I kissed her, she didn't resist. When my hands moved over her body, she responded in kind. I thought I'd try that thing the older guys kept talking about—French kissing—but somehow, I fumbled that one. Soon after, she leaned back, adjusted her clothes, and said, "I'd better get home."

I knew she was my girl. And she was my girl for almost four years.

But I never sped in the Mustang again when she was in the car.

- - -

AFTER TOM CAME back from 'Nam in 1966, it was debatable who was more affected by the experience—Tom, who'd been there, or Dylan, who became involved in the anti-war movement on his college campus.

Tom did not do well after he came home. He had changed completely, and I missed the way he had been before. He was there, but he wasn't there. He was in the house, but he didn't seem to register what was going on half the time. It was breaking Mom's heart; heck, it was breaking mine too. He seemed constantly haunted; shut inside of himself. He, who had such great plans to open his own restaurant or start a record shop, hadn't been able to go back to work or school. He tried to work at a family friend's restaurant but hadn't lasted long because he was too weird. It was like he was living in another place, although his body was present and accounted for.

They said he was too sick to fight any more, so that's probably a good thing. But he couldn't work; he usually couldn't even have a normal conversation.

Tom sat at home, watching TV, the television turned up loud because he was somewhat deaf after his experiences over there. And we had to be careful about what we let him watch. No news, no war movies. Even "Hogan's Heroes" got him upset. "Ed Sullivan" was okay. "American Bandstand"—things like that. He watched the new comedy called "The Smothers Brothers" and the "Carol Burnett Show"—very funny shows—but he didn't laugh much.

I tried to sit with him and talk to him. I'd always gotten along with Tom the best—Allan was a bit geeky sometimes, and Dylan was totally over the top, becoming more so as his family became richer and richer, and university activism kicked in. Tom had never had pretensions, he was smart but not too smart, more interested in being the life of the party than needing to excel.

At least, that was how I remember the pre-Vietnam Tom.

Once he was back, I'd sit down beside him on the couch in our living room, with its heavy drapes, in the armchair that smelled of smoke because both Mom and Dad were addicted to cigarettes.

"Mom always liked you best," said TV comedian Tommy Smothers to his brother Dick.

"No, Mom always liked you best," I chimed in, looking at Tom for a reaction. But there wasn't one. Just a blank stare as he met my eyes briefly; then looked back at the TV.

He'd gone from being gaunt to having a bit of a belly, from so much sitting around watching the boob tube and drinking beer. It was hard to get him out of the house—when Dylan was home from university, he'd sometimes come with us. But with Dylan away at college in San Francisco, and with Tom so… damaged, I'm afraid the old gang wasn't what it used to be before and during the war years. Allan and I would drive around and hang out, but we were using my parents' old Country Squire station wagon and didn't have nearly as much fun as we did in the Mustang. We missed Dylan and his rec room. And Tom. I saw a lot more of Mary-Anne during those years.

Mom and Dad were overwhelmed by the changes in Tom. The worst was the nightmares. On more than one occasion, he woke the whole house up, screaming. "There were little kids there, and mothers," he said, the only words that we could understand among all the hysterical sobs and yelling. "We killed them, and they were just little." Even Mom couldn't calm him down, and he resisted when she tried to hold and comfort him.

We figured Tom must be reliving some of the worst scenes from the war. He'd wake up sweating and screaming, "No, no, no!" He'd lash out as Mom and Dad tried to control his flailing arms and kicking legs. It took ages to calm him down and convince him that he was in quiet old Hermosa Beach, not the jungles of 'Nam. I got so I was pretty good at handling this part. I would talk soothingly, quietly about how we lived in a good place in Southern California—how he never needed to experience all that stuff again. I would sit with him sometimes, perched on the side of his single bed in his room. I wish I'd sat with him more often.

One day, I had a brainwave. I got out his guitar and started to play. I wasn't that good, but I had mastered enough of the chords to play along with simple songs like "Where have all the Flowers gone?" and "Blowin' in the Wind." Both those songs talk about war, and I hesitated when I played the first one. But there was no bad reaction from my brother. I saw the angry crease between his eyebrows go slack, and his face started to relax. Eventually, his foot started to tap in time with the music. That was enough for the first time I played.

I started playing guitar every chance I got. I handed it to him to see if he wanted to play, but he didn't take it. But one day he started to sing. His voice was deeper and raspier than it used to be. Mine was slightly higher than his, and I could harmonize.

"You sound like Bob Dylan," I said.

THE BOMBER IN THE BASEMENT

And for the first time in a long time, I got a smile out of him.

7: CORPORATE WIFE
(Katie, January 1977)

THE LAW FIRM John now worked for always had its Christmas party in January, saying people's schedules were way too full in December. (I think they got a better deal on the venue by celebrating during the off-season.)

It was the day of the John's office Christmas party, and I didn't think I had ever been this nervous. It was John who made me nervous—he'd bought me a dress he thought would be suitable after rejecting all the clothes in my closet, including the beautiful going away outfit I had worn at our wedding. The new dress was gorgeous and cost way more than I would ever pay. John said it was my Christmas present. It was white satin, with a plunging neckline that made me feel sort of undressed. I felt much more comfortable wearing it with the short, white cape that I could fasten around my neck. My opinion was that the dress would have looked a little better on someone who was more well-endowed than I was, but John seemed to like it and that was what counted tonight.

I wore nylons—ones that cost $10 for one pair and came from Holt Renfrew—same as the dress. I was so scared that I would get a run in them—not that anyone could see them as my dress trailed to the ground. I'd put a pair of the three- for a-dollar ones I usually wore in my purse just in case. John insisted I wear heels, even though they made me about six inches taller than him, rather than just two or three. I don't usually wear heels, and the thought that I might trip made me more anxious than ever. And he'd told me I should take my glasses off—I kept those in my purse too and felt more than a little vulnerable because I couldn't see properly up close without them. I vowed that I'd be like John and get contacts soon—that way I could see what I was doing in situations like this.

I'd curled the tips of my long hair with a curling iron and was wearing it down—John's request again. He didn't like it when I pulled the front pieces back or wore it in a ponytail. I was wearing makeup, and that also felt strange and unfamiliar. I had earrings on too, clip-ons and they hurt!

The pep talk John gave me in the taxi that took us from our house in Little India near Greenwood and Gerrard to the Sutton Place at Bay and Wellesley didn't do anything to ease my tension.

"Don't bore people by talking about environmental stuff," he said. "People aren't interested in your job—as a matter of fact most of the other wives don't have to work. Talk about stuff like the weather, or fashion, or Florida or golf. I think most of the people there play golf."

"So, it's okay to mention that we got married at Markland Woods Golf and Country Club," I said, with a touch of sarcasm.

John hesitated. "I don't know if I'd bring that up," he said seriously. "I think they mostly golf at Rosedale."

I wasn't exactly graceful getting out of the cab—I had a hard time seeing where I was going without my glasses. One of my spikey heels caught on a grate and I had to pull it out. Thank goodness it didn't break off! I had to manoeuvre the folds of my long, white dress and my longish coat up and away from Toronto's omnipresent filthy winter slush, remnants of a snowfall a few days back.

"Why did you bring that purse?" John asked in a stage whisper. "You shouldn't have brought that purse—purses are supposed to be small. Maybe you could leave it at the coat check."

"I need my purse," I whispered back, though I got his point. It was a well-used dark and shabby purse, at odds with my pristine floor-length white gown and curled hair.

Oh, but the hotel was so beautiful. John's firm had spared no expense, taking over the whole Stop 33 restaurant at the Sutton Place, with its floor-to-ceiling views of the downtown bank buildings, a big gap between, and then the CN Tower. I never got tired of looking at the tower and was glad we lived in a house where you could see it from the back bedroom.

If I stood still, I could imagine myself fitting in to this luxury lifestyle, as I took a glass of wine and a shrimp and cucumber canapé. Then I felt awkward, as it was hard to hold my wine glass and my purse and eat a canapé at the same time. Plus, everything up close looked a bit blurry. I dangled the purse and ate the canapé. Good. It was much easier once I just had the purse and the wine.

"Oh, there's someone I'd like to say hello to," said John, patting my arm and rushing off without me to join a group of men, who looked like they were probably the firm's senior partners.

"You must be Kate," said a very short, beautifully turned-out blonde woman. She was about my age, but tiny and dainty, the kind of woman who always made me feel like a giraffe.

I held out my hand, thankful that I was no longer holding the canapé.

"Gillian Perry," she said. "I work with Johnathan."

"Oh," I said. "Nice to meet you. So, what do you do at the office?"

"I'm articling, just like Johnathan."

I giggled a little – the wine was making me a little lightheaded. "We never call him Johnathan at home. He's always been just plain John."

She gave me a look I couldn't read. I sensed I'd said something that wasn't entirely appropriate.

"So," she said, taking a sip of her wine. "I hear you write about environmental issues."

So, John did talk about me at work after all. But he'd said not to get onto that topic. "Um," I said, all my interviewing skills deserting me. "I'm a journalist. I graduated from Ryerson."

Again, I'd said something not quite appropriate. Maybe it was because Ryerson wasn't a university…? Maybe she was one of those people who thought college degrees didn't quite measure up? It seemed I couldn't say anything right to this woman.

"Isn't this a beautiful hotel," I said, trying for a neutral topic while flipping back a piece of hair so it wouldn't dangle in my wine.

"Yes, it is," she said. "Good to meet you," she said, insincerely I thought. And then she walked away to talk to someone else.

"Johnathan," I thought to myself, suppressing a giggle, thinking of John's dreams to rise through the ranks to become a judge. The Honourable Johnathan Lloyd McKittrick. Too funny.

And then I made the mistake of taking a step forward, my heel got caught in the hem of my dress and I tumbled to the floor, wine glass smashing into a million little pieces, purse wide open exposing, among other things, my 33-cent nylons.

The rest of the evening passed in a blur, as I worked hard to fade into the woodwork, sitting on a chair so I didn't collapse on those high heels again. There was an older gentleman—well, maybe not too old, maybe 30 or so with his hair clearly receding in the front— who took pity on me and kept bringing me food.

"My name's Alex Johnson," he said, his manners courtly. "By the way, that's a beautiful dress."

Alex Johnson sat down beside me, all concerned. "Are you

okay?" he asked. "It looks like you took quite a tumble."

I shook my head and smiled. "Nothing hurt except my pride." I reached into my purse and took out my glasses so I could see him properly. He had a smile that reached up to the friendly crinkles around his eyes

"So, you're Johnathan's wife?" he asked, looking around the room for John who was talking to a much older gentleman who radiated confidence and charm. "Oh, there he is. He's talking to James Kilbourne. He's a senior partner."

It figures, I thought. The new John seemed obsessed with getting in with the bigwigs. But I knew he wouldn't be talking to Mr. Kilbourne for long. "You have to circulate," he'd told me during his pre-party pep talk. "Work the room."

To heck with that, I thought, reluctant to risk falling again on those high, wobbly heels. Sitting here, sipping wine, and talking to Mr. Johnson was quite pleasant.

"So, I hear you write about environmental control," Alex Johnson said to me.

"I'm assistant editor of ECO," I said, surprised to see that he was nodding.

"I know it," he said. "For a while I thought about becoming an environmental lawyer, but instead I decided to specialize in family law."

I was baffled. "Why did you switch?" I asked.

He took a moment before he answered.

"Well, there's a lot happening in the environmental field, but there's also a lot happening in family law. The Divorce Act of 1968 changed everything. Before then, the courts presumed that everyone was in a traditional nuclear family relationship, working dad, stay-at-home mom, and children. When parents divorced, the courts almost always awarded custody to the mother. But things are changing. I've never married, but lots of my friends who did are now getting divorced. And it's a new world out there, with more women working and single parent families on the rise. And stay-at-home dads—I only know one personally, but that's a trend too."

"Hmm. I hadn't thought of all that," I said, looking at him with a bit more interest. "And not everyone gets married," I added, pondering all this for the first time. "My friend Allison, out in B.C., is living with a guy. They just had a baby, and they may or may not get married, or maybe they'll wait until the baby is older."

He nodded affirmation. "So that's why I switched specialties. And how about you? What's going on in the environmental world?"

I could see John trying to catch my eye. He was making a horizontal circle with his finger, code for "Don't get bogged down with any one person. Work the room. Circulate. Mingle."

I raised my eyebrows and shook my head. I was quite happy where I was. And I didn't even care that I was breaking his other rule regarding talk about my work.

"Well," I said and then dove in. "Right now, we're writing about everything from Pollution Probe to sewage treatment, and of course, the environmental effects of the proposed Mackenzie Valley Pipeline."

John was wrong. This guy wasn't bored with my work. There was actually someone at his company party who was interested in both the environment and the new family law regulations. He didn't just want to talk about golfing at Rosedale and other pretentious chitchat. He handed me a business card, which I stuffed into my inappropriate purse.

Thank you, Mr. Johnson, for making this evening bearable, I thought to myself.

"Johnathan" made a point of ignoring me for the rest of the

party, not bothering to introduce me to any of his colleagues, and reluctantly escorting me to a cab for the 20-minute ride home.

"So," he accused me when we were safe in the cab and only the driver could overhear us. "You didn't circulate. You didn't meet the important people. You just got stuck in a corner with some guy."

"And you ignored me the whole time—you didn't help when I had my accident either."

"I was too embarrassed," John said, looking away.

"And that guy's name is Alex Johnson. We had a great talk about family and environmental law. I actually had a good time," I said. "Wait a minute, don't you know him?"

The look John gave me was stone cold. "Of course, I know him," he said. "But he doesn't even belong to our firm. He's on his own, and he has a family law practice. Maybe he used to work for Kilbourne, but he doesn't any more. "He's not important," John added.

I didn't think my debut as a corporate wife had gone particularly well.

8: DYLAN'S RADICALIZATION
(Barry, 1966-67)

- - - - -

HOME WAS KIND of depressing in the year following Tom's return from overseas. Tom was still sitting like a vegetable in front of the TV. Sometimes I could get a smile out of him by bringing him an O'Henry bar or watching his favourite shows. He was gaining weight because he never went out; just sat there most of the time, or ate, or slept. His face was pudgy now—he sure didn't look like my handsome brother, and he didn't act like the hero who had always looked out for me. It was taking its toll on Mom and Dad too. They were fighting more, and Mom's face had aged a lot. I could still get Tom to smile when I played guitar, but in the big scheme of things, it was a small victory.

One night, Tom and I were hanging out in the living room, and he seemed reasonably happy for a change. He was working on the knots we had learned in Scouts, and it brought back wonderful memories of Scout Camp, with the smell of pine trees and the joy of sitting around a campfire and singing.

"Round turn, two half hitches," I said, challenging him to make the knot, which he did, no problem.

"Do you remember some of the others?" I asked.

And of course, he did. Sheet Bend. Double Sheet Bend. Bow Line. Trucker's Hitch. Taut Line Hitch. Prusik Hitch. Double Fisherman's Knot. Clove Hitch. Sailor's Knot. Square Knot or Reef Knot. We had the best time we'd had in months as he demonstrated them all for me.

- - -

ALLAN AND I found him the next day, suspended from a tree in a park near our home. He had used a knot I didn't recognize from Scouts—I later found it was called a Hangman's Knot.

I DON'T KNOW how you describe grief, for of course that is what we all felt after losing Tom. For me at first it was a physical feeling—a headache, a lead weight in the pit of my stomach, extreme tiredness, a feeling that my thinking was fuzzy and might never be normal again. At first, I tried to avoid thinking about Tom—tried to avoid the triggers that would make me very aware that my best buddy, the guy who would ride me down the hill on the handlebars of his bike, the guy who was so into Scouting and had a raspy voice like Bob Dylan—would never be coming back.

Tom's death spelled the end of my family as we once knew it. Dad seemed to grow smaller and quieter by the day. He no longer wanted to work with me on cars or fix things around the house. We sold the 409—Dad's idea, not mine. Mom tried to keep it all together, but her efforts were half-hearted. The housework was suffering. She didn't have the same sharp wit that she had before, but she did have a sharp tongue, often aimed at her remaining teenage sons.

I don't think Mom had a lot of patience with me and my style of mourning, which was basically to sleep a lot, refuse to do chores, and sneak off to drink or do drugs with friends, including Mary-Anne, each night. I rarely got up before noon. I skipped classes and eventually dropped out of school. That wasn't a thing us Bronsons were supposed to do. Bronsons had to work or be at school. Mom thought that I shouldn't be wasting my time if I wasn't in school. She called the machinist I was working for and got me a full-time job with him.

Allan doesn't show his emotions much, but I knew he was hurting too. With his personality, mourning meant that he concentrated on one thing and one thing alone. Luckily, that thing was the undergraduate chemistry degree he was taking at UCLA. He was probably doing better than the rest of us in coping with Tom's passing.

I remember one day in particular. I came out of my room and looked around the house for the first time in months. I noticed it was dirty—and Mom had been such an obsessive housekeeper. I mean, that's what Moms did in the '50s and '60s. There were dishes stacked in the sink with blobs of food all over them. The couch wasn't aligned at a perfect 90-degree angle to the easy chair like it usually was. The pillows were piled in a heap at one end of the couch, not neatly and symmetrically arranged the way Mom liked them. There was dust everywhere.

But the biggest shock was seeing her plants—Mom had a pile of houseplants in the south-facing window at the front of our house. It wasn't exactly a solarium, but it was a big window and it had lots of plants. I didn't know all the fancy Latin names (Allan did). I knew them as the rubber plant, the elephant ear plant, the Wandering Jew, the Dracaena (now there's a good, fancy word) and the one I used to call Phil when I was little and couldn't say big words. Its real name was Philodendron.

I'm sure they hadn't been watered in weeks and they were all covered with dust. Phil's leaves were drooping and turning yellow. The others didn't look much better.

Years later, when I was far away from my family and missing my mother, I would kick myself. Why didn't I just dust and water those plants? Why didn't I wash the dishes and help Mom, who surely must have been suffering as much as I was? Why didn't I straighten those pillows on the couch? It would have made our relationship so much better, maybe taken some of the edge off the fights that had become the sum-total of our relationship.

But I was a stupid teenager then and didn't think of anyone but myself.

After a few months, my mood changed to anger. Anger at a world that made a gentle, kind person like Tom kill children, and messed up his brain, all because Nixon wanted to fight communism by waging a war in Vietnam. I was worried too, that I would be called up in a year or so.

My mood was exactly in sync with the anti-war movement that was gaining momentum across the country.

DYLAN HAD GONE off to college in 1966, attending San Francisco State University. Allan also went to college on a scholarship, but he went to UCLA and commuted on LA's less-than-ideal transit system from home. Our family couldn't afford the cost of out-of-town learning. But Allan was a year ahead of Dylan because he had skipped a grade. The schools did that a lot in the '60s.

Dylan went to SFSU because he liked the sound of their recently formed Experimental College. The college had free courses taught by students, professors, and community members. His parents thought it was a bad idea—they would have preferred that he study law, medicine, or engineering at a less-radical university. Certainly, they could have afforded it. But Dylan told them it was SFSU or bust. And his parents, who had never been particularly involved in what he did, let him go. Dylan had no idea what he wanted to do with his life, so he took psychology.

I don't think he went to class regularly. From what I heard

from his parents, he passed everything, but his grades were nothing to write home about and he was not what you would call a serious student.

At first, all we heard about was the drugs—freely available in the house he shared with other stoners from wealthy families who went to SFSU. Throughout high school, he'd told us about the trips he'd taken doing tabs of acid, but it was always a hassle to get drugs and there was always the possibility of getting caught in a deal. No such problems at SFSU, Dylan said. At the experimental college, they were even conducting studies of whether drugs like LSD could enhance creativity. Some of the results were favourable, or so Dylan said, as he shared a spliff with the rest of us on a trip home.

Tom's suicide happened in January 1967, and our first trip to SFSU happened in June.

On a beautiful weekend, we decided to take a trip up to San Francisco to find out what all the hype was about. Allan and I decided to go together. We took turns driving the 1957 Country Squire station wagon Mom and Dad had lent us for the weekend. No Mustang for our family. Just a bit of a beater of a family car with wood-grain panels and sluggish automatic transmission. Dad and I had worked on it, but no amount of effort could make that car anything but a workhorse.

But even though the Country Squire wasn't the best car, the drive was amazing—up the Ventura Highway with cliffs rising to the right of us and the cliffs to the ocean plummeting to the left. Past the sprawling Hearst Castle (no relation to Dylan). We left after Allan had finished work around 5 p.m. at his summer job. At San Luis Obispo, we switched to the coastal route, and had to stop at Morro Bay, home of that huge volcanic rock and three-stack nuclear power plant, because it was such a long drive. We pulled off the highway and onto the beach. I remember that trip as one of the highlights of my teenage life. Allan and I weren't similar at all, but we did get along okay. In a more grown up, teenage way, he still had me on his team. We thought about sleeping in the back of the station wagon—certainly there was room. But instead, we opted to sleep in our sleeping bags out under the stars, with the sand as our mattress and a clear sky with stars above us.

While the trip there was relaxing, the scene at Dylan's Haight-Ashbury house was exhilarating—I think that's the word. I felt like I'd arrived somewhere special. It made our hearts beat faster and filled us with the excitement of being at the centre of things. And we were at the centre of things. We were in the midst of what was already being called "The Summer of Love." I heard later that there were 100,000 extra people in San Francisco that summer. Dylan had already filled us in on the Human Be-In that had taken place at nearby Golden Gate Park in January. He ragged on about a guy called Timothy Leary, who told everyone to "Turn on, tune in, drop out."

Among all the hippies there, my hair, which caused me so much grief with my boss in Hermosa Beach, seemed rather short, and Allan's growing-out crew cut was way out of place. Dylan's hair had been growing steadily since he left home the previous September, and now reached his shoulders. He looked good as a hippie. When I first met him as a kid in Hermosa Beach, Dylan had short, sandy hair and looked pretty average. For a while, he was a player on the junior football team. When he didn't make the senior football team, he went through his surfer dude stage, and as his hair grew out, it showed some blond streaks. Caused by the sun? Peroxide? Beach Boys move over—Dylan was a pretty good surfer dude like the ones on the beach near home. Now, his hair was even longer and more streaked and he was a hippie wearing a bandanna around his head, a tie-dyed shirt, a suede vest with a fringe, loose cotton pants held up by a string, and sandals.

The old multi-storey wooden house smelled pleasantly of marijuana. Allan wrinkled up his nose—unlike mine, his friends were mostly science geeks who didn't use. I don't remember all the names of Dylan's housemates, only that one of them, George, seemed to be strung out on something. He kept muttering about the counterculture, the establishment, ban the bomb and other things we didn't catch. Dylan talked about these things too, but he was more understandable.

I felt strangely at home on the bottom floor that three-storey place on Lyon Street. It was old, like extremely old, 1800s maybe? Early 1900s? It was made of wood and was in every way different from our stucco bungalow in Hermosa Beach. While Mom and Dad's décor was strictly Sears-inspired, everything about this place was weird—in a good way. Beads were strung from the doorway in place of a door. There were old fashioned, flower-patterned carpets everywhere. Pillows on the floor served as seating. Mattresses were spread on the floor for sleeping. Blankets hung on the walls as decoration. There were Tiffany lamps—now those had cost someone a few bucks. And plants everywhere, both indoors and out.

The furniture came from what my Grandma used to call "the olden days." It was old and shabby. There were a couple of chairs, although people rarely sat on them. They were curved, and the padding was coming out. So, Dylan and his friends just covered them with blankets.

Dylan's part of the house was a commune, and everyone pitched in. Even Dylan. We were a bit surprised that he was helping make food and wash dishes and stuff laundry in the machine. At home, he was never expected to do any of those things. And within our little group, he was more likely to ask us to step and fetch it.

We helped ourselves to the chilli con carne someone had made and reclined on the pillows on the floor. For the first time, I understood why someone would want to leave home and live in a place like this one.

"So, how's everyone coping with Tom gone," Dylan said, once we were nicely mellow on dope and chilli (except Allan. He dug into the chilli, but he didn't smoke weed.)

How are we doing without Tom? Well, that was a bit of a conversation stopper.

"Our family sucks," I said. That came out a bit harsher than I'd meant. The marijuana was making me less inhibited. "Dad's wasting away, Mom and I don't get along any more, and Allan… well, how are you doing Allan?"

"Our family sucks," Allan repeated, nodding. He was a bit mellower than usual. Allan didn't usually smoke weed, but he'd probably inhaled a lot of our second-hand smoke.

There was a comfortable pause in the conversation.

"We see a lot of soldiers going off to 'Nam," Dylan said, speaking like me, slowly, languidly, also mellow after smoking weed. "A lot of soldiers ship out of here to 'Nam. They're so happy and excited about going. We give them flowers sometimes.

"But we know they're not going to come back as the same people."

Yes, Allan and I knew that firsthand.

As the night progressed, Dylan talked to us about Tom, linking his rotten war experience to the activism on campus. It was the establishment that forced us into this rotten war, he said. A war with no purpose in countries no one cared about. A war that destroyed our best young men… like Tom. "Think about it, Scottie. Think about it, Allan," he said.

The concert held over the next few days, a bit of a drive

away in Monterey, was unbelievable. Looking back ten years later, I realize that Allan and I participated in history. It was the Monterey Music Festival that kicked off the Summer of Love. We heard Jefferson Airplane and the Grateful Dead and a guy called Ravi Shankar who played this weird Indian music on a sitar.

- - -

WE WENT BACK to see Dylan a lot that summer—partly to escape the sadness that was in our home. Allan came along—not sure why as he wasn't really into the hippie scene but home was like a heavy blanket, smothering everything, smothering joy. Allan came to escape, like I did. And he was always close with Dylan, despite the fact that they were polar opposites. I think he liked talking with Dylan, even though he had this annoying habit of waving his hand in front of his face when he felt the marijuana smoke was getting too much.

Mary-Anne came sometimes too, which made sleeping on the beach or sharing a room in the commune a bit awkward, since Allan was just a few feet away.

That was such strange summer. The summer I was sixteen and could drive legally. The summer Mary-Anne and I truly became a couple. A summer marked by trips to Dylan's hippie house, smokes, tokes and beer, music that endures even now, and that strangely welcoming first floor apartment with the beautiful terrace out back.

- - -

BY THE END of the summer, Haight-Ashbury was changing; so was Dylan and so was his home. Haight-Ashbury was the centre of the universe; everyone wanted to be there, and the area was going downhill. There were just too many people; even Dylan's house had a few extra roommates, which meant we no longer had our own room when we crashed on the mattresses on the floor and had to share with strangers.

And that summer, our feelings changed too, helped in no small part by our need to come to terms with the reasons behind Tom's death.

At the beginning of the summer, we were hugging the soldiers and sending them off to war. By the end of the summer, we despaired at the soldiers coming back, broken in their bodies and in their minds—like Tom. They were fighting a war that no one believed in any more, a war with atrocities that were ruining our young men. Over the summer, Dylan's priorities changed from peace, love and getting high, to seeking revenge for the awfulness that was the Vietnam War. We stopped talking about cops, referring to them as "the pigs."

9: THE PUB
(Katie, January 1977)

- - - - -

I'VE BEEN STRUGGLING lately to keep happy. I'm usually the kind of girl who greets people with a smile, unless I'm absorbed in something, like writing for example. But lately life has been a bit too much to handle. John is never home, and when he is, he seems preoccupied, impatient. A far cry from my friendly rival in high school, or the cutie who'd proposed in legalese.

I'm not enjoying my job as much as I used to. I have been working with Rosedale Publishing since 1972, when I started as a summer student while I was at Ryerson taking journalism. I worked with Moira, the office manager on a directory that included an Associations and Societies section. My summer job was to come up with as many Canadian associations as possible. I drove my family, John and my best friend Allison nuts, because I was forever on the lookout for new associations. I'd jot down names of associations on signs we passed, walking down the street or in the car. I went to the library and searched for the names of associations in the classified sections of telephone directories from every city and town that had a directory at the library. Once I had the names of associations, we had to verify them—name of association, address, president or executive director and phone number. First, we sent out a massive mailing, and I'd developed a great filing system for the replies. If they didn't respond to the mailing, then I'd have to call.

I'd done well—when I started that summer, the section had just 32 pages. When I finished at the end of August, we had it up to 178 pages of fully vetted, accurate listings.

While I was at Ryerson, I had a part-time job with Rosedale updating another directory that listed government contacts in the federal government, and all 10 provinces and two territories. My job was to update the Ontario Government section. The job paid $200 a month, and since I was living with my parents, I was swimming in cash.

The following summer, I met my mentor. Her name was Elizabeth and she looked like a pixie, tiny with short brown hair and a heart-shaped face that radiated curiosity. She was the editor of ECO, and I was the editorial assistant. It was my first real journalism job, and I wasn't even 20 years old yet. Elizabeth had two decades of work experience behind her —10 years as an engineer and 10 as a writer and editor.

It was a great honour to start as an editorial assistant when I was just 19 and hadn't even finished school. It was a lot of work, learning to write about a new subject that takes in everything from solid waste management to the environmental protests about the Mackenzie Valley Pipeline, Pollution Probe and the well-intentioned but sometimes crazy things that Greenpeace was doing. But I was already interested in the environment, and Elizabeth drove me to delve more deeply when we received press releases about various stories. No topic was too mundane to pique her interest, and she could even make the least glamorous part of our beat interesting—who knew that there were several possible ways to process the sewage sludge that came from our cities? She knew that because of her engineering background. And unlike some engineers, she could explain things simply and bring that subject to life. Like me, she felt nothing but disgust for those cities that still dumped their waste into the ocean, soiling one of our most precious resources. Even Toronto. Up until 1910, all the city's sewage flowed directly into the lake. Since then, the city has built several sewage-treatment plants, the largest of them at Ashbridges Bay, where I take Quincy for a walk. But if it rains or snows too much for the system to handle, then untreated sewage is released into Lake Ontario. Elizabeth made me acutely aware of this problem and the work to be done.

I had two summers working with Elizabeth, enjoyed them thoroughly, and was promoted to the position of assistant editor. Then she left to join one of those associations I had listed in my directory. And by the time I graduated and went to work for Rosedale full time, she was gone. Her replacement was a big-boned, stern-looking woman who wore her hair pulled back in a tight bun. Her name was Margaret, and she was now my boss.

We didn't click. And worse than that, she seemed to view me as a threat. I'd come up with what I thought were great ideas for ECO, and she'd shoot them down. While Elizabeth would give even a lowly summer student assignments that were interesting, in and among the day-to-day departments like People, News Briefs, Products and Coming Events, Margaret limited my role to those departments and proofreading. While Elizabeth and I would have long and lively debates about grammar and punctuation, checking the Globe & Mail Style Guide or Strunk & White Elements of Style, Margaret seemed to have her own style guide, which was mainly in her head and totally inflexible. She leaned toward British spellings, "programme" instead of "program" for example, instead of Canadian spelling, which was a bit of a mishmash of American and British words laid out in the Globe & Mail guide. It bugged me because the idea of our newsletter was to keep things short and succinct. The other newsletter editors didn't even put periods between short forms—but Margaret insisted upon it. Sigh.

We didn't like each other; we didn't respect each other; and I was seriously unhappy at my job.

But I did like the other RPites (sounds like Arpeeites), our affectionate name for those who worked at the company. No close friends, but everyone was nice, and they all said hi when I walked in the front doors and through the office. Gordon, the boss, was a positive and upbeat person—he did a lot to keep morale up.

Margaret seemed to expect me to work overtime a lot too. "You don't have a family and children," she said when I protested or said I had something else to do. "Working late now and then shouldn't be a problem."

So, I was working long hours and hating most of them.

I didn't see much of John these days, and I wouldn't have seen much of him even if I were home. The law firm forces him to work insane hours. John kept saying it was all part of the process of becoming a lawyer—kind of an initiation that seemed to be lasting for years. He had always been ambitious—and I guessed I wouldn't have been attracted to him if he wasn't.

But still... I kept thinking back to that Christmas party, where I had made such an ass of myself. "Johnathan." I still giggled at how pretentious that was—the only person who had ever called him that before was his mother. When he'd done something really, really, bad. That moniker alone showed how much he had changed.

Good thing Barry kept more reasonable hours and could feed and walk Quincy. Poor pup. I think he's becoming more attached to Barry than me, and that makes me blue too. Plus, it's winter. The coldest winter on record they're saying. And it was rarely sunny. I'll be blunt about it. I hate cold, dark miserable Canadian winters.

Every morning, I get up and have a cup of coffee and sit on the blue corduroy couch in the living room until sanity sets in. I will be blunt again. I am not a morning person. I don't usually see John since he goes downtown to his law firm at the crack of dawn. I don't usually see Barry come up through the kitchen, since he starts work earlier than me, and doesn't eat breakfast. So, it's very quiet—just Quincy and me. Once I'm fully awake, I eat some cereal (same kind every day) and take Quincy out for a walk. He needs exercise since he is such a large dog. And he won't pee or poo in the back yard. He needs a walk, and he needs an audience. Lately, I've been dragging my buns. It's such an effort to put on hat, mitts, boots, bulky heavy coat, scarf, or neck warmer. Quincy doesn't mind the cold. He's part German Shepherd and part something else. Bernese Mountain Dog, maybe? That would explain his love of the cold. He frolics off leash in the grounds of the sewage treatment plant near our house, staying close and coming when called—he's that well trained—and I plod along with him until he's done his business and it's time to go home.

 Next, it's the streetcar that runs along Gerrard and Carlton to the College subway. I take the Yonge line three stops north to Rosedale. The streetcar ride is boring and too long. I keep myself amused by looking at the houses along the way; they get older as we get closer to downtown. Broadview, Regent Park and finally Cabbagetown, a neighbourhood that's starting to be "white painted" or going upscale. That's not happening in our neighbourhood.

 Or I think about babies. It's one of my favourite daydreams. John and I had grown up together since we were kids. It seems like it's time for us to have kids ourselves. My Mom had me by the time she was my age. Will the babies be girls or boys? Girls, I hope. I had always planned to have girls. I tried out different names—Dawn Elizabeth, Kyla Janine—to see how they could roll off my tongue. Boys' names didn't have the same musical quality. We'd probably be more conservative about those. Maybe John (not Johnathan!) after his Dad? Or Robert after mine.

The streetcar/subway route was long, but not nearly as long as it would have been if we lived in out in the boonies in Etobicoke near Mom and Dad. It was always a relief when I finally got to work.

Up the elevator to the third floor. More coffee. Sometimes I had to make it because writers and editors use coffee like it is rocket fuel—the very thing to get those creative juices humming—and we often run out before 9:30 when I start work. I don't even need to measure how much coffee I need to put in the top to get the new urn going—I've been making that coffee since I started working as a summer student almost five years ago. It's now second nature.

After that second cup of coffee, I'm good for the morning, the afternoon and usually I get a second wind into the evening. I drink lots of coffee to keep me going. My only vice. I don't drink much alcohol, don't smoke cigarettes, I'm not addicted to drugs, and I certainly don't smoke dope.

I have my own private cubicle, so that's a good thing—I'm especially glad I don't have to share with Margaret. Some people like to have the radio on when they write, and some of the people I went to school with are working in open concept newsrooms, where there's constant clacking of typewriter keys and loud voices. I don't think I could handle that. I like my cubicle.

Today, I looked at the pile of mail on my desk, the source of story ideas for ECO. My job involved going through the mail, and then typing up a list of story ideas for Margaret, who would likely reject most of them and then assign me the boring stuff.

There was something from Pollution Probe and something from Greenpeace, both home-grown Canadian organizations. More on The Berger Report, which had come out recently, outlining the effects of the Mackenzie Valley Pipeline on the

First Nations up north. Canada Centre for Inland Waters was holding a waste disposal conference—not the most glamorous part of my beat as they mainly dealt with sewage sludge and settling ponds, etc. And Toronto was still contemplating snow melters to deal with the snow next winter. I'm not sure how those fit into my environmental newsletter—certainly they are newsworthy but are they energy efficient and environmentally friendly?

Maybe Margaret would let me go to the CCIW conference. Not the most exciting subject for a conference, but it would be great to get out of the office and drive my car to their Burlington headquarters.

Pollution Probe had some new suggestions for recycling in the home—not really suitable for my business audience but very relevant for John and me personally. Reduce, reuse, recycle. There's curbside pickup for all kinds of recyclable things —aluminum cans, bottles and jars and newspapers—in The Beach neighbourhood, not too far from us, and Moira from the office lives there and lets me put recycled things by her curb. (She's not into recycling, but she respects the fact that I am.)

Most interesting of all was an article about wind buggies. How cool! They looked like tricycles, but they hugged the ground, and they had sails to power them. The one in my news release was called a Land Buggy. They were definitely environmentally friendly and energy efficient.

I'd love to see a wind buggy up close…

I went out at lunch and headed for a bargain store near Bloor and Yonge, just a 15-minute walk away. They had pants on sale for just five bucks! Unbelievable. It took a few minutes to find my size, but I did. A beautiful pair of lime green slacks with a checked pattern. And for six dollars, a lime-green T-shirt to match. Bingo!

Nevertheless, the long hours and incompatible boss are taking their toll. I'm always tired. The doctor says it's because I have iron-poor blood, so I'm taking pills for that. And today, by 4:30, I'd had it.

The day wasn't over yet. Gordon, the boss, had a special mailing he wanted to send out for the Directory and Almanac our company produced, and it was all hands on deck. Each of our newsletters needed to be collated, folded, and stuffed into envelopes, but the two Compugraphic operators handled those as part of their jobs. Sometimes we could hear them singing as they worked. Linda, in particular, had a beautiful voice.

But this was different—while our newsletters cost hundreds of dollars per subscription and went to a group of subscribers that numbered less than a thousand each, this mailing was unusual, and would go out to 4,000 people. When there was a mailing like this one, everyone's help was needed.

Gordon had a system—he laid the pages that had to be collated from front to back along the length of the boardroom table. The collators put the pages together and then stacked them, one collated piece laid horizontally on top of one laid vertically and so on. Then the folders did their job, careful to place each piece, folded in three, the same way so that they could easily be inserted into envelopes with the address showing through the window of the envelope. Gordon had the envelopes ready with their flaps open and facing toward the inserts so the envelope stuffer could put them in the envelopes with one fluid motion per piece. The last bits were annoying—using a plastic tube filled with water to "lick" the envelopes, and then putting stamps on them. I always tried to be a stuffer or a collator.

The system was brilliantly efficient, and it was something of a rite of passage. Everyone at Rosedale learned Gordon's system for sending out a mailing. I wasn't sure how Gordon had come up with it. Was it a time/motion study from his engineering days? Or did he come up with it when he was stuffing envelopes himself, finding ways to make the boring job go faster until he had it optimized. Certainly, I had invented ways to make the job go faster—counting mostly or keeping track of the number of pieces I had processed each hour and trying to beat my average.

It took eight of us, the boss included, two hours to stuff all those envelopes. By then it was 6:30 or so. The envelopes were neatly lined up in boxes, ready for the mail, and the boxes were stacked and put into bigger ones. Margaret had begged off, saying she would miss the GO Train that she used to commute to Oakville.

We all heaved sighs of relief when we were done, and were more than receptive when Gordon said, "Let's go to the pub. Food's on me."

One person begged off, saying she had to catch the subway home, but six of us were game. I knew that if John were true to form, he wouldn't be home for another two or three hours. And Barry was in the group too. I figured we could take the streetcar home together and I would be safe. It was, as my Dad would say, the big, bad city.

- - -

THE PUB WAS Korenowsky's, located a block south of Bloor and about halfway between Yonge and Church Streets, one subway stop or a 15-minute walk from work. There was a core gang of five or six people who went there often, usually on a Thursday night after work. I'd never been invited before. In fact, I'd barely even registered that people went and I wasn't invited. I did what I'd done all through high school and university—kept my head down and worked hard. But this time was different because the boss was coming, and he was treating.

So, I thought I'd give it a go.

We walked to Korenowsky's. I paired up with various people as we trudged down the icy, snowy sidewalks. With Moira, who ran the office, her best friend Linda, who did typesetting on the Compugraphic machine, Mark, one of the other editors, and Shazma, our accountant. I even talked to Gordon for a bit.

I talked too much—I always talk too much when I am nervous or in an unfamiliar situation. I know I talked too much because people kept moving away after I'd talked their ear off and then I'd repeat the process with someone else. Barry ended up walking beside me and by then I realized my mistake and didn't talk at all.

The pub was warm after our too-long walk in the bitter cold. I ordered a coffee while everyone else shared pitchers of beer.

"I don't drink much," I told the group when they asked if I wanted some beer. Which went over like a lead balloon.

Gordon gave Moira some money to pay for our food, teased a few people, had a beer and then left—reluctantly I thought—to head home to his wife and kids in the community just north of Rosedale.

At first, I just watched everyone, and felt like a fish out of water. Why on earth had I decided to go? The cigarette smoke was overpowering, especially since almost everyone else at our table smoked. Barry had a cigarette now and then, though he wasn't an addicted smoker. He was quite considerate about that at home. He always stood outside the back door on the rare occasions when he smoked. And he had a coffee can for any butts.

I concentrated on the live music, which was very good. The singer was doing "Leaving on a Jet Plane" by John Denver, one of my favourites. I almost sang along, but was glad I didn't when somebody said, "I hate John Denver. His songs are so sickeningly sweet."

"Who's your favourite singer?" Moira asked the table, as I steadfastly kept my mouth shut.

"I like jazz," Linda said. I knew that. I'd heard her humming jazz tunes at the office.

"The Bee-Gees," said Shazma.

"The Who," said Mark, who was a little older than the rest of us.

"I saw The Who once," said Barry; then looked as though he regretted the words.

"Really? Where did you see them?" Moira asked.

"Um. Out west," Barry said, and didn't elaborate further.

Finally, I had something to share with them. "I saw The Who too," I said. "In Toronto, when my favourite cousin came down for the summer. They were the opening act for Herman's Hermits back in 1967."

"What? That's amazing," said Shazma. I liked the way she talked. She came from Pakistan, and her voice was like velvet with a trace of an English accent from the international boarding schools she had attended. She was exactly my age, she was smart, and she was beautiful, with long, dark hair that curled around her shoulders and down her back. I liked her name too. She had told me once that it meant "rare moon."

"Herman's Hermits?" someone else said. "Really?"

Apparently, they were just as uncool as John Denver, but my story intrigued the group.

After that, the conversation flowed more easily. I got up the nerve to have some of the draft beer that was being passed around. The pizza and chicken wings Gordon had ordered arrived, and I had some of those too.

"So how do you like working with Margaret," asked Moira,

when the subject had turned to mild office gossip. She had a way of talking that showed that even though the question was serious, she had a bit of a smile showing she already knew the answer and had a strong opinion—not necessarily in Margaret's favour.

I rolled my eyes a bit and shrugged my shoulders.

"She's a tough old broad," Moira said. "You ever get fed up with her, come work with me on the directories. You did a great job on them when you were a student."

Later, when we were all slightly tipsy, Moira leaned back in her chair and mused, "We're all a bunch of misfits. You know, I think you have to be a bit odd to work at Rosedale.

"None of us has a traditional life, really. We work crazy hours when we're on deadline. We're not punching a time clock; we've got weird interests. I don't think any of us were on the football team or cheerleaders when we were in high school. We're mostly single; none of us has kids. We don't live in the suburbs, but in these quirky little apartments in houses."

"I'm not quite a misfit," I admitted, talking before I'd thought things through, as usual. "I'm married and I've got a house."

Moira gave me a friendly hug. "But you're odd, honey. You fit right in."

JOHN WAS NOT happy when Barry and I got home around 9:30 p.m. For once, we were later than he was. Barry said goodnight and went right downstairs.

"You smell like smoke," John said, clearly not happy with me. "You should have a bath before we go to bed."

I bristled. "Well, I went to a pub and all pubs have smoke,"

I said. "And it wasn't like I was missing out on time with you because you weren't here. You were at work."

"And you're drunk," he added.

"So? You have a few too many sometimes when you go out with people from work," I retorted. (I never would have said that if I hadn't had a few myself.)

"You should go have a bath," he repeated.

"Is that all you can think about, the smell of smoke?"

"No, all I can think about is that my wife goes out on the town and smells like crap, and I'm tired and want to go to bed and don't want to smell smoke and beer all night."

I couldn't think of anything to say back that wouldn't make things worse.

Chastised, I went to the bathroom, brushed my teeth, and drew a bath in our claw-foot tub with the fake pink tile panelling around it.

10: EARLY EXPLOSIONS
(Barry, 1967-69)

SO, MY LANDLADY, the kind but wacky one, had a fight with her husband recently. This wasn't totally out of the blue. I heard about the disastrous Christmas Party—I thought it was kind of a funny story. He was pretty upset after we came home from the pub. And she's pretty upset that he's always working and never home. These houses built in the '30s aren't great in terms of soundproofing or insulation, and there's a vent between the floors, so I could hear every word that was spoken upstairs in the living room.

John had recently landed a promotion at a major Toronto law firm, and Katie was really excited, John less so.

"That's super, John! That's what you've always wanted," Katie said enthusiastically.

"Yes, it's what I wanted, but we're going to have to make a few changes," John said.

"You'll be making a lot more money! We can do stuff to the house—maybe fix the bathroom, reinsulate? That would help us save on gas."

"I'll be making more money, sure, but I'll also be working more hours. There's a learning curve, and we're expected to come in early and stay late—even more so than when I was articling."

Katie was quiet. What he'd said wasn't terribly unexpected.

"And there's something else," John said, pausing as though he were mulling over the most tactful way to say something. Katie was quiet, waiting. That was unusual.

"You're going to have to change your image," John finally said.

"What?"

"Okay, I'm working all day with people who wear collar, tie and jacket to work, three-piece suits for the guys and suits with high heels for the women."

"The lady lawyers?" Katie asked.

"Not just them—the secretaries too. Everyone at the firm has to dress for success."

"And?"

"And we're going to be dealing with clients who have lots of money and dress well. Not like a hippie. Not like you did in high school. Not with stuff from bargain stores. We're going to have to go out and get you a new wardrobe. Like I said, dress for success."

I didn't hear anything from Katie. Not a good sign.

"And that hairstyle of yours has to go," John continued.

This time I did hear Katie. I heard muffled sobs, and I could picture the tears running down her cheeks as the words sunk in.

"I mean, you've got the basics—you're tall and slim…"

But those words came too late. I could hear her footsteps and sobs that became louder as she ran from the room and pounded up the stairs to the bedroom. I could hear Quincy following her—I hoped he'd help her feel better.

I now had an opinion about my landlady's husband. John. Was. A pompous asshole! Not the first lawyer I'd ever hated. Dylan's Dad had been the first.

BY LATE 1967, I had been out of school for a while. I had finished Grade 10 of the tech stream (barely) and my part time machinist job had evolved into an apprenticeship. Mary-Anne had finished as well and got a job as an apprentice hairdresser in a place that advertised Unisex hairstyles (for men and women).

The job with Harry in his small pattern-making shop suited me a lot better than school did. I needed my high school diploma if I were going to be a full-fledged machinist or tool-and-die maker, but my grade 10 meant I could be a metal patternmaker, shaping rough metal castings or blocks into patterns using the tools in the shop. It was demanding work—I needed to measure things to a thousandth of an inch; otherwise, they wouldn't work. But I was good at it. And the money was great. I earned a lot more working full-time than I had as a student part-timer. Instead of fetching things and cleaning the shop, I was starting to actually do the work. Harry was a good teacher, even though he still hassled me about my hair now and then.

I had the best of both worlds, living at home rent-free and earning good money, more than my college boy gang were earning with their lame summer jobs.

Going up to San Francisco to see Dylan on the weekends was a bit of a juggling act. Allan and I and sometimes Mary-Anne would head up on Fridays after we had finished work and school, and come back on Sunday night. I had to make sure I was sober for work, which was hard due to the way we our spent weekends at Dylan's. Sometimes I had a massive hangover headache on Monday mornings, which wasn't the best idea when you were measuring things to a thousandth of an inch.

Our trips to San Francisco weren't as much fun as they used to be. There were homeless people in the street, asking for money or drugs. The streets were dirty; there were way too many people around. But Dylan was still our best friend, even though he too was changing. He was angry. He was angry about Tom, which was kind of weird because he hadn't even visited Tom that much in the six months before he died. He was angry about the war, and he and his friends started talking about ways to stop it. There was already lots of anti-war protesting going on.

I was angry too, and deathly afraid that I would be drafted. The dreaded age was 18 and I was almost 17 now—just a year and a bit until I could be drafted. I was prime draft material too, as I wasn't in college or university, and they did need skilled tradespeople in the war. Allan and Dylan were old enough, but they were both in college.

I read LIFE magazine all the time, and the photos of the war were now gruesome ones. They even had photographers in the trenches. Even when I was a 10-year-old, eagerly looking at the pictures in the magazines Mom and Dad kept on our coffee table, LIFE was talking about the realities of the brutal war in Vietnam. I didn't think too much about it then. The Vietcong were the bad guys and the American GIs were the good guys. It was just like when we were playing. After all, I was a boy and it was the very early sixties, when all our games, indoors or out, involved fighting and guns. I liked it when their body counts were higher than ours.

Later on, there were pictures of people with heavily bandaged faces, helicopter pilots with mortally injured comrades, jungles on fire, and women and kids among the pictures of the "enemy." When Tom came back, all of a sudden, the war took on a different meaning. He'd been in those fiery jungles, seeing those women and children and perhaps killing some, and it had damaged him, permanently it seemed. My brother didn't die in the war physically—but ultimately, the war was what killed him.

The conversations changed, as we ate pizza, passed joints, and drank beer seated on the pillows and mattresses that served as chairs at Dylan's communal house in Haight-Ashbury. By the end of the Summer of Love, the Students for a Democratic Society had held a huge anti-war rally in Washington. Joan Baez and Judy Collins were there. I loved their music—they sang some of the tunes I had played on guitar for Tom.

I guess Dylan was attending at least some of his classes, because he had one of the profs from school visit us that night. That prof reminded me of Tom, or my Dad, because he took the opposing side just to get an argument going. At least I think he was testing everyone—Dylan would never have invited him if his views had been as contrary as he sounded. And among the group was Andy, brother of somebody, home on leave from the war.

"So, what do you think? Is [President] Johnson doing a good job," asked Larry, the prof, as he took a good, long toke from the joint being passed around.

"Don't think so," said Dylan dismissively. "What the hell are we doing in this war anyway? The North Vietnamese are just trying to get rid of foreign aggressors … us. They just want to run their country the way they see fit. I don't see why it's any of our business."

"Yes, but what if communism spreads? Do you want the U.S. to become communist?"

"Fat chance," said Dylan. "Senator McCarthy rooted out all the communists years ago. The war isn't a threat to us. It's just a waste of talented young Americans. And you've seen those photos… innocent Vietnamese peasants are getting caught in the crossfire."

"They're not innocent; even the kids are being recruited to fight the Americans," said the professor.

Beside him, Andy, the soldier on leave was nodding ever so slightly.

"That's not true," said Dylan.

"What about you," asked Dylan, turning to the soldier. "Are you happy to be going back to 'Nam?"

The soldier took his time to answer, drawing on the joint as it was passed to him. "No, I'm not eager to go back," was all he said.

"We can help end this war," said Dylan. "The protests and everything are helping, right?"

Again, the soldier drew slowly on the cigarette, pausing before he answered. "I think it will take a lot more than protests to end this war."

That was in 1967, at the end of the magical summer that was turning sour.

There was a five-page spread in LIFE magazine that fall, showing blown up bodies of U.S. soldiers in War Zone C. Apparently, those guys had come across a sign that said, "American who read this die," and then they were blown up.

By early 1968, the views on the war had changed again, as the North Vietnamese launched the Tet offensive. I guess we won, because the North Vietnamese didn't get the South Vietnamese to turn over to their side. But the whole thing was gruesome. The picture that affected me the most was in the newspaper—a photo of the South Vietnamese police shooting a prisoner in the head, a guy that looked just a little older than me. You could see the expression on that guy's face as the bullet was hitting him. The photographer caught the exact minute that he died. It was a powerful photo.

We started to see demonstrations by former veterans, many of them more obviously crippled than Tom, with wheelchairs and crutches, some with no legs. They were throwing away the medals they won in the war; that something was wrong with the war was obvious.

We started participating in the protests. It was heady stuff—

all those people who felt like we did. Protest signs. Marching. Shouting. Raising our fists in solidarity. I was particularly good at making the protest signs—the skills that made me so good at mechanical things and detailed work extended to my printing. The signs had various slogans—"End the War!" "End Imperialist aggression in Vietnam." "Free all anti-war GI prisoners." "I don't give a damn for Uncle Sam. I ain't goin' to Vietnam!"

We thought we were making a difference.

11: A CUP OF COFFEE WITH KATIE
(Barry, January 1977)

- - - - -

IT WAS SATURDAY. My landlady was in the kitchen, soaking the labels off bottles and cans so that she could recycle them on the curb at Moira's place, a mile or so away. She was wearing green checked pants and a long-sleeved lime green t-shirt to match—an outfit that made me think that maybe John had a point about the way she dressed.

Her hair was still wet, but although it was wet, even I could tell she had hacked it off herself. It's only halfway down her back now, one part is definitely shorter than the other parts and it doesn't look good. On the plus side, the plastic beaded elastic thingy that held it back was gone. Katie's eyes and face were wet too. I could tell that she had been crying.

I wanted to just sneak downstairs and mind my own business, but she sobbed more loudly when I entered the room, and I knew that wouldn't be possible.

"What's wrong," I asked tentatively, not sure what her reaction would be.

"Oh, Barry," she said, still looking down and scraping the label off a can. "John wants me to get a haircut, and I cut it myself and it looks awful," she said. "I hate hairdressers. They never do what I ask them to. I've been growing my hair since I was 14, and now I've ruined it."

I gave her a look that I hoped was sympathetic, but I didn't know what to say. I knew something about hair issues too…

When she raised her red-rimmed eyes and looked straight at me, I knew I had to say something.

"Um, I'm not exactly an expert when it comes to ladies' hairstyles," I said, shrugging my shoulders. "It's still pretty long," I added lamely. "Maybe you can put it in a ponytail," I added.

She returned to her task, scrubbing at the glue on the can with a wire net. It looked like she was taking her frustrations out on that poor can.

"He hates me," she sobbed, her tears falling into the sink. "I've known John half my life and we've never had fights like this before. It's like he's looking at me and I'm not good enough. I just don't measure up. He doesn't like my looks. He doesn't like my clothes. He's the one who said I should cut my hair," she repeated, winding a strand around her finger with her soapy hand.

The can was totally clean, but she was still scrubbing. I have never been good at handling situations like this. I wished I could retreat to the basement, but something kept me rooted to the spot.

I looked over to the Formica table and thought about what my mother would do when someone was as upset as Katie. My mother, who I would probably never see again.

"Um, maybe I can make you a cup of coffee," I said, knowing how much she loved the stuff. "Maybe we should sit down at the table."

She turned off the tap and dumped a bunch of other cans into the water in the sink to help soak off the labels. And then she sat down at the table. I found some Kleenex and gave it to her. Quincy, who had been sitting mournfully in a corner of the kitchen, came over and rested his big head on her lap. Stroking his massive head seemed to calm her down just a little.

Crap, the dog was better suited for this than I was.

"Can you make me a cup of tea?" Katie asked between sniffles.

"Um, I don't know how to make tea," I said. "Do I just boil the kettle and put the bag in the cup?"

"I thought you came from Vancouver, the home of Murchie's Tea. Home to lots of people from England…" She had stopped crying for a second, and I realized she was trying to tease me. She didn't know how sensitive I was on the subject of Vancouver.

"My family didn't drink tea," I said. "But we did drink lots of coffee. And most days when I get into Rosedale, I make a pot."

"I think everyone at Rosedale makes a pot… Coffee it is, then," she said. "Sometime I'll have to teach you how to make a proper cup of tea. You don't just put a bag in a cup," she added disdainfully.

I putzed around the kitchen, finding the coffee, cups, cream, sugar and spoons, with a bit of direction from Katie. I usually made my own coffee down in my room, and I don't drink nearly as much as she does.

"So tell me about the house," I said just to change the subject. "How did you and John come to live here?"

Get her talking about something else. That was the technique my mother used. To calm us down, she would get us talking about something ordinary, something safe.

Katie told me about how she didn't want to live in the suburbs, that there were certain things she and John looked for in a house, that their real estate agent didn't understand them, and that they'd come to the east end of Toronto because it was less expensive than the west end.

The tears started to dry up as she got into her story. It had too many details, and she talked too fast, but at least she wasn't crying. She wiped the last of the sniffles away with her sleeve of her lime-green top.

It wasn't until later that I had the idea. Shazma at work was well-dressed and gorgeous. And she was about Katie's age. Maybe she could help Katie "dress for success."

12: PREPARING FOR THE BIG ONE
(Barry, 1969-70)

SO, NOW I'M getting into the reasons why I can never see my mother again. Or Tom, of course, and probably Dylan and Allan.

First, we started protesting on our weekends in San Francisco, or on road trips with Dylan to other places. We were among the millions of young people across America protesting the war. Dylan was super involved, writing anti-war articles in campus underground newspapers and posting paper signs on every available surface. We would also make our own cardboard signs mounted on sticks and march and yell slogans. At first, it felt good—American democracy at its best. In other countries, we could be arrested or shot, but here we had freedom of speech.

Until we didn't. In the early days, the cops stood by to keep things under control, but they didn't hurt anybody. But then, people started being arrested. And the cops started using their shields and batons. That's when we started calling them "the pigs."

The protest that caused us to look at more radical measures wasn't even about Vietnam. It was about some park people had created in Berkeley. A bunch of people had planted stuff in the so-called "People's Park" and the university wanted to take over the land. People had been occupying the park for weeks, objecting to the takeover. So, on May 9, 1969, we protested. It wasn't even a weekend—it was a Thursday, but by then Allan and I thought nothing of making the trip to San Francisco to help Dylan in one of his causes. But that day, the police didn't just stand there and keep the protest contained. They used tear gas and rifles loaded with birdshot against the young protesters. One guy died, many were injured, and we heard later that another one was crippled for life. It was like we were in Vietnam and the pigs thought we were the Vietcong. And this was America!

Dylan was hit hard in the head by a baton—I'm sure he had a concussion, and the wound was bleeding. Allan and I had to support him as blood streamed from his head wound. Worse than that was the abuse that was hurled at us as we limped through the streets. "Fuckin' hippie communists. Serves you right!" said one older man with a crew cut, glaring at us with pure hatred. "You hippies don't know a thing about Vietnam. You should be proud to serve your country," said another younger man, possibly a recent vet. Hell! We weren't even protesting Vietnam that day—it was all about saving a plot of land that people like us had nurtured and cared for.

Maybe it was the blow to the head or maybe it was the anger we were all feeling against the establishment, and in particular the pigs. But Dylan's focus changed completely. "Nobody messes with Dylan Hearst," he would say angrily. "Fuck the establishment. Fuck the pigs! Fuck Nixon! Fuck Vietnam!"

The dialogue in the crowded house in Haight-Ashbury changed again. "I think it will take a lot more than protests to end this war," the young soldier visiting the house had said. It was Dylan who decided what those next steps would be.

"We could blow something up," said Dylan, and it was partly because we were high on something much stronger than marijuana that I nodded and accepted that this was indeed a good idea. And for me, my agreement was fuelled by fear. If this war continued, I could go to that horrible place, shoot mothers and children, and end up like Tom.

Dylan became more and more radical, but it was Allan who had the logistics all figured out. Bombs can be made from all kinds of common stuff like fertilizer and fuel oil. We could make the bombs and drop them from the air or maybe do an explosion using a truck—he hadn't totally figured that one out. But he had some targets in mind. What better way to fight the war than to blow up the places that researched and made weapons?

Dylan was stoked. Instead of just protesting the war, he could finally do something about it. And thanks to his Daddy's generous allowance, he had the funds to make it happen.

- - -

WE STARTED MAKING bombs. It was Allan and Dylan who led the charge; I like to think I was a reluctant participant. But I did participate. I can't change that, and I really can't justify that now. Except to say that for me it was all about Tom, all about ending the Vietnam War, and all about my fear that I would have to go to Vietnam too.

There was more to our reasoning. Part of the reason why Allan and I got involved, was because of what our Dad had told us years before. "The people of Germany had no idea of the death and destruction their bombs were causing until the Allies started bombing their country. Then it hit home. When they started dropping bombs on places like Dresden—well, that was a turning point in the war." Dad talked about Japan too—how the atomic bombs in Hiroshima and Nagasaki on Japanese soil, were what ended the war in the Pacific. In the same way, President Nixon and his cronies had no idea of the destruction their bombs were causing in Vietnam. They were turning a blind eye to it all. What better way to drive the point home than to release bombs here in the U.S.? Preferably blowing up military targets.

Preferably places whose destruction would deliver the anti-war message loud and clear.

Allan had the technical know-how to put bombs together, and I don't think it really registered with him that bombs can cause damage and kill people. Building a bomb was just a challenge to him—a way to use his inventive mind and scientific know-how.

And Dylan—well, Dylan was a natural born leader who constantly recreated himself. When we were little, Dylan came up with ideas for games, Tom helped direct what we'd do, and Allan and I would play our parts, whether it was Cops and Robbers, Hide and Seek, or Mother May I. Tom sort of tempered Dylan in those days—if he came up with something that was too dangerous or too crazy, Tom would usually talk him out of it.

In high school, Dylan played football and then surfed. That's when he got the Mustang and started driving faster and more dangerously. His hair got longer and blonder and he had lots of girlfriends. He'd go all the way with them and then ditch them. I think one girl even got pregnant. Dylan was like a magnet—people couldn't help but be drawn to him. But I didn't like the way he treated those girls. I would never have treated Mary-Anne like that.

Mary-Anne—I probably won't ever see her again, either.

"Scottie, the problem with you is that you're too easily led," my mother said to me after a conversation where Dylan's name was front and centre. She probably had a point.

The People's Park protest was our last in San Francisco. After he flunked out of school yet again, Dylan's parents finally got tired of funding his student career in San Francisco—they told him he had to return home. He enrolled in a college—one of the lesser-known ones, not UCLA or anything. So, we had to find a target in L.A.

If Allan was the technical guy, then Dylan specialized in P.R. He wrote articles in campus newsletter and followed the moves of the Students for a Democratic Society, and later, the more radical Weathermen. The Weathermen believed that by stoking violence in the U.S., they could distract the politicians enough to get them to withdraw from Vietnam. Dylan was a good writer, and he had always been persuasive. I'm sure he got those talents from his lawyer Dad, who was always being quoted in the news. His Dad was using his talents to promote the status quo; while Dylan wanted everything to change.

My role in all of this was to be the gopher. They sent me to buy the stuff we needed in our bombs, using a fake I.D. that said I was older than I looked. I like to think that I didn't really pay much attention to all of Dylan's speeches and writing and all of Allan's technical manoeuvring—though I probably should have. I kept recalling my Dad's words about World War II Germany and Japan, and my own mantra. I was doing this for Tom.

At first, we were really lousy at doing bombings. We left a bomb in a mailbox in front of the local army recruitment centre in downtown L.A., but the timing was off, and it failed to blow up. The next time, we got the timing right, and the bomb did explode, but then it fizzled out because it was raining. Raining? California was supposed to be in a constant drought. Go figure. The third time, we got the wrong building. We were supposed to be bombing the ROTC building to protest their military scholarships, but we ended up bombing a gym instead.

That was all in 1969.

Nineteen-seventy was a new year—we needed better planning and organization if we were going to make our point. Back to the drawing board. Go big or go home, Dylan said. We started working on a plan to bomb one of the research centres involved with Dow Chemical, the L.A. Research Center. They were the ones making those napalm bombs that were ruining the lives of everyone exposed to them.

Then the Kent State massacre happened in early May, and that was a good reason to speed up our plans. It was People's Park all over again. This time the National Guard killed four protesters. And this time, they were protesting Vietnam.

Go big. Dylan came up with the idea of using a van—a vehicle not tied to any of us, preferably unregistered or with a fake license plate. We could load it up with bomb materials and then light the fuse. Allan knew exactly what should go inside the van—huge drums of fertilizer and fuel oil. That would create quite a blast. All we needed was to figure out how to get five things—van, fake license plate, fertilizer, fuel oil and dynamite—and a place where we could put together such a massive bomb. We needed a hideout of some sort.

13: THE SUPERINTENDENT & THE HAIRCUT
(Katie, Feburary 1977)

BARRY WAS NICE when I was so upset about John, even if he has no clue how to make tea. And he had a good idea—I should talk to Shazma about changing my looks a bit to make John happy.

Shazma was smart as well as beautiful. She had one accounting degree and was studying at night for another, and she did the books for the company. She wasn't beautiful in a Barbie-doll way with ordinary business suits and blouses and a lacquered bob to match—she had strong facial features and I think she got her clothes at a Vintage store or something. She always looked well dressed, but her clothes weren't the same as everyone else's. You could tell they were high quality, but they were also unique. And that hair—thick, curly, long and black, the exact opposite of mine, which was brown, straight, limp and only sort-of long, since I'd hacked off half of it with the scissors.

It took me awhile to get up the nerve to ask for her help, but then I remembered how nice she'd been at the pub. We were the same age too, the youngest two in the office. Maybe we'd have some things in common.

I asked her to go for lunch at Luigi's Trattoria, the Italian place on Yonge between Bloor and the Canadian Tire store. We had what was probably too good a time, as we had wine with lunch, and I found it very hard to concentrate that afternoon!

We're going to go shopping on Saturday, and she's going to make me an appointment at the unisex hair salon, House of Lords, on Yonge Street. They're the most popular place in Toronto these days, and they've catered to rock stars like Mick Jagger. Not that I want to look like Mick Jagger. I have a photo of the Charlie's Angels star, Farrah Fawcett, who has a hairstyle I like. The idea is to hand it to the stylist (not hairdresser) and let him or her work their magic. I must admit that I'm nervous—I haven't had a haircut in almost 10 years, other than my lousy, self-administered one. But I trust Shazma. And hopefully, John will be happy. In the meantime, I am wearing my hair in a ponytail. It doesn't look noticeably horrible.

And I will investigate getting those contact lenses…

- - -

MOM AND DAD came over to our house for dinner on Friday night. I made lasagna from scratch. I'm learning to cook better now that John and I are out on our own. My specialty is anything made from hamburger, as that is the cheapest meat around. Lasagna was an experiment, but it turned out well. The recipe was from The Joy of Cooking, a big thick book I got when we had the housewarming party with our friends just after we moved in last fall.

Dad didn't notice my hair, but Mom did. "What have you done," she asked. "It's okay," I said. "I have an appointment for tomorrow to get it fixed."

She didn't look too convinced. Mom and I have never seen eye to eye on fashion or hairstyles. She thinks I should have a short, poufy "do" that "frames my face"—a style more suitable for her generation than mine!

Enough about looks—they really shouldn't be so important.

Dad, being the Superintendent of the division responsible for our area, talked about the crime rate, asked to see our locks, and gave me all sorts of unsolicited advice about staying safe in the neighbourhood, which had its share of robberies and even a few assaults. No murders recently, though.

I tried to bring the conversation around to topics that were near and dear to my heart, such as environmental control, energy conservation and getting more women into business.

Thank goodness John took over the conversation, talking about his boss, his fellow lawyers, the long hours he had to work and his recent promotion. Mom and Dad liked John. While they had commented about him being a geek when we first got together, they had always been in favour of the relationship. And John's approval rating shot up dramatically when he entered law school. They thought I had married well. He was a young man on his way up in the world, and for people like them who grew up in the Depression, that was what counted.

I was glad John was home. I was glad John was talking. But I was still smarting from his remarks the other night.

Barry came in while we were having dinner. He has to go through the kitchen to reach his room in the basement.

For the first time, I saw him from Mom and Dad's point of view: gangly, shy, with longish hair and more than a little scruffy.

"This is Barry. He rents the basement apartment. Barry, this is my Dad, Robert, and my Mom, Virginia."

Mom held out her hand for a handshake. "Ginny, actually. You can call me Ginny."

Barry shook Mom's hand and then held out his hand. Dad gave it a powerful shake.

"So, are you a Toronto guy, Barry?" Dad asked. Dad wasn't great on small talk. He was more used to interrogating suspects and giving orders to staff.

"Yup, I've lived in Toronto for a while, now," Barry said,

nodding his head lazily.

"And before that," Dad prompted.

"I'm from out west," Barry replied.

"Vancouver?" Barry nodded almost imperceptibly. I had never actually heard him say he was from Vancouver, but everyone seemed to have that impression.

"Ever been to the East Side?" Dad asked.

"Yeah," said Barry. There was a gap in the conversation. "Nice," he said.

Dad's look was hard to read.

Barry was never much for small talk either. "Well, I'll be going downstairs now," he said. And opened the door to the basement, nodding good-bye shyly, with a little wave.

Dad watched the door for far longer than it took Barry to close it and go down the stairs.

"That guy's not from Vancouver. The East Side of Vancouver is a haven for druggies and prostitutes. It is not 'nice'," Dad said.

"Well, he did live in a commune for a while, so maybe his standards are a little different from yours," I said in Barry's defence.

Dad looked straight at me. "He's not from Vancouver," Dad said, with a penetrating look right at me.

I didn't know what to say.

"And he has a bit of an accent too… Not sure what kind, but it's there."

Thank goodness John intervened by talking more about work, and a case that had a tie to Vancouver. I was grateful that Dad and John could find common ground; they had a pretty good relationship.

Mom and I were okay, even though she always thought I should do things like cheerleading and joining a sorority when I was growing up, but I couldn't say that Dad had a good relationship with me.

ON SATURDAY, I met Shazma outside the Bloor-Yonge Subway and we walked to the House of Lords, the "in" place to get a haircut in Toronto. I wore my green velour tracksuit under my puffer jacket, while Shazma had on flared jeans and an untucked shirt, when she took off her sheepskin coat. She looked every bit as gorgeous in her casual clothes as she did in the long dresses, peasant blouses and calf-length skirts she wore to work.

Shazma flipped back her hair and looked at the photo of Charlie's Angels, including Farrah Fawcett, who had the long, curling hair look I wanted. Shazma had a look that was similar, except her hair was black, not ash blonde like Farrah's. She showed it to the stylist, who ran her fingers through my lank, mouse brown locks. "Let's see what we can do," he said.

14: DRAFT CARD
(Barry, 1969)

MY LANDLADY IS still a bit strange, but she is looking a lot better these days. The haircut makes a big difference, even though she moans on and on about how they cut her hair too short. It's shoulder-length with bangs, and it looks a lot better than when she pulled the top part back and put that silly-looking elastic bauble thingy in it. And she's working on ditching the glasses for contact lenses too.

John told her she looked nice, but he's still an ass. He still works all the time and is never home. He still criticizes her for everything. He doesn't seem to mind all the strange energy-conserving stuff, but he tells her she talks too much (which she does) and that she must get new clothes before he can take her to functions where she will play the role of corporate wife.

I'm not sure why those two got married. Must have been something left over from high school or college… They sure didn't seem like a good fit now.

I missed the Sky-Fi sound system one of the other renters, Eric, had scored in the "commune". (No idea where he got it and I didn't ask. Probably contra for some drugs or something.) And even though I had the TV, my radio was primitive. But both TV and radio served the same purpose: they were loud enough to drown out John and Katie's bickering upstairs.

IN FEBRUARY 1969, I had to register for the draft. It was the law—all men over age 18 had to do it. I didn't want to register, but I did so reluctantly. After Tom's experience and all those full-page photos in LIFE magazine, the war had no appeal whatsoever. Hard to believe that just five short years earlier, Dylan, Allan and I had cheerfully wished Tom well on his big overseas adventure.

They couldn't actually draft me until I was 19, though, so I had one more year of possible freedom. But once I turned 19, I was a perfect choice for the draft. The government was ramping up the whole draft process and closing the loopholes that had got people out of it before. The biggest group of draftees was men who were between the ages of 19 and 25, who weren't deferred for some reason or other. I wasn't in college, and as of this year, the focus was on drafting 19-year-olds. If this continued, I would be prime to go to war next year. I had one chance—that was to go to college to become a tool and die maker. I could do the work no problem, given my mechanical abilities and attention to detail, but I didn't have my grade 12 and that was a important qualification.

What to do? Go back to school to get Grade 12? That would take two years and I'd be way older than all the kids in my class. Only then could I enroll to be a tool and die maker.

I didn't want to go to war, and that made me very receptive to Dylan and Allan and their protest plans.

15: THE WIND BUGGY
(Katie, March 1977)

I'M NOT SURE what's got into John these days. He's so irritable and critical. I'm not sure what I'm doing wrong. We always got along so well, all through high school and college. But now that he's becoming a real lawyer, it seems like everything I do is wrong. He liked my haircut, but he didn't like the clothes I bought with Shazma. Too hippie-dippy, he said, and I really didn't like the nasty way he said it. All I could see is that maybe they were a little casual for a lawyer's office, where they all wore suits—three-piece suits with the vest and all, and ties and matching handkerchiefs; skirts and stilettos for the women

All of a sudden, John was very particular about his ties. He had lots of them even before he started this new stage of our lives. But none of them would do. And he couldn't just buy something off the rack at Eaton's any more. He liked Frank Stollery's, the upscale men's store at Bloor and Yonge. The ties there cost about three times as much as they did at Eaton's, and I personally couldn't see any difference.

It was Saturday. I'd prepared a fast and early dinner for us to eat—spaghetti and meatballs, using spaghetti sauce I'd made and frozen. I also made some Caesar Salad. My family has a special recipe for this, with real egg yolks, bacon bits and croutons, and it's one of John's favourites. After supper, I thought we would go to the park at the foot of Park Lawn Road, where they were demonstrating some wind buggies. We'd have to eat quickly, because the wind buggy demo started at 5:30. John had promised me that he'd leave work by 3:00 p.m. and get home by

4:00. Yes, John was working on the weekend. It appears lawyers work every day (and night) of the week.

I'd been sneaking stories about the wind buggy into the News Briefs section of ECO. I wasn't crazy enough to think it was an energy-saving alternative to the car, but I was just crazy enough to want to see how it worked. Sort of like a sailboat on land, as far as I could tell. Sailing on land would be fun! Even though my heart knew it wasn't practical, I got a kick out of imagining a wind buggy parked on our street among the Hondas and Pintos and our rusty Maverick.

And it was such a beautiful day, one of the first following what had been a cold and nasty winter. The sun was out, and a breeze was blowing. It was a perfect wind-buggy-demo day.

I'd set the table with care, even though it was to be a quick meal. If my mother had taught me one thing, it was the importance of setting the table properly and sitting down to dinner as a family. Our family had always eaten in the dining room, and we often went to her place on Sundays for roast beef and potatoes. There was no formal dining room in our house, rather a round table and acrylic chairs in the large, wallpapered kitchen. (That wallpaper had to go. It was a large-weave plaid design overlaid with pears and apples. Not quite my style. Not quite my mother's style even; maybe my grandmother's. We had bought the house from an old couple, who probably hadn't changed the décor in decades!)

The table was set, the spaghetti and Caesar salad were served. But where was John? At 4:00 p.m., I started pacing the kitchen. At 4:30, I called his office. No answer. I nibbled on the spaghetti and Caesar salad myself. By 4:45, I was royally ticked off. I had to let off steam somehow. I stormed down the stairs to tell Barry what had happened. The tears rolled down my face as I railed on about how unreliable John had become. And then it all came pouring out—how I couldn't do anything right, how John was never around any more, and how such a beautiful day was being wasted by him working at his bloody office again! "Is he sleeping there?" I asked Barry.

Barry looked taken aback to say the least. I guessed he didn't have sisters, so he wasn't familiar with emotional women like me.

"I'm going to go anyway," I ranted. "If I take the car, I can get there on time."

Barry shook his head, no. "You're in no mood to drive," he said, from where he sat on the bed. "Maybe, I should go with you."

"But you don't drive," I said.

"I can," he said with a glint in his eye. "But you're right, I don't have a license. Makes no sense since I can't afford a car.

"But I can go with you… maybe calm you down a bit.

"And Quincy could come too," he added. "He always makes you feel good."

I looked behind me to see Quincy's mournful face. My moods always made him sad too. I gave him a big hug and felt marginally better.

"I've never seen a wind buggy," Barry said.

"Okay, just let me clean up the kitchen a bit," I said.

"And put some sunglasses on," Barry added. "So people don't see you've been crying."

Ten minutes later, the three of us were seated in our 1970 Maverick, which had a great engine, but was more rust than car. Quincy panted in the back seat, his head leaning into the front, between the two of ours. We passed John coming from the bus stop on the way home. But I didn't care. I was angry with him at that point.

THE WIND BUGGIES were very cool. I didn't get to drive one, but I did get to admire them, sitting on a grassy hill with Barry and Quincy, as they sailed like land-bound ships across the parking lot, the drivers maneuvering the sails just as they would on the sea.

We took Quincy for a walk on the park trails after the demo was finished. It was twilight, and we could see that new landmark, the CN tower, across the water, along with the big bank towers—the three TD ones, designed by some famous Dutch architect, van der something, and the Bank of Montreal tower. There weren't just banks in those towers—John's legal firm was in one of them. But I didn't want to think about him. It just made me madder and madder.

It was nice walking with Barry and Quincy. He didn't talk much, and for once I didn't either. There weren't many people there, so we could take Quincy off his leash, and watch him bound along the trails. A big dog like that needed to run, and it was heart-warming to watch him. At times he seemed like the old dog he was supposed to be—70 in dog years, and that was old for a big dog. At times, I noticed the gray in his muzzle, the yellow on his old teeth. But at times like this, he was no different from the puppy who had come into my life when I was just 14.

We got home around 9:00 p.m. John had gone to bed already. I guess that when lawyers aren't working, they're sleeping. No in-between time, really. So, I brought out the lasagna, and heated it up in the oven. I got the Caesar salad out of the fridge. It was a little soggy, but not too bad. I reset the table and pulled out a bottle of white wine.

"Do you drink wine?" I asked Barry. Funny, I didn't even know if he did, although he had lived at our place for almost four months. I knew from the pub that he liked beer, but I had no idea whether he drank wine.

"I'll have a glass," Barry said.

"So, tell me a bit about yourself," I asked in my best journalistic interview voice once we were sitting down with a glass of wine. I didn't turn the lights off and light candles as I might have done on special occasions with John. That would be overkill.

Barry looked a bit shy and uncomfortable with my questions. I guessed he didn't like being the focus of the conversation. "Not much to tell," he said.

"Where do your parents live? Do you have sisters or brothers?" I persisted.

"My parents aren't around, and I don't see my brothers," Barry said briefly.

"Why not?" I asked him.

"We just don't get together," Barry said, and that was the end of that topic of conversation.

He turned the conversation around to me. "How about you? I don't think I've heard you talk about any brothers or sisters, so I'm assuming you are an only child," he said.

"That's right," I said. "I'm an only child. The apple of my parents' eye."

"I believe that," he said, nodding slowly.

"I was being ironic," I said. "They actually don't approve of anything I do, other than the fact that I married a lawyer."

"And how about Quincy?" he asked, stroking the big mutt's silky ears, the only part of him that didn't look like a German Shepherd, as they flopped downward, more like the ears of a Lab or a Saint Bernard. Those ears gave him a friendly look, even though he was huge and powerful.

Okay, he'd happened on one of my favourite subjects. "We found him by the side of the road," I said. "Not far from Highway 427, on the other side of a fence, on the grounds of the high school near our old house. I went home and somehow convinced Dad to take the car around to pick him up. My best friend, Allison, stayed there to make sure he didn't get away. I can't believe someone left him there. He was such a cute little guy. But they must have known that someone would find him at the high school. They didn't leave him on the highway or anything."

I was in a much better mood now, having a nice dinnertime conversation after a pleasant walk in the park. Quincy, whose moods always reflected my own, had curled up on the floor beside the table, his head resting on Barry's shoe.

It was only later, after I'd crawled into bed beside John, that it hit me. John and I were not doing well. And tears ran down my cheeks as I thought about all our dreams, the kids we planned to have who would have his dark, curly hair and my height. And then my mind started going new places as I lay awake in the dark. Do lawyers really work those long hours? Or was there someone else in his life? John was snoring, immovable; he had always been a deep sleeper.

16: THE BIG ONE
(Barry, March 1970)

- - - - -

MY POOR LANDLADY is going through a tough time. She keeps trying to please that stupid lawyer husband of hers, and nothing she does is good enough. She keeps talking about how they have known each other forever from their time in the leafy, quiet, and probably totally boring suburb where they grew up.

That suburb probably wasn't so different from Hermosa Beach—other than the climate and the freezing cold, no beach and trees that were totally different, of course. Our suburb had cookie cutter homes, and wide streets designed for cars, not people. The only reason our suburb wasn't boring is that I hung out with Tom, Allan and Dylan, we had wheels, and I was always doing stuff with kids three to five years older than me. I sure didn't compete for marks in school. I hung out with the tech kids, smoked in the back of the school or in the washrooms, and quit school as soon as I could.

When I came upstairs on Saturday afternoon, she was bawling her eyes out because John was supposed to be home and he'd let her down. Again. I've always been a bit of a sucker for tears, and sometimes it's gotten me into trouble. My Mom tells everyone that even as a toddler, I would give someone a hug if they were crying. I remember I would give Mom hugs if she was upset, up until Tom came back from Vietnam. We had that kind of relationship until I was about 15. And then I became a rotten teenager, and Dylan turned out to be a "bad influence" or "the wrong crowd."

I would give anything to be able to give Mom a hug right

now. In some ways, she's lost all three of her sons. Tom's gone, and Allan and I can't go home. She still has Dad, of course.

Mary-Anne liked my hugs—she was volatile sometimes and I guess I was a calming influence. When I wasn't doing dumb stuff with Dylan and Allan.

Weird or not, my landlady has always been nice to me. So, I asked her what was wrong and ended up going with her and Quincy to see the wind buggies. I actually had a good time. It was perfect weather for the buggies—there were two of them—a sunny but windy and cold March day. We walked Quincy afterward. That dog is so cool. Sometimes when I miss my childhood in Hermosa Beach, I think of the little dog we had as kids. Sometimes Quincy comes to visit me in the basement and puts his big head on my knee when I watch the boob tube, as Dad used to call the television.

- - -

IN MAY, 1970, we found a place to build our bomb. It wasn't far from a secondary highway, down a barely passable trail and hidden by a grove of trees. We had no clue who owned it, but that didn't matter as long as no one could see what we were doing or link it to us.

"Are you sure this location is going to work?" asked Allan, as he sat on an upturned tree stump surrounded by dry grass, doing calculations and sketches on a pad of graph paper. Dylan was lounging against a tree, while I sat cross-legged on the ground.

"There's never been anyone here, any time I came here," said Dylan. "It's a great place to bring girls… totally deserted," he quipped. I didn't respond with the smile Dylan expected. I was not totally on board with how he treated the women he dated.

"What do you think, Al? What do we need to do this?" Dylan asked.

Allan didn't like being called 'Al,' but he would tolerate it from Dylan.

We stood there awhile, while Allan deliberated. He wasn't one to give quick answers—he'd only talk when he was ready to do so. Dylan nudged Allan's shoulders a bit, and Allan responded with an irritated shrug.

"We'll need a van," he said finally. "A really big van."

"How about a Travco RV?" I said. "Or one of those Ford Econoline vans?"

Allan was still on his own train of thought. "We could strip out the insides and have barrels of ammonium nitrate and fuel oil in there. Then we'd need something to blow it all up remotely."

"Allan, what kind of van?" I was persistent. If there was one thing I knew about, it was cars.

He was still lost in his own little world. "Yeah, Econoline," he said absent-mindedly.

"How will we get the van?" I asked.

Dylan looked at me as though I was a moron.

"We'll steal one, of course," he said.

I could do that. I could do it for Tom.

- - -

JUST WHAT THE target would be was something we debated all the time. We thought seriously about bombing Dow Chemical or Monsanto, makers of Agent Orange, or one of the army induction centres. We focused on an army induction centre in downtown L.A., where soldiers were screened for army service, but rejected that target. It would be too hard to unleash a van full of explosives in the middle of the city without blowing ourselves up too. And we didn't really want to risk hurting any soldiers—the point was to show that war was wrong, not hurt the poor suckers who had to go off to war. Besides other groups had already targeted that place with protests, so the security was probably tight around that building. We needed somewhere that would make our point; that was in a large, open space; and wasn't well guarded. We planned to set off our bomb late at night, when the explosion would have maximum visual effect, but wouldn't kill anybody.

A tall order. And then we realized that our answer was in the hills close to the Dylan's university campus—a research facility that developed warheads was located very close by. In May 1970, Allan got himself a summer job at the facility. We figured that if we could park a van loaded with explosive materials in the loading dock area of the building, and then light a fuse from a distance, it would do significant damage. At night, of course, when no one was working.

Allan was a big part of our plan. He'd arranged with one of his professors to work at the research facility. He was smart enough, and he looked straight and clean cut enough that no one could possibly expect that he was involved with radicals like Dylan and me. And he was free to work there any time of day or night.

Early Sunday morning, June 28, 1970, was the date we chose. A fitting date, as it was Tom's birthday. Tom, of course, had cared less and less about birthdays and living in general in his final months. It was a month after the National Guard had shot four protesters at Kent State University. Even though that event had taken place far away in Ohio, it fuelled the rage of protesters all over the States, including here in California.

We'd packed a van with dynamite, and barrels of fuel oil and ammonium nitrate fertilizer. It was tricky to get all that stuff. We got the van. We didn't have to steal one after all. We got it cheap from a guy through the want ads. It was a clunker, but I enlisted Dad to help me fix it, and got it to work just fine, so that Allan could drive it to his summer job. Stripping the insides made sense because Allan sometimes needed to transport stuff for his job. I felt kind of bad that Dad had worked so hard to fix the thing, when there's no way he would knowingly have helped with our plan.

It was my job to get the ammonium nitrate fertilizer from farm supply stores, telling the storekeepers that I was working with my uncle on a farm for the summer, and that I needed bagged ammonium nitrate fertilizer. Allan was specific—we needed the kind that contained 33.3 per cent nitrogen. I don't think anyone suspected my ultimate purpose, even though the kind of fertilizer we wanted was usually used to blast holes for agricultural ponds. I bought it in lots of different stores, one bag at a time, so the quantities weren't suspicious. We paid cash too—and that helped if any of the people at the stores had qualms about selling it to me. All together, we bought 1,500 pounds of ammonium nitrate fertilizer—or 30 50-pound bags. The bags were super heavy, but we could fit a few at a time into the back of the van, and then take them to our assembly site.

If we were to follow Allan's plans, we needed 50 gallons of fuel oil, but more importantly, we needed five or six of the 55-gallon drums that fuel oil generally came in. Allan and I canvassed several service stations about fuel oil and getting some of those big drums. No one had the drums, and they looked puzzled about why we would need them.

Luckily, we'd started early in our search for the drums,

because they proved so hard to buy. And then one day, Dylan came upon a deserted construction site with several empty barrels. Late at night, shortly before the bombing, all three of us loaded those barrels into the back of the van. Then we went to a Texaco and bought the fuel oil, carefully measuring it into the drums so that each one contained an equal amount.

We returned to our assembly site, and then added the fertilizer.

And dynamite? Well, we left that to Dylan. I really didn't want to know where he got the dynamite, because it probably wasn't legal.

On the Friday night, we'd brought a few beers up to the assembly site, and we toasted our plans before heading home to get a good sleep and be ready for the next day. I personally could not sleep a wink. It was the adrenaline, the anticipation. At 4:10 a.m., still tossing and wide-awake, I calculated: in 24 hours, it would all be over.

- - -

ALLAN HAD DRIVEN the van into the parking lot earlier on the day before the bombing—no problem as he'd driven that van in there before and it was on the security list of approved vehicles. He parked in a normal parking spot and went inside to do some work. He stayed late, checking before he went out that he was the last to leave. At 3:30 a.m., long after the researchers had left for the day, he parked the van close to the building's loading dock. He'd done that before to load and unload stuff for his job, so he figured no one would think anything of it. They knew nothing about the cargo it carried. And then he joined us, hundreds of feet away hiding in the bushes, where Dylan held the detonator that would make it all happen.

The building was darker than the night, just a few lights left on for security purposes. The three of us huddled in the chilly June evening, under an evergreen bush whose dried out needles scratched our skin. The soil beneath our feet was covered in needles that had dropped during an unusually dry spring. The only sound was the whoosh of cars going by on the nearby freeway.

Quiet, but not for long. Our hearts were pounding; adrenaline was kicking in. A whole year of planning and a couple of false starts were tied up in this operation. It was almost time.

That building was evil, an instrument of war. People inside were researching more efficient ways to kill innocents and to permanently scar the lives of those charged with defending the western world from communism. Allan knew first-hand about that after playing his part by working in the building.

We had checked the building carefully, timing the blast for a Sunday at four in the morning to make sure no one was inside. I had muffled my voice and called building security on a nearby pay phone—then dashed to join Allan and Dylan in the bushes. No need to perpetuate the killing—just a need to tell the world that the war was wrong!

We had planted the bomb in the van—it was a large, but crude affair using a detonator, along with fuel oil and ammonium nitrate, not as easy to make as it sounds. But not beyond our capabilities, especially those of Allan, who had two degrees in chemistry.

Dylan's hand shook as we backed away and he pressed the button on the detonator. We all ducked, to shield ourselves from the blast.

The explosion was more than we could have hoped for, filling the skies with light lapped by furious flames.

THE BOMBER IN THE BASEMENT

We called the police, as planned, and left to celebrate at an all-night diner after putting some distance between us and the blast.

And there we found out that things had gone horribly wrong.

17: ON THE RUN
(Barry, June 1970)

DYLAN'S MUSTANG WAS our getaway car, and I got to drive. Looking back, it was probably kind of stupid to use a red Mustang convertible as a getaway car, because it stood out so much.

But we didn't care about any of that. We were higher than kites even though none of us had quaffed a beer or smoked a doobie all day. We wanted to make sure we were sober and sensible so we could pull off the bombing. But after two hours driving on Interstate 5 north from L.A. towards San Francisco, where we planned to spend the weekend, it was time to celebrate. We turned on to Highway 99 where the Interstate ended, pulled over at a roadside diner near Bakersfield and ordered some coffee. There was an old black and white TV set hanging from the ceiling, tuned in to the news. They had footage of the blast, and it looked spectacular.

"Police are still seeking two people who had not signed out and may have been working in the building at the time of the blast," the reporter said. "They are Allan Bronson and Edward Sung, who had been working in the labs that were destroyed by the blast.

"Guards have identified Allan Bronson as the driver of the burnt-out van used in the blast. Sung is missing and presumed dead. Police are looking for a red sports car seen in the vicinity around the time of the blast."

Two photos appeared on the screen. Allan recognized his work tag photo, and Ted Sung's as well.

"I had no idea he was still working," whispered Allan to Dylan, his face crumpling as the enormity of what we had done sunk in.

No one was supposed to die.

Dylan passed Allan his L.A. Dodgers cap and pulled the brim low on his forehead. We suddenly realized how vulnerable we were; how easily we could be recognized. My mother wouldn't have approved of the cap, I thought briefly. In 1970, wearing a cap in a restaurant was considered the height of rudeness, but right now it was more important that the waitress not recognize Allan from his picture.

"We'll have three coffees," Dylan said, taking care not to look the waitress in the eye. She was young and pretty, if a bit tired-looking, and normally Dylan would have flirted with her.

"To go," Allan added from beneath the cap.

"I'll make you a fresh pot, hon," she said to Dylan. It took all our patience to sit there at the table while she made the coffee—if we ran, or even showed the wrong emotions, that would give us away for sure.

- - -

COFFEES IN HAND, we regrouped at the back of the restaurant, behind a dumpster, talking in whispers, far away from the Mustang that was such a target, and out of sight of the highway. What a rookie mistake, choosing that car to escape in. My Dad's old Country Squire station wagon would have been a better choice, or maybe a Ford Pinto. A white Pinto. There were lots of those around.

"No one was supposed to die," said Dylan, speaking for all of us.

"Did you know that guy," I asked Allan. "Did you see him

leave? Maybe they're wrong and he'll end up safe at home."

Allan shook his head miserably. "There are a hundred people working in that building. The place looked deserted. I didn't see any lights on."

Dylan surreptitiously looked toward the side of the diner, where the Mustang was parked. "First thing we have to do is get rid of the 'Stang," he said. "And we have to split up."

Dylan took the Mustang, and I took a good long look at my favourite car, knowing he would have to destroy it. Would he set it on fire? Push it into a lake or a pond? Put it in drive and have it fall off a cliff? I felt sad about the car, all the while knowing I would feel even worse as what we had done became more real. We were protesting the war—protesting what killing people had done to my brother, Tom. And yet, we had probably managed to kill someone too.

Dylan drove off down the highway; Allan started walking north and I started walking south. I had to see Mary-Anne one more time before I went on the run. She'd stopped coming with us when we started planning the bombings. I knew she didn't approve of Dylan and the way things were headed. But she'd been my girl for the past four years—I couldn't just up and leave. I stuffed my long hair up into my ball cap and put out my thumb.

- - -

I GOT THE truck driver to let me off a couple miles from my house—in Redondo Beach, not Hermosa. By then it was mid-afternoon. I didn't dare go home. If they knew that Allan was missing, and possibly involved, the pigs would surely be watching our house. Heck, they might even have realized that Mary-Anne was our friend. Her house might be off limits too. So, I walked to the hairdressers on Pier Street, where she worked. I wasn't 100 per cent sure of her work schedule, but figured she would probably get off work around six. I hung out in the back behind the dumpster to wait.

It was way after six when she came out the back door of the shop, keys in hand to lock up the place, and I emerged from my hiding place, looking around to make sure there was no one else behind the building.

"Scottie," she said, surprised, and gave me a big hug. "How's Allan? I've been worried sick. I saw on the news that he might be dead after that bomb blast at his work.

"Weren't you supposed to be picking him up there, and doing something with Dylan?"

I motioned to her to be quiet; then came up close to her and whispered.

"Allan's alive, but I'm in big trouble, and so is Allan and so is Dylan," I told her.

"If you and Allan are in big trouble it's because of Dylan," she said.

"How much do you know about the bombing?" I asked, checking again to make sure we were alone.

She looked down at the uneven pavement for a minute before she answered. "I saw it on the news, that there was a bomb blast and Allan was missing along with another guy. He works at the place that blew up, right?"

I wondered how much I should tell her—I knew it would change her opinion of me forever. But I needed help. I needed a plan.

I looked over at her carefully to gauge her reaction. "You know how we've been planning something big to protest the war? "

She nodded her head warily.

"We set off the bomb."

"The one that's on the news?" She let out a little cry and turned away. "Scottie, no!"

"We were supposed to blow up a building. We chose to set the bomb at four in the morning on a Saturday so no one would be there."

"No," she cried again, pushing me away when I tried to hold her. "I can't believe you did that."

"Mary-Anne—you have to help me. We did it for Tom. The police will soon know Allan was involved and it won't take long before they start looking for Dylan and me too. We've all gone our separate ways, but I have no idea where to go next."

There was lawn chair with plastic loops outside the back door to the hairdressers, where employees could sit and have a smoke. I knew because the ground was littered with cigarette butts. Mary-Anne collapsed in that chair, her head in her hands. I could tell she was debating whether to scream at me and tell me to go to hell, or whether she might be able to help. For the first time, I noticed that she was looking sick. She looked like she could be sick to her stomach at any moment. Or maybe it was what I had just told her that made her look like that.

"Please," I said, appealing to all that we'd shared since I first met her four years ago.

She looked up at me. She wasn't happy, but she seemed to have made her decision.

"Come back into the shop with me," she said.

- - -

WE DIDN'T TURN any lights on as Mary-Anne led the way to the bathroom at the back of the shop. "Wait a minute," she said in a hoarse whisper as she walked over to where her station was set up, and felt around until she found some scissors, a comb, and an electric razor. She looked pale. I'm sure she would much rather be safe in her bed at home, than dealing with me. She shut the door behind us, stuffed a towel over the door crack and then turned on the bathroom light. She wasn't gentle as she hacked my hair off and then buzzed it with the razor. I felt strange; I hadn't had a buzz cut since I was a little kid.

"You hide out back, while I go to get you some of my brother's I.D., maybe his draft card or his driver's license," she said in a whisper that still sounded slightly hostile.

"You should head to Canada, pretend you are a draft dodger," she added.

"I am a draft dodger," I said, referring to my own draft eligibility.

She gave me a look that I couldn't quite read, and then headed off.

I curled up behind the dumpster, purposefully reaching for the bristles that replaced the longish hair that had become my identity over the past few years. I caught a few hours of sleep behind the stinking dumpster on the cold, hard pavement. Then Mary-Anne drove back with her brother's driver's license. "I couldn't find the draft card," she said. "And I figured if I just took the one thing, he'd just think he'd lost it.

"There's cops all over our neighbourhood," she said. "I had to run the car with no lights and use all the side streets. You have to get out of here right away," she said.

She looked at me quizzically. "You do look different," she said. She kissed me quickly—I couldn't tell if she was still mad or not. Then she passed me two $20 bills, so I figured she wasn't totally done with me.

"Go to Canada," she said.

"I still love you," I called as she headed out in her car with the headlights off.

And that's when I became a draft dodger on my way to Canada.

18: JOHN IS GONE
(Katie, April 1971)

- - - - -

JOHN HAD A big deadline and was going to be working all weekend, and I had been invited to visit my parents' place in suburban Markland Woods. It was the weekend of the Police Games, and my Dad was participating.

I had a kind of off and on relationship with my parents, even though I was pretty sure that if they had to choose between John and me, they would choose John. Smart guy, on his way to becoming a big-time lawyer. They sort of liked him even in high school when he looked like a nerd. I think they liked the idea that their plain and studious daughter could attract a boyfriend. Once he went to law school, their approval rating went way up. They liked him even better since he looked so professional these days. Sometimes I thought my parents felt John was slumming by hanging out with me. At any rate, they were disappointed when John didn't come.

The weekend went quite well. Mom and I went shopping at Cloverdale Mall, picking up some bargains while we were there.

Dad had tickets for the Miss Toronto Beauty Contest, held on Saturday night at Exhibition Stadium in conjunction with the Police Games. Okay, so as feminist, I have trouble with the Miss Toronto pageant, because it objectifies women, judging them on their looks. I find the swimsuit portion particularly obnoxious, but some of the ball gowns are pretty. Lots of people felt like that. A few years ago, some feminists protested the contest, with the slogan, "Liberation, not Degradation."

But in recent years, they'd added a talent component, where

the contestants sing or dance or play piano, so that makes a bit of a difference.

My Dad got free tickets since he was part of the police games entertainment, as an officer on one of the teams that had a mighty tug of war that evening. The Miss Toronto pageant and Police Games brought back all kinds of memories for me. This year, I went with just my parents, but other years I had brought my best friend, Allison, who was now in Vancouver, and recently, John.

I was in a great mood when I got home on Sunday afternoon. John wasn't home yet—he was probably still at work. I got busy making his favourite meal, spaghetti with individual home-made meatballs; he was usually home at a decent time if he worked Sundays.

My hands were all slimy as I made the meatballs for the spaghetti he liked so much, when Barry came upstairs looking all gloomy.

"What's the matter?" I asked him. "Want to come up for spaghetti and meatballs later on?"

He didn't answer. He couldn't meet my eyes. I knew right away that something was wrong.

"Barry?" I asked.

He took a few minutes to form his response; obviously there was something he didn't want to tell me.

"John's gone," he said.

"What?"

"He's moved out. Take a look upstairs. I saw him clearing his clothes and stuff out of here on the weekend."

I just looked at him, not understanding.

"Look upstairs," he repeated.

Barry followed me as I dashed up the 14 steep stairs to the second floor and burst into our bedroom with the sloping ceilings and bay window. We had mirrored closet doors—his half and my half. John's half of the mirrored closet was open and his clothes were gone.

"I'm so sorry, Katie. He brought a U-Haul and loaded all his stuff in there. I think he must have bought or rented a car because obviously, he couldn't have taken yours."

I sat on the bed, unbelieving. Yes, John had been absorbed with work a lot. Yes, we had fought more than usual. Yes, I was sick of him always ragging on me about my clothes, my hair, my flawed personality.

But this was John. We had known each other since high school, played together in the school band, sung together in the choir. We'd been rivals, friends and then lovers. We were planning to have kids together—well, I was planning that; he was less enthusiastic. But why would he possibly want to leave our home?

"Did he say where he was going?" I asked Barry.

"He didn't say," he replied.

There was a long pause, where Barry didn't say anything and I was incapable of saying anything, probably because I was in shock.

"There was a woman with him. I think she was driving the car," Barry offered. "Short? Blonde hair?

"I'm so sorry, Katie," Barry added, still refusing to look at me directly, although none of this was his fault. "If you need some help eating that spaghetti later, I'm downstairs."

It was only when I heard his feet going down the fourteen stairs to the basement, that I lay my head down on the kitchen table and cried. I'm a good crier—my parents always said my tear ducts were leaky—but usually when I cried, John would come and comfort me, or try to talk me through what was going on. I could count on it.

But he wasn't coming to comfort me now.

SO, WHAT DO I do? John is gone and I don't know what to do about it. I don't even know for sure where he is, although Barry's comments gave me a real good clue.

On Monday morning, I called his office. His secretary put me right through—she wasn't the one, as she was in her 60s and due to retire soon. She didn't match Barry's description at all. I was almost sure it was Gillian, the tiny, perfect blonde, whom I'd met at the Christmas party at Sutton Place.

"John?" I asked him, trying to keep my emotions at bay. "What's happening? Can we talk about it?" I could almost hear him stretching the long telephone cord as he went around his desk to close his office door.

"This isn't the time or place to talk about this, Katie," he said firmly.

"But what's happening? How could you just leave?"

"It's a long story," he said.

"Do you want to get together and talk about it?" I asked.

"No," he said, and hung up the phone.

So much for his famous negotiating skills as a lawyer. That was just plain rude.

ON MONDAY, I'D taken the day off work, which turned out to be a bad plan. I just couldn't stop crying. I felt sick to my stomach and retched in the toilet. I walked around the house, disoriented. I loved this house. I wanted to stay here. What would happen now that John had moved out? I looked in his closet, now completely bare except for a couple of hangers with the dry-cleaning paper still on them. I kept walking aimlessly until my head hurt and I figured I had better lie down.

I lay down on my bed and just felt worse and worse. There was a horrible ache in my stomach that told me things weren't going to get better anytime soon. The pillow was sopping with tears, but I didn't even have the energy to get up and change the pillowcase.

Quincy jumped up on the bed beside me, 100 pounds of warm and sympathetic dog. He tried to lick my tears—probably because they have salt in them. I pushed his face away, but kept my arm around him. Technically, he wasn't allowed on the bed. John didn't like it.

But John wasn't here.

My parents called, but I couldn't face them. "I'm not feeling well," I said. "Can I call you back tomorrow?" They love John. If he's left for good, they'll think it's all my fault.

It probably is all my fault. Maybe if I'd paid more attention when he told me what he expected of a corporate wife. Maybe if I was prettier. Maybe if I could talk more about the legal stuff he liked so much. Maybe if I toned things down a bit, as he'd told me a hundred times, maybe not be so hot to trot about all my environmental causes.

But no, I couldn't tone things down. That was me. Those are things that I believe in, and I thought he believed in them too. He's changed, and he wants me to change, and maybe it's not too late. We've known each other so long and shared so much.

And then I thought about the girl at the office. The "other woman" as they say. I was positive I was right about who it was.

19: THE FUGITIVE
(Barry, 1970 & April 1977)

WHAT AN ASS, I thought to myself as I watched John and two guys in golf shirts and designer jeans load all his stuff into the U-Haul that the woman was driving. He doesn't try to work things out with his wife, who has her quirks but has loved him for years and would do just about anything to please him. He just up and leaves. While she's visiting her parents for the weekend, so he doesn't have to tell her face-to-face. He didn't take much stuff—just clothes including the two three-piece suits he wore every day to work, his home office desk, chair, electric typewriter, files and a bookshelf.

He saw me watching, but he didn't say a word and neither did I. It was a standoff. Looking back, I should have asked him where he was going. And then I saw the driver, a petite, efficient-looking woman with blonde hair—a beautiful fair-haired, stuck-up version of Mary-Anne. I saw him put his arm around her waist, possessively. And while I didn't know where he was going, I knew the reason he was leaving.

BACK IN CALIFORNIA in 1970, I was embarking upon a new life as well. My second night on the run wasn't much better than the first one. I had a new haircut, but my clothes were the same ones I had been wearing the day of the bombing. The first day, I walked from Hermosa Beach to Santa Monica Beach. It took me over four hours. People looked at me differently, and I realized that was probably because I looked like an army guy now—either a veteran or a recruit. It felt strange, but as the day dragged on, I became more comfortable, realizing there was no way anyone would recognize me. Seeing the haircut, people thought "army guy," not "potential bombing suspect."

When I got to Santa Monica, I took my $40 and went to Sears. I got some lunch at the counter. Their roast beef dinner set me back $1.10—the first decent meal I'd had since the bombing. I spent the rest of the first $20 bill on a new shirt, some Wrangler jeans and a blanket. I'd been to Santa Monica several times with Dylan and Allan. We didn't always go to Hermosa Beach—sometimes we tried other beaches too, with the goal of meeting some girls, not a problem in Dylan's Mustang, which attracted lots of attention in car-crazy L.A. I was hitched up with Mary-Anne, Allan was too nerdy to attract much attention from girls, but Dylan had what it took to get lots of action. Some nights he'd drop us off in the 'Stang and then head off with some good-looking girl. His relationships didn't last long, and he wasn't always nice. But he never had any problem finding willing partners.

Santa Monica was filled with the homeless, some of them screwed up army vets like my brother, Tom, before he died; some just down and out, pushing their possessions around in shopping carts. The shopping carts nestled in the bushes provided my first hint of the number of homeless in this beautiful beach town with its awesome pier. I guess I looked like I belonged. The haircut fit in; they didn't know my particular trauma wasn't due to the war, but to the growing realization of what we had done and the position I found myself in now. I also looked like I had some street smarts, so that nobody hassled me.

In my rush to get out of Dodge, I had only thought about Mary-Anne. And she had come through, helping me with the disguise, the I.D. and the money, and giving me the idea of heading to Canada. I wouldn't be seeing her for a long time, if ever again.

There had been no question of going home; Mary-Anne had said the place was surrounded by cops all wanting to know about Allan—and possibly me and Dylan too. But I wished I could have somehow sent Mom and Dad a message, let them know I was still alive and where I was headed. But I really couldn't do that either, as it would just put the pigs on my trail.

My parents were good people; they'd done their best to raise us and pass on their values. And now, directly or indirectly because of the war, they had essentially lost all three kids.

I stuck to myself, spreading the blanket and making my bed under some shrubs and plants in a hotel garden, the hosta plants shielding me from view. It was better than the pavement at the back of Mary-Anne's hairdressing shop, and it smelled better, but it was a small space, and I couldn't really move around much without crushing those hostas. My dreams were of the explosion, but my thoughts were all twisted together; it wasn't about blowing up the research building, it was about blowing up our home in Hermosa Beach, with my family, Mary-Anne and Dylan all inside.

I awoke way too early—around five a.m. according to my watch and lay there, paralyzed, heart pounding, anxious and worried about how I would get to Canada, how I would avoid the cops who had probably figured out that Dylan and I were with Allan at the time of the bombing. I couldn't linger in Santa Monica, although I could probably blend in here for a while. It was just too close to home. I would have to join the thousands of draft dodgers making their way to Canada.

By 6 a.m., the sun was up and the beach began to come to life. I saw some guys pull up in a truck with rakes and hoes, and figured I had better skedaddle before they realized I was sleeping in among the shrubs. I was a homeless person now, I thought, rubbing my two-day beard, feeling grubby and dishevelled. Get a plan, Scottie, I told myself. No, not Scottie Bronson any more. I pulled out the I.D. Barry. Barry Douglas Gillespie. Draft dodger, heading to Canada. The I.D. was blurry enough that it could have been me. And I'd met the actual Barry several times. He was older than me, but not by much; there was maybe 18 months between him and Mary-Anne. His birth date was Feb. 15, 1950. So, he was a year older than me. I'd have to commit that date to heart, and get used to not answering if someone called me Scottie.

With one eye on the gardening crew, I packed my few possessions into the centre of the blanket and grabbed the four corners. All I needed was a stick and I could really look like one of those hobos riding the rails in the Dirty Thirties. Then I remembered the Sears bag from yesterday's purchases. That would do for today, but I'd soon have to get something like a suitcase or a knapsack of some sort to hold my stuff on the way to Canada.

I was so hungry; that roast beef dinner at Sears was a long time ago. I shouldered my load and walked east, up Olympic Street until I came to a coffee shop with a penguin on its sign. I got a donut and coffee to go, not wanting to linger and attract attention. The radio was tuned to a news station that was talking about the bombing, about how Edward Sung was a family man who left a wife and two teenage girls. He'd been working late so that he could leave on a family vacation the next morning. Shit. They hadn't found Allan's body, and the guard had identified him as the driver of the van.

I walked the short distance to the Santa Monica pier, followed the pier to the end and sat on a bench eating my donut and savouring the coffee. My breakfast, such as it was, had set me back another dollar. I'd have to find another way to get food or a way to get some funds; otherwise the second $20 wouldn't last very long.

The pier was relatively quiet with just a few runners who paid no attention to me. There was a guy swimming. The water was probably warm enough this time of year. Maybe that was a way to get clean. There was smog in the distance, hiding the hills on the north side of the beach, but the sky where I was had turned blue and cloudless. The weather was in the high 60s but getting warmer by the minute. I knew I'd be sweltering by noon. The coffee calmed me down a little. The donut put something in my belly. I decided I could clean up in the Sears bathroom, since I still had the bag and the receipt for the clothes.

By 10 a.m. I had hit the road, a little cleaner than before, wearing my new duds. I stood at the side of Highway 2 and put out my thumb. The best—and perhaps only—way for me to get to Canada was to hitchhike.

- - -

AFTER A SHORT trip along Highway 2 to the 405, I lucked out. The guy who picked me up was a trucker named Bill, who was going up Highway 99, then turning west toward San Francisco. He lived in the back of his truck, and it smelled like it, but he was nice enough. I think he found the long miles lonely, and he kept up a steady stream of chatter, not requiring much of me but to nod and make affirmative noises now and then. Thank goodness. Normally, I would have asked him all kinds of questions and provided some information about me and my family and why I was making this trip. But what could I say? I wasn't me any more, and anything I said could land me in front of a judge and in jail.

Eventually, he ran out of words and turned the radio on,

country and western music of course, but there were news stories at the top of the hour. The police had determined that Allan Bronson was not killed in the blast and in fact was wanted for murder. They said me and Dylan were wanted as co-conspirators as well. They had found the getaway car, the Mustang, burned out and hidden in a clearing among some trees. I mourned for the Mustang. But that was just the beginning of my sorrow. I hadn't had a chance to say good-bye to my parents; Mom's last words were something about Dylan being a bad influence, and to make sure Allan was okay. I probably wouldn't see Mary-Anne for a long, long time. How could I even get in touch with any of them?

Sunny Scottie was no more. I was sunk in despair. I didn't know what to say to anyone. I was afraid to talk in case I would reveal my true identity. I took advantage of the let-up in conversation to close my eyes and laid back in the passenger seat, and once again slept a troubled sleep.

I awoke as we were nearing the turnoff for San Francisco, and I asked Bill if he had a road map. He did of course. It was well thumbed and ripped where the folds had been opened and closed too often. Turned out I didn't need a map quite yet—Bill was quite good at giving directions.

"Where you headed after this?" Bill asked.

"North. To Canada," I said.

"Well, awhile back we turned from 99 onto I-5. I'll be taking it north and then turning onto State Route 50 to go to San Francisco. You'll want to get back over to the 99. The I-5 doesn't go through yet."

"So how do I get there?"

"When I turn west onto 50, you'll go the other way, towards Manteca. Not too far. Less than a half hour. I'd stay the night if I were you. Not as safe hitching at night, unless you get a nice trucker like me." He grinned, showing his stained teeth. His smile spread right up to his eyes, and I could see how the unshaven face and greasy hair might be overlooked by the family he talked so much about.

"You goin' to Vancouver?" he asked.

I nodded.

He looked at me more seriously and handed me the map. "Take this. The highway's still a work in progress. Best you know where you're going."

When I protested, he insisted, pushing the map into my hands. "I don't need this bloody thing. If I don't know the roads by now, I'm sunk." He lobbed an apple at me. "Here. Take this too—we haven't had much to eat today. First place I'm gonna hit in San Fran is a truck stop for some good food."

I caught the apple. That breakfast on the Santa Monica pier was a long time ago.

"Good idea going to Canada. And all the best," he said. "I lost a brother in 'Nam."

We had more in common than he knew.

Bill let me off by the ramp that turned onto State Route 20 east—and I quickly got another ride to Manteca. I didn't want to go anywhere near San Francisco. Take the highway straight north to Canada. That was the route I had planned for myself. I hadn't realized that parts of the Interstate weren't complete yet. I folded the map so it was small enough to fit in the back pocket of my jeans—no easy feat, but I figured I had better keep it handy. I didn't want to have to root around in the Sears bag that held the rest of my possessions.

Manteca wasn't a very big place, but it did have a main street, and I was able to find a restaurant, blowing more of my cash so I only had $17 left. I saved some money by drinking from a public fountain, wishing I had a container of some sort so I could take more water with me.

It was too small a place and too public to find a place to sleep, so I walked out of town and settled for the night in an almond grove. The trees were planted in neat rows—not the best configuration for someone trying to hide. But there was a pile of wood that could shield me from the road, and I hunkered down behind it. Since it was late June, the blossoms on the almond trees were long gone, but I figured it would be a while before the nuts were harvested.

There was nobody around, so I spread my blanket on the ground, which was, thankfully, quite dry. I picked a few almonds from the tree above me. If I were going to preserve my funds, I had better try all possible sources of free food. The almonds were bitter. I'd heard the green ones with fuzzy stuff were good to eat, and I loved the almonds I bought in the store. But these ones were almost inedible.

My mind turned to camping trips that Tom, Allan and I had taken with the Scouts, an hour-and-a-half east of our home in Hermosa Beach. Ninety minutes made a world of difference. That drive took us from Southern California to a landscape that was probably more like northern Canada, with mountains, trees, and lakes. Tom was big on survival skills, and he taught all of us how to scour the ground for edible plants.

Allan, of course, was very attentive and soon knew and identified those plants even better than Tom did. Right now, I wished I'd paid more attention.

Allan, I thought, edging into depression territory. I would not be seeing Allan for a very long time. I'd lost two brothers now. Allan and I had been thrown together after Tom died. It wasn't a natural pairing—we'd both related better to Tom. But we'd stuck together; we'd been through a lot together. He wasn't much into feelings and affection, but he always had an answer for any situation we got ourselves into. And right now, I needed some answers.

It was my third night on the run and counting. My stomach felt a bit queasy after eating those unripe almonds—not a taste I was used to. My body felt every bump in the ground through the blanket. And my head was kind of messed up too. I kept thinking about the guy who'd died—the guy our bomb had killed. My night was restless and troubled. He wasn't supposed to be there. No one was supposed to die.

Day four, and I managed to land a long-distance ride. I grabbed a muffin and a coffee from a place in Manteca, used their bathroom to clean up a bit and then caught a ride up to Stockton, and stuck out my thumb again near the junction of state routes 99 and 88. I figured that would give me two options—going north to Canada or going northeast to Canada. Normally I would walk backwards with my thumb out, just to give me the illusion of moving somewhere. But today I stood in the one spot, figuring I could double my chances of being picked up.

I saw a VW microbus slow down and stop just down the road from me. I ran toward the car, thinking they had slowed down to pick me up. But no, a closer look showed a flat front tire on the driver's side.

As I drew up to the van, the driver got out and so did the passenger. Both women. One quite muscular and mannish, and one softer and more beautiful. And both about ten years older than me.

"Car problems?" I asked the muscular one, the driver. "Need help with that tire?"

"Ah… no," said the driver. "I can handle it. And we don't pick up hitchhikers."

"No problem," I said, as I watched her struggle with the

spare tire mounted on the front.

"Here, let me help," I added, pulling it off easily. "I'm a mechanic."

She looked angry, not grateful, as I handed her the tire. Maybe she was one of those women's lib types who wanted to do everything herself. Or one who hated the old 1950s idea that a woman's place was in the home.

"Got a jack?" I asked. Maybe I'd make more points if I showed her how to do it herself.

I demonstrated where to position the jack and how to pump it; then let her take over. I handed her the wheel and showed her how to take off the first nut and let her do the rest. She was on her own as she placed the spare tire and replaced the nuts. When she finished, she looked grim. "That should hold for a while until we can stop and get it fixed," she said.

And grudgingly. "Thanks."

She got into the car and pulled away, the passenger yelling, "Thanks," before she got into the car. As they pulled out, I figured out that they both had accents—Canadian accents. And the car had Canadian plates.

I sighed and stuck my thumb out again.

A few minutes later, I saw the microbus coming towards me. It went past me and found a safe place to make a U-turn.

"Get in," the driver said gruffly.

"Where are you headed," I asked her.

"Tronno," she said.

Her name was Buffy and the other girl was Dawn. I rode in the hippie van with them for ten days. I helped them with car maintenance and put my $17 into the communal till.

I never did see Vancouver, although that was where I had been headed at first.

And that was how I ended up in Toronto, Ontario, Canada.

I'D TOTALLY LUCKED out by running into those two women. Dawn was sweet and generous almost to a fault. "No problem," she'd said when I offered to pitch in my $17. "If we need it, we'll take it. But we have lots of food and lots of money." Maybe not the best thing to say to a hitchhiker. How did she know I wasn't an axe murderer who'd kill them and steal everything they had? I wondered if she'd be so generous if she knew what I'd done; that I wasn't just going to Canada because it was an interesting stop on my world tour or as a draft dodger; that I wasn't who I seemed. I was a fugitive on the run.

Buffy took a bit of getting used to. She drove a panel van back in Toronto, doing deliveries for a flower company. Women drivers were something of a novelty in those days, but I guess the fact that it was a flower company sort of balanced things out. She wasn't as easygoing as Dawn; in fact, she could be argumentative and gruff. But I could see her as a truck driver; I could easily visualize her slinging pots and flowers into the back of a vehicle; then lugging them into the stores. She talked a lot about parking in Toronto—how she had to double-park most of the time, and she regaled us with the ways she'd managed to talk down angry car owners and even the traffic cops; and then make a quick getaway when needed.

I could relate—I'd spent my life in L.A. and San Francisco, sometimes downtown, and knew all about unbelievably awful parking. And I knew more than I wanted to tell her about driving a getaway vehicle.

But basically, they were on vacation, so they were in a good mood most of the time. I think they felt that having a guy with them would make them safer. And I did have some talents when it came to mechanical breakdowns.

The sleeping arrangements were a no-brainer. The two of them were an item and slept on a double mattress on the floor. I stretched out on the rumble seat at the back of the van. It didn't quite work for my five-foot-eleven body and my legs hung over the edge. But hey, it sure beat the pavement by the dumpsters outside Mary-Anne's salon, the middle of the hosta plants at that hotel in Santa Monica, or the almond grove. I sat quietly in the back during the day, looking out the window and listening to the two of them chat or argue as we racked up the miles between Stockton and Lake Tahoe. I often referenced the map Bill had given me, fascinated watching the miles roll by and plotting our journey.

I figured the less I said the better. It was hard for me. I wasn't naturally a quiet person. I was usually playing the clown and trying to be the life of the party. I was relieved when we crossed the state border into Nevada. I was free of California—and that would make it more difficult for the pigs to catch up to me. The van was Buffy's baby, and she wouldn't let me drive. I was happy about that, since the only license I possessed wasn't mine, and I sure as hell didn't want to show it if I was pulled over by the cops.

I slept soundly that first night and way past noon the next day—sheer exhaustion. But my sleeps after that were much more troubled—I had mixed up dreams where the guy who was killed blew us up and I saw mangled bodies of Tom, Allan and Dylan. It was a dream… it didn't have to make any sense. And then I saw myself in Vietnam, witnessing all that Tom had seen, and more things my mind had retained from all those LIFE magazine articles.

I was talking in my sleep too. One night, Dawn asked me, "Who's Tom?"

OF COURSE, WHEN we stopped for lunch or dinner, the news on the TV was all about the bombing. They had figured out a long time ago that Allan was alive and probably the one who was responsible for the bombings, and that he must have had help. They'd talked to my parents and had figured out that I was supposed to be with Allan at the time. They had put two and two together and realized the Mustang must have been the getaway car. That it was found, all burnt out, and that it was registered to Dylan's parents.

In the latest news report, Dylan's parents were quoted, and they were a couple of jackasses.

"The car is ours, but the Bronson brothers must have stolen it. There's no way our son, Dylan, could have been involved. He's a student—he's a good kid," Dylan's dad said. Dylan's dad, who I'd only met a few times because he was hardly ever home. Dylan's dad, who was a fancy lawyer and earned gazillions of dollars. Dylan's dad, whom the police seemed to believe was a credible witness at the time. They showed a picture of Dylan that was taken back in high school, when he was in surfer dude mode and looked like a cross between a male model and the boy next door. Dylan's mom just stood beside his dad, not saying anything, but looking perfectly made up as usual.

My parents had given the TV people a more recent photo of Allan and me. Allan looked nerdy as usual, and I looked like a hooligan with long, scruffy hair and an early attempt at a beard. At least I didn't look anything like I did now.

My heart almost broke as I listened to my parents make an impassioned plea for Allan and I to "just give yourselves up" and come home to California.

THE BOMBER IN THE BASEMENT

"I'm not sure I get all the protests and stuff that is going on," said Buffy. "I mean, the Vietnam War is bad, and I get all the draft dodgers coming to Canada," she added with a backwards nod toward me. They'd decided on their own that's what I was doing, and I didn't correct them. "But violence? I mean, what possible good could those bombers do by torching that building? Why would people do that?"

Oh, I had so many responses to that. Try losing a brother to the Vietnam War, and not because he was killed and went out in a blaze of glory, but because the war had ripped out his soul and left him permanently damaged. Try seeing your brother suspended from the tree in a nearby park, with horrible bruising on his neck and his tongue all hanging out and dry. I will never forget that image. Dad, Mom and Allan won't forget it either. And it was all because of what happened to Tom in Vietnam.

"What do you think, Barry?" Buffy asked.

"The war is a terrible thing," I mumbled, and then went quiet.

"But you shouldn't destroy things and take people's lives in the process," Dawn said, with great conviction.

"Right," I said, wishing for the thousandth time that I hadn't done just that.

It was during that ride that I started to realize that if I didn't say much, people would just make their own assumptions, which were often far from reality. If I just stayed quiet that would work most of the time. When I did speak, I talked in generalities that wouldn't reveal my true background and would allow everyone to draw their own conclusions.

Buffy and Dawn assumed I was a draft dodger because of the haircut, and that I probably had strong feelings about the war, but preferred to keep them to myself.

And they respected that.

Buffy was a bit of a newspaper junkie, and she made a point of getting a local newspaper each place we stopped. It didn't matter if we had a national newspaper or a local rag, our bombing always dominated the news. The stories that gripped my heart were the ones about the researcher we had killed, Edward Sung. He was in his 40s, a family guy with teenage kids not that much younger than me. He'd come to the U.S. from Hong Kong, seeking a better life in the U.S. Those teenagers were cute—sweet girls with long black hair, ages 16 and 18. The guy we killed looked like an older, Chinese version of Allan, with coke-bottle glasses, but he was better looking than Allan and had black hair, not dirty brown like all the Bronson boys. Ironically, I bet the two of them would have got along famously, since he was a quiet and serious science genius, and a doctoral student. And the guy who died wasn't even researching weapons of war—his specialty was something totally different aimed at curing cancer. Allan would understand what it was—I didn't.

Other articles talked about the valuable and irreplaceable research that was taking place in that lab—how science in the U.S. had been set back years by the notes and books destroyed in the blast. The research we ended up destroying was not war related. The war research was being done on the top floor, which was relatively undamaged.

Still, thanks to Dylan's articles in student-run underground newspapers, the warning I had given to building security from the phone booth, and the call I had made to the cops, there was no doubt in anyone's mind that the bombing was done to stop the war.

Salt Lake City, Omaha, Des Moines. I was sorry we'd missed Denver—I'd heard a lot about the Mile High City. I even secretly liked the singer, John Denver, though I'd never tell Dylan, who was mostly into acid rock. I spent a lot of time scanning the map Bill had given me, partly to stay quiet and not engage in conversation, and partly because I enjoyed it.

We stopped in various places, sometimes in KOA campgrounds, sometimes just at a convenient place off the road. We played tourist sometimes, and drove on through at other times. I refused to let Buffy or Dawn take my picture with their brand-new Polaroid camera. They figured my reluctance had to do with the draft dodger thing.

My eyes were glued to the great outdoors. The trip took us through some beautiful country, rugged at first and then filled with farms and cattle and crops. I'd never been outside California, so it was all new to me. We drove around Chicago—no way did Buffy want to tackle big city traffic. It was too much like work.

So, we stayed at a campground on the east side of Lake Michigan, a beautiful place with a nice beach. Not quite a California beach, but with warm water and sand. For a while I forgot where I was headed and why. I swam in the lake, remembering our sun and surf days when I was a teenager, before Tom came back from Vietnam and life got complicated.

Buffy and Dawn were eager to get home after that, so we drove on through. At one point we had a choice of going across the border at Detroit, or at a much smaller place called Port Huron, Michigan.

"Let's go through Port Huron," I said, worried as hell about this border crossing, and figuring the Detroit police would probably be on the lookout for me.

"Why?" asked Buffy.

"They've got riots in Detroit. It's not a safe place, and it's probably a bitch to drive in," I said.

"You're right," said Buffy, and we headed to Port Huron.

My stomach churned and my head felt overwhelmed as we

headed there, but my fears were unfounded.

"Born?" The agent asked Buffy and Dawn.

"Tronno," said Buffy.

"Tronno," said Dawn.

"Tronno," I said, doing my best to sound just like Dawn and Buffy did. It was just one of many blatant outright lies I would tell in the next several years, whenever being quiet didn't work.

Was I imagining things, or did he look with a bit of suspicion at my abnormally short hair? Did he know I was lying? Did he think I was a draft dodger, but ignore it? I'd heard some Canadian border guards were sympathetic to draft evaders.

Either way, he turned back to his booth and said, "Have a nice day."

I was in Canada!

20: POWER TRIP
(Katie, April 1977)

LIFE IS JUST too much to take lately. John doesn't show any signs of wanting to come back. I've called him at work a few times, hating myself whenever I did so. He hasn't answered my calls. Home is just so depressing with the clothes in John's half of the closet missing, and his desk, typewriter and the bookshelf gone from his half of our second bedroom that served as an office. Quincy misses him—I don't know why since he didn't spend much time with his dog. But that dog could mope better than any animal I'd ever met, and Quincy, while affectionate, also seemed depressed.

So that was home, which was punctuated by a dreary ride to and from the office on the streetcar during a winter that wouldn't go away, interspersed with long bouts of work, which were even more depressing.

Margaret was on the warpath today. I mean, she was always in a bad mood, but this time she was actively seeking me out to berate me.

"What's this story?" she said, waving a short article I'd written by adding some of my research to one of the News Briefs. I thought it was a good article—it put together some of the news about the Mackenzie Valley Pipeline with information from one of the environmental groups that was opposing it.

"We had the news clipping for News Briefs, and I know the PR person for that environmental group, so I just put two and two together, and wrote the article."

Margaret was livid. Her face was starting to turn red. "I

didn't ask you to write that article! I'm your boss and I decide what you should or should not do."

I kept my mouth shut—I didn't want to make matters worse by speaking.

"You're on a bit of a power trip, aren't you?" she yelled. And then she ripped it up. The only copy of that story, I'd so painstakingly put together on my IBM Selectric typewriter.

I couldn't help it. I burst into tears, as she huffed out the door. It all welled up inside me—all the pain of John leaving, all the dreariness of the interminable winter, and all the frustration of having a bad boss after blossoming as a writer under a good one.

"Well, that wasn't very nice," a voice whispered.

Moira, who had the office beside me, poked her head into my cubby hole. She had overheard the whole thing. "You're a good writer—I saw what you wrote when you worked with Elizabeth. Margaret's just a frustrated old biddy," she added. "And I know you care about ECO too—anyone who's willing to truck their recycled cans and bottles over to my place, has to be committed to environmental stuff."

Not many people could put so much expression into the words, "frustrated old biddy" as Moira could. She wrinkled up her whole face with distaste and exaggerated each whispered word. I gave her a half smile and sniffled a bit.

"She's not that popular around the office," Moira added, still whispering. "I'm not sure the management even likes her," she said, inclining her head in the direction of Gordon's and Hugh's offices.

"You could come back and work for me," she said, grinning. I smiled—we both knew that even though we'd had a great time when I'd updated the directories with her, that my true ambition was to be a writer and editor with my own publication.

"Or I could put in a good word with Gordon," she suggested.

I shook my head—I thought that was probably a very bad idea.

"Or you could talk to Gordon," she added. That idea was better. I'd have to give it some thought.

"And you should come to the pub tonight," she added.

"Oh, I don't know…" I said.

"They're doing Karaoke," she said.

That sounded good. I liked to sing.

But she hadn't finished talking to me yet.

"Enjoy your 'power trip'," she said with a grin, mimicking Margaret's bossy tones.

Yes, I'd go to karaoke.

WE HAD A good turnout at Korenowsky's—me, Moira, Shazma, Barry, Linda (the typesetter, who was also Moira's friend) and Mark (the older editor). I felt much more at home with this group by now, and didn't need any prompting to help down the pitchers of beer we ordered. No boss this time, though Gordon hadn't cramped our style too much.

We clinked glasses, and Moira said: "I'm surprised you're associating with us, Katie. I heard a rumour that you're on a 'power trip'."

"What????" several of my office mates said in unison.

"It's got to be true," said Moira, milking the attention. "It comes straight from Margaret," she added, rolling out the name with emphasis and a sly smile.

"Oh, Margaret…" The groans told me just how much my co-workers loved my despicable boss, i.e., not at all.

"Well, here's to your 'power trip'," said Mark, raising his glass again, and everyone joined in.

The karaoke part was fun. I had always liked to sing, and belonged to the choir at my high school. I played piano too—we had an antique piano from my grandmother at our place in Little India, leaning against the fake brick wall. (That fake brick has got to go!) But at least I didn't have to worry about getting home safely, since Barry and I would take the streetcar together. And I wouldn't have to worry about John hassling me about the smoke and telling me to take a bath. I cheered a bit at the thought.

I didn't think I'd ever grasp my co-workers' taste in music. John Denver was not cool. Herman's Hermits were not cool. Then why were they urging me to get up and join them in a Peter, Paul and Mary song, 'Blowin' in the Wind'? Surely folk singers were not cool… It turns out that song was written by Bob Dylan, and that placed it squarely in the 'approved music' category.

"Dylan always said it wasn't a protest song, but it was," said Mark, who knew about these things. "It may have been the biggest protest song of the '60s."

I was happy to join in the singing—it was one of our choir songs during high school—and I didn't need karaoke for the words. We started out as a group, but it turned out that my voice was one of the stronger ones. I tried to pipe down so the other voices could be heard, but Moira encouraged me, cupping her ear, and nodding to show she wanted to hear me. The other voice that stood out was Barry's. His voice was mellow and deeper than mine—and while he started out quietly, he ended up singing a very tuneful tenor harmony. The others stopped singing, and we sang the last verse as a duet—my higher voice blending well with his lower tones.

At the end of the song, I saw something I'd never seen before. He tried to hide it, but Barry's eyes were swimming with tears.

21: KENSINGTON MARKET & MIMICO CREEK
(Barry, April 1977)

MY LANDLADY IS not doing well because that twerp of a husband has left her. I'm not totally unhappy, though. John had never really acknowledged me as anything more than someone whose money helped pay the bills. I instinctively didn't like him much right from the beginning. And sometimes my instincts prove to be right.

I wanted to cheer her up a bit, so I suggested we go to Kensington Market. She loved it—that crazy place with live chickens on display, where you can barter with the vendors over the price of produce. At first, she didn't believe me when I told her you could do that, but she got into it pretty quickly. And she was good. My landlady does like to argue. And she chatted up some of the vendors, asking what they fed their chickens and whether they used pesticides on the crops they were growing and what they thought of GMOs. Turns out there are a lot of people who feel as strongly about these issues as she does. She's good at interviewing people; even when there's a language barrier, she can sometimes get them to open up.

All in all, it was a successful day. No tears from Katie for a change, but I don't know what she's going to do about John and the house.

I think Katie is lonely and needs to talk. I've been invited up to the main floor of the house a few times for something she calls "Happy Hour," consisting of drinks and pre-dinner chat. Her living room doesn't look anything like the one in our family home in California—the colours and furniture are totally different for one thing. Our California home had a lot of green in it—various shades of green, everything from pale green to a sort of greeny-blue. (I'm not that knowledgeable about decorating colours. My Mom was. She was constantly reading Ladies' Home Journal and House Beautiful, and it wasn't unusual for me to come home and find out she'd moved the furniture around. The couches were kind of modern and streamlined and the set came in pieces, so that she could arrange them in different ways.)

This house was darker, with orangey-brown panelled walls that were not unattractive. They were a warm shade of brown, and I could tell the wood was substantial, not the cheap sheets of panelling that are so popular these days. The couch and chair were blue corduroy and there was a story behind them. They were from the office next door to Rosedale Publishing, a consulting company that was far more posh than RP. The consulting company was moving to another (probably classier) building, and they were selling off their couch and matching chair for a real bargain price—$100 I think. Both Katie and one of the co-owners, Hugh, wanted it, so they tossed a coin and Katie won. The couch was really comfortable—large and deep enough to accommodate my long legs, with cushions that weren't too hard or too soft. (Do I sound like Goldilocks in The Three Bears here?)

My landlady sat across from me on the chair, and overhead was a macramé lamp that hung from the ceiling. Maybe not real macramé, as Katie had simply taken a lamp frame and vertically wound rows of macramé string around it. It looked nice. Katie was clever that way.

There was a fireplace too—not a real fireplace, but one of those electric ones with a rotating disk that mimicked the look of fire and blew out hot air. We didn't have a fireplace at home in California, but there was one in Dylan's family room. It was a modern affair that looked a bit like a black dome attached to the ceiling with a large black tube. I liked Katie's fireplace better, even though it wasn't the real deal—I could imagine it would be cozy during the really cold winter months, and it was welcome even in the current unpredictable April weather.

When I entered the room, Katie wasn't wearing her glasses and she looked as though she was weeping. Her eyes were red, and she kept rubbing them.

"Contacts," she explained. "John and I both got them, but mine were more complicated and are harder to get used to."

All part of her self-improvement projects to please John, I'd bet.

I wasn't familiar with contact lenses, even though three out of five people in our family wore glasses. Allan and Dad shared the same style of heavy, black-rimmed glasses—and neither of them cared a wit about fashion. Mom had stylish glasses shaped like a cat's eye.

One evening, Katie asked me upstairs, not just for Happy Hour, but to stay for dinner and finish some spaghetti and meatballs she'd frozen. She had made the meal when she and John were together, and there was plenty for two people. The spaghetti was a welcome change from cooking on my hot plate in the basement. My other standby was samosas from Little India on Gerrard Street—they were cheap and much more satisfying than my own home cooking.

"So," she said, with an overly bright smile. "How are you enjoying your work at Rosedale."

"Actually, it's one of the nicer places I've worked," I said honestly. "And I like the pub nights….

"You should come more often," I added. While the Rosedale

gang went out to pubs quite regularly, and I tagged along sometimes, Katie had only been there twice: that evening when Gordon came too, and the time we sang Karaoke. She had always said John didn't approve. Too bad. John was gone now, so maybe she would like to join us.

"I might do that," she said.

There was an awkward pause—neither of us was much good at small talk. With me, I just wasn't in the habit of offering too much information. With Katie, every conversation sounded like an interview. Which helped her at work and made her a very good editor, but didn't make her an easy conversationalist.

"So where did you go to college?" she asked me, not a question I welcomed.

"I didn't," I said honestly, without being too specific. "I dropped out after Grade 10."

She looked at me with something like incredible disbelief.

"Really? Why?"

"I didn't enjoy school. I was bored. I wanted to earn money, so I worked as a machinist.

"But I'm taking high school correspondence courses," I added, and I noticed her interest was piqued. "I'm going to graduate soon."

KENSINGTON MARKET BRINGS back memories for me. Buffy, Dawn and I landed in Toronto not far from there in 1970. They live in a house off College Street that has a rainbow painted on the front porch. Dawn's work, I think. The house is big with a main floor, three bedrooms on the second floor, a loft in the attic and a grungy, low-ceilinged 1920s basement. There are other people in the house as well—a couple of guys, Eric and

George, and another girl, Bonnie. Buffy and Dawn share the attic room. They plopped down a mattress and a double-wide sleeping bag for me in one of the bedrooms, unpacked their stuff and ran down to Kensington to get the ingredients for a delicious roast chicken dinner. It reminded me a lot of Dylan's place in Haight-Ashbury. I mean, Toronto wasn't San Francisco, but it was an older house, downtown with lots of nooks and crannies, and unrelated people sharing the space. Sort of like a commune, Dawn explained to me.

I couldn't stay long, though. I didn't want anyone to be able to link me to my past in California. During the long drive to Canada, I had spent plenty of time hunched in the back of the minibus, thinking about what I would say when people asked about my past.

As little as possible was my answer. I would be as quiet as possible and say as little as I could.

I'd have to work on a Canadian accent. I didn't even want people to know I was American. That would prompt way too many questions about the war. Was I a draft dodger? That sort of thing. While I was in the car, I teased Buffy and Dawn about their Canadianisms—the way they sometimes ended sentences with "eh?" or "right," almost as though they were seeking my approval about what they said. As far as they were concerned, the alphabet ended in zed, not zee.

"You can stay with us for a while," Dawn said. "We have an extra mattress or you can sleep on the chesterfield."

"The what?" I queried.

"The chesterfield, you know, the couch. What's the matter," she asked as I grinned from ear to ear. "Haven't you ever heard that word before?"

"No," I said, shaking my head. "We don't have any chesterfields in the States."

"You'll like Canada in the summer. It's more than 70 above most of the time."

"Seventy above what?"

"Seventy degrees. I'm talking about the weather, stupid."

Or, "Northern Ontario is great for fishing. You can catch a lot of Pickerel."

"Pickerel? What's that?"

"It's a fish, dumbo. A fish that grows really big and you can find it in the lakes of Northern Ontario."

It was long after our road trip that I realized she was talking about Walleye.

There were differences in the way Dawn and Buffy pronounced some words as well.

"We'll take State Root 80 for some of the way," is what Buffy said when she outlined our travel plans.

"Ra-out," I said. "That's the way we say it in the States."

"Want a pop," Dawn said, pulling a Coke from the ice bucket they carried in the minibus.

"Soda," I said. "In the States we call it 'soda'."

And this one was my favourite. "Where did you say we were headed again?"

"Tronno," said Dawn and Buffy in unison.

"Humph!" I teased them. "I thought it was pronounced Tor-on-to."

I'm a good mimic. I used to make Tom, Dylan and even Allan laugh with my imitations of various TV entertainers. I made Dawn and Buffy laugh as I tried "talking Canadian" back to them. I picked up some of the Canadian idiosyncrasies, turning them over on my tongue as the miles rolled on by. By the time I got to Canada, I figured I might not pass for a Canadian, but maybe—apart from my military haircut, which was thankfully starting to grow out—I wouldn't stick out as an American.

THE MATTRESS WAS comfy (I never did get to sleep on the chesterfield), and Dawn and Buffy's housemates were nice, but I couldn't stay. They knew I came from California, and if things ever clicked together, they could tie me to San Francisco at the time of the bombing.

Buffy and Dawn were so kind. They said they were sorry to see me go; that I was welcome back any time; and Buffy even slipped me five $10 bills—that crazy, colourful currency they use in this country.

So, I hit the streets. And for the first time since that night in the almond grove off the highway in Manteca, I was truly alone.

AFTER OUT TRIP to Kensington Market, Katie and I started going to different places on Saturdays. We'd enjoyed our trip there, and Katie told me that it was her turn. She would take me to one of her favourite places. We drove in her Maverick to a neighbourhood near Burnhamthorpe and Martin Grove Road in the Borough of Etobicoke. She parked in front of a modest postwar bungalow.

"That's where I used to live," she told me. "Then my parents moved to Markland Woods when Dad started getting promotions at work."

As a cop and now the Superintendent for our area, I reflected. I knew all about Katie's Dad's promotions at work.

"The lots here are really big—Dad fought in World War II and the war vets were given these large, deep lots. They called them wartime lots, and they're half an acre. I always loved this house—I wasn't crazy about moving to Markland, but then again, when I moved there, I met John."

Good, she had said his name without bursting into tears.

We walked through the treed neighbourhood, crossed Martin Grove, and descended a steep hill to a medium-sized creek. We followed a path that was simply last year's grass crushed by people's feet, with lots of mud. I was glad I didn't care about messing up my already grotty shoes.

The weather was warm for April—a month that was highly unpredictable in Toronto. It had actually snowed a week or so ago, when the Toronto Blue Jays baseball team had made their major league debut. There was sun today, and the weather was "50 above," or plus ten in the metric system Canada had adopted.

"You know my name's not really Katie," she told me, as we avoided mud puddles along the path.

I didn't know that. She signed her byline on the newsletter as K.T. McKittrick, and I'd always assumed the K stood for Katie.

"It's really Kathleen, or Kathy," she said. "But there were three other Kathys in my Grade 1 class, so we ran out of names. There was Kath, Kathy and Catherine. It was confusing. I didn't like 'Kathleen,' so I called myself Katie. It worked for a lot of reasons. My Mom had read me the book, 'What Katie Did,' and I liked the lead character. And it worked with my initials—K.T., 'Katie'."

"What's the 'T' stand for," I asked, glad that she seemed to be chattering away like she normally did. She wasn't sad and she wasn't thinking about John for a change.

"Thompson. That's my maiden name.

"My friend Allison and I used to come here all the time," she said. "We were studying explorers in school, so we pretended we were explorers too. Samuel de Champlain. Etienne Brulé—he's probably the one who discovered this creek. There were islands in the middle of the stream, and we'd name them—usually after our favourite pets."

We passed an island that was really nothing more than muddy grass raised slightly above the rushing water.

"What's that one called," I asked her.

"I don't know," she said. "The islands have totally changed since Allison and I came here. I think the water is slightly less polluted though—I think we've made a little progress in that department."

I was still staring at the island. "Let's call it Quincy Island," I said, gratified when she grinned back at me.

"Quincy Islet is more like it," she said. "It's pretty tiny."

The islands had changed, but some of her other memories hadn't.

"Look," she said, running halfway up the ravine to where tree roots had trapped soil that had otherwise eroded, forming an overhang—almost a cave. "I can't believe it's still here. Allison and I used to play in here—we used to call it our Fort. We'd bring our toys and our candy, and stay in here for hours. It was our special place. We could hide out from her pesky little brothers."

I scrambled up the hill after her.

"Let's see if we can still fit," she said, crawling into the cave like space. I crawled in after her, but it was tight. She leaned against me, and the feeling wasn't unwelcome. Somehow it just felt right. The view out the front 'door' was a nice one, with the creek in the distance and some weeping willow trees taking advantage of the moist soil by the creek.

"The Fort's not much good in the rain, though," Katie said, crawling out about 10 minutes later. "It's pretty open."

22: PANHANDLING
(Barry, 1970)

I WANTED TO get far away from Dawn and Buffy, so I kept walking, first east toward the city centre, and then south. I thought I would try to get a job, maybe as a handyman somewhere.

I used the money they had given me to get a hotel room—$40 bought me a week at a walk-up room on the fourth floor of a building in a ratty downtown neighbourhood. The extra $10 was for food. The room was little more than a sink and a bed—with a shower down the hall. I figured I should be able to find a job in a week. I tried a few of the apartment buildings in the downtown area, but they all wanted a driver's licence, a resume, some references and a fixed address. How was I supposed to come up with any of that stuff?

Around that time, I figured I had better get myself a new name—it was a long shot, but the police could be looking for a Barry Gillespie if Mary-Anne spilled the beans about giving me her brother's I.D. And I couldn't show a California address. I kept the Barry part—I was getting used to that name—but I decided I would call myself Barry Barton. There had been a kid in my class back in California with that last name. I figured it was ordinary enough that people wouldn't remember it, but not as obvious as Smith or Jones, or John Doe.

Each day, I would take a shower down the hall from my room, making sure my hair didn't stick up in weird directions. I kept my two T-shirts in good shape, folding them carefully each night, washing them in the sink after two wearings. Same with socks and underwear. I couldn't do much about my one pair of jeans.

I was growing a beard too—I'd never had any problem producing facial hair. It meant I didn't look clean cut for the job interviews, but it did make me look less like the WANTED photos that were starting to circulate for Scott Bronson of Hermosa Beach, CA, whom police were seeking for bombing the research centre in Los Angeles. Dylan, Allan and I were on America's Ten Most Wanted List. I was wanted for sabotage, destruction of government property and conspiracy. Police were calling it the largest act of destruction of government property in U.S. history. There was a $100,000 reward as well.

As time went on, our cause began to seem less noble—less an act of protest to avenge the deaths of Tom and thousands of other American boys whose lives were destroyed by Vietnam. The dead researcher made all the difference. No one was supposed to be in that building, but they were. I didn't spend hours poring over the articles in the paper—that might have made Dawn and Buffy suspicious. But it was hard to miss the glaring headlines in enormous type: **VAN BOMB KILLS ONE AND INJURES FOUR. FUND SET UP FOR VICTIM'S FAMILY. CALIFORNIA TRIO WANTED FOR LARGEST U.S VAN BOMBING. CALIFORNIA BOMBERS MAKE AMERICA'S 10 MOST WANTED LIST. $100,000 REWARD FOR INFORMATION LEADING TO THEIR ARREST.**

The last two headlines were scary—it meant that police all over the U.S. and here in Canada too, wanted to catch us and had our pictures. And anyone who knew about us could become rich very quickly.

The papers didn't seem to get that we were protesting the Vietnam War, although I had made it very clear in the calls I made to police and security. And the Vietnam War people in the

U.S. didn't seem to be rallying around us either. They seemed strangely quiet about the whole thing, as if maybe we'd gone too far. I hoped they'd eventually come around.

When I left the hotel, I was homeless, penniless, and hungry. My Sears bag was getting tattered and had a hole in the bottom. I was glad to find out that they had Sears in Canada, so I didn't look too obviously American. As I walked the streets, I saw musicians with their guitar cases open for donations. Some of them were good and some were just awful. I could play guitar and I had a pretty good singing voice. But I hadn't brought my guitar. It was sitting back in my bedroom in Hermosa Beach gathering dust since Tom had passed away. There were flower vendors, and food trucks that sold hot dogs and sausages. But I didn't have any flowers, and I didn't have a truck.

There was one option open to me. Panhandling.

It was certainly never an option I'd ever considered before. I sort of thought that by being handy I could get a job anywhere. Finding a spot to panhandle was a bit tricky—people seemed to have taken over certain good places like Bloor and Yonge, Queen and Yonge, and the street corners on the seedy part of Yonge Street south of Gerrard. These people could be quite violent if you took their spot. I tried a few places and got chased away—fearing I'd be beat up or worse, killed by the other panhandlers. There was no sense of camaraderie—it was each man for himself. Or each woman. There weren't very many women.

I finally found a place near University and King. Most of the time I didn't have to fight anybody to get that spot. I started walking north along University with my hat out, trying not to look too threatening but also to attract their sympathy by walking slumped over, like I was down and out. That part wasn't really all that difficult. I was down and out. It was horrible. People avoided looking at me, or if they did, it was as though I was a piece of dog shit. At the end of the day, I was up a couple of dollars, enough to buy a meal at Fran's on College Street, the only food I'd had all day. I still looked pretty good—I'd had a shower at my hotel just that morning.

But then what? I had no money, no place to stay. I knew nobody in Toronto other than Dawn and Buffy, and I wanted to sever my ties with them.

I found a park bench and lay down to sleep around 10 p.m. when it was finally dark outside. I was roused quickly by an aggressive drunk who said in no uncertain terms that I was on his bench. I was glad I'd brought a kitchen knife from Dawn and Buffy's place—it looked as though I might need it. So, I moved to a spot under a tree, covering myself with the blanket I'd bought in California and using my Sears bag full of possessions for a pillow. The weather wasn't too bad that first night—it got a bit chilly for a California boy like me, but my blanket helped. I had survived my first day as a panhandler.

But as the summer wore on, panhandling took its toll. There were some nice days when the temperature stayed in the 70s or low 80s, but other days that were blistering hot. My face looked an unhealthy red—I'd never been one to tan easily, not great if you lived in California and even worse if you were stuck outside all day during a hot, humid Toronto summer. Going to the bathroom was a major job hazard. I didn't smell so good after a while, and I'd been turned out of restaurants when I tried to use the bathroom. I'd go down to the lake or the Don River and try to wash, but that water there was totally polluted. I'd drink out of drinking fountains and try to splash water on my face. The beard didn't help, although my hair was still pretty short and I did look less and less like my WANTED picture as time wore on.

By September, the nights were getting cold, not chilly. Rain was a huge problem. The Sears bag was waterproof, but my blanket wasn't. And once it got soaked, I didn't have anywhere to dry it. One day, I commandeered a bench that was usually used by someone smaller than me. When he came to claim his bench, I snarled at him. I probably looked quite scary by then. Tall, skinny, red faced from being outside all the time, with a shaggy beard and uncombed hair. He backed off and I dried my blanket.

And then the police started to crack down on panhandling.

That made me rethink everything I had decided about contacting the draft dodger community. They may not be totally on board if I told them about the bombing, but I needed help. I could just tell them the draft dodger part. Maybe they could get me some I.D. And then maybe I could get off the streets and get a job. I got in touch with the Toronto Anti-Draft group, and told them I had left the States because I was afraid of being drafted. It was true. It wasn't the only reason I had left the States, but it was one of them.

After using my last dime to call them using a pay phone, I walked north on Yonge Street until I found the building they were in. They couldn't have been more helpful. In fact, I think they might have been helpful even if I had told them the whole truth. They arranged to get me some new I.D. "Can I keep the Barry," I asked. They came close. Lo and behold, they found some guy named Gary who was close to me in age and looks. Garry Ballantyne was my name now, but I stuck to Barry with the unlikely story that it was a combination of my first and last name. I was happy to get rid of Barry Gillespie's drivers' license, since it was just a matter of time before the police interviewed Mary-Anne's family and realized it was missing.

Next came finding a place to live. I had no experience of Toronto in winter, but I had heard that it was freezing cold. Not a good time to be living on the street. The Anti-Draft people were nice—they put me up in one of the hostels and I was able to get clean for the first time in weeks. Once it was clean, my hair didn't look too bad. It had grown out a couple of inches from the crew cut Mary-Anne had given me, and brushing it made it look a little shaggy but sort of respectable.

I needed a place to live. 'No fixed address' did not look good on a job application form. There must have been a subconscious reason I kept the name Barry. I went back to the rainbow house on Baldwin Street and asked Dawn and Buffy if I could stay for a while—I'd get a job. I'd pay rent, I told them. After all, they could link me to California, but not L.A. And they liked me. We'd bonded on our long road trip across the U.S.A.

It wasn't a commune as in living off the land and growing our crops or anything, unless you counted the tomato plants that were past their prime when I came back in September. The bare plants with some tiny green tomatoes were all that remained of Dawn's gardening efforts. We did pool some of our money for food and rent. And there was a transient nature to the place—Dawn and Buffy welcomed a lot of strays, people who needed to crash somewhere for a few days. Friends in the lesbian community who were going through rough times. And we did do some drugs—soft stuff like grass and hash. No LSD trips for these hippie commune people.

So maybe it wasn't really and truly a commune, but saying I lived in a commune was a good conversation starter.

As Barry Ballantyne, I got a few jobs. The best one was doing maintenance at a small motel in the west end on the Lakeshore. I made a friend of the owner, Tony, who wasn't nuts about my lengthening hair and overall scruffy appearance, but appreciated the fact that I could unclog a toilet, paint a room or apply tar to the huge asphalt parking lot.

Back in California, the investigation continued.

It turns out that no protesters had ever detonated a bomb the size of ours. We knew the Econoline van was large; we knew the barrels inside the van were industrial size. One of our main problems had been getting them into the van. And we knew they were filled with a lot of ammonium nitrate and fuel oil. But apparently there was more than a ton of that stuff in the barrels. And we got the explosion part right this time too—the news reports were saying it was the biggest vehicle bomb ever released on U.S. soil. That meant there were all kinds of levels of government out looking for us—the FBI, the California state police and the local L.A. cops.

I followed the news in the papers, cast-offs left on park benches or on the tables in the fast-food joints that were my staple meals in the early days. Sometimes guests left papers lying around at the motel when I worked there, and I'd stuff them in the backpack I'd bought to replace the tattered Sears bag. At the commune, they got the Toronto Star and they watched TV a lot, so I followed the news that way.

As the weeks and months went by, things looked worse and worse. We'd missed our target yet again. We didn't destroy the war-related research labs at the LA Research Lab; we'd hit some targets that had nothing to do with the bombs that were being dropped on innocent people in Vietnam. Story after story dealt with the costs of damage to the heavy-duty research equipment in the labs we'd destroyed—heartbreaking stories of how scientists at the research centre had lost their entire careers' worth of findings on things like curing diseases or coming up with better crops to feed the world.

And then there was the guy that died. There was a lot of sympathy for him, of course, and the public had raised $40,000—enough to buy a house or a small fleet of cars—for his family.

He wasn't our target. And in addition to that, a few people had been injured. One guy was in a wheelchair for life; a woman had lost an eye. All because of us.

Our message seemed to be lost in all the outrage over the damage to people and property. While there were some radical university student newspapers that supported our cause, there were just as many mainstream publications, in the States at least, that said we'd gone too far.

Was I sorry we had done it? No, we needed to do something to draw attention to the death of Tom and the experiences faced by millions of other veterans. But I was sorry those people had been injured and that the one guy had died. We had never intended that.

America's 10 Most Wanted had put out posters for each of us. The posters talked about each of the three of us this way:

CAUTION: SCOTT DOUGLAS BRONSON IS BEING SOUGHT IN CONNECTION WITH THE DESTRUCTION BY EXPLOSIVES OF A BUILDING IN WHICH ONE PERSON WAS KILLED AND SEVERAL INJURED. HE MAY BE ACCOMPANIED BY ALLAN GEORGE BRONSON OR DYLAN THOMAS HEARST. CONSIDER DANGEROUS.

The only good thing about my Wanted poster is that I looked nothing like the long-haired, clean-shaven teenager in the picture. And I was no longer the same height shown in the poster—I'd grown at least a couple of inches. Not fun, when you're homeless and trying to fit in jeans that became too short, but a good thing if the cops were on your tail.

The FBI wanted us for conspiracy and the bombing.

The state of California wanted us for murder.

The cops had found the place in the woods where we had assembled the bomb. Apparently, we had been careless—there were receipts that tied us to the purchase of fuel oil and the big drums, and unusual quantities of ammonium nitrate. When the vendors were shown the receipts and photos of the three suspects, they had no trouble identifying Allan, Dylan and me.

They had found enough evidence to track down the van we used in the bombing. We'd put a phony licence plate on it, but the ownership could still be tracked to Dad.

And Dylan had made a mistake—apparently, he had contacted his parents from a pay phone in New York State and asked them to wire him some money. But by the time they tracked down that lead, Dylan was long gone.

There were plenty of leads but none of them useful. But the cops had figured out that we would head for Canada. Why not? Canada seemed to be turning a blind eye to draft dodgers and even deserters.

And then, in 1973, I got to read about my brother in the papers. Apparently, the RCMP had taken a suspect in custody, who was willing to deal, saying he knew where Allan Bronson was hiding.

It turned out that Allan was hiding in plain sight. He'd changed his name—he was now known as James White and was working at a library. His employers thought he was a nice, intelligent young man—perhaps a little on the quiet side—and they had no complaints about his work. His landlord said he was a good tenant who had a job and always paid on time for his single room. Allan looked nothing like his picture on the Most Wanted poster. On the poster he had longish hair and a beard; the person the Toronto police arrested had short hair and was clean-shaven.

Police staked out his house, waiting for him to come home from work. They arrested Allan without incident, much to the surprise of the house's other residents.

One down, two to go, the cops were quoted as saying.

23: SIR JOHN'S DINNER
(Katie, May 1977)

IT TOOK ABOUT a month, but I finally managed to get John to go to dinner and explain himself. This did not go well. I insisted we go to Sir John's in the brand-new Eaton Centre on Yonge Street as it was in between John's law office and the Rosedale Subway stop. And I knew John had been dying to go there—it had just opened, it was self-serve and it reportedly served good steak at a price well below the city's high-end steakhouses like Julie's Mansion and Barberian's Steak House.

I walked there along Yonge—it took about half an hour, but I needed the time to calm down, and to bridge the gap between work and my horrible personal life.

On the way, I tried not to think about John. Walking helped a bit—May in Toronto is beautiful, and even in downtown Toronto there were blossoms in view. I knew the area well—I made a habit of getting out at lunchtime and going for a walk, often to a destination like the Belair Café, just across the road, or Kentucky Fried Chicken on Bloor, or Burger King, just south of Bloor. I walked by Ramsden Park, where I often read and ate my lunch on a spread-out blanket, to get a break from the office. It was grassy; there were blossoms on some of the trees. Then I walked past Luigi's Trattoria where people from work went if they wanted a fancy Italian lunch with a glass of wine. Then came the huge Canadian Tire store. Behind the store and beyond the subway, there were glimpses of the Rosedale Valley Ravine.

I passed Yorkville, which was changing from a cool, hippie

place into a shopping destination, since developers had bought up the properties on the street that had once been a hotspot for singers like Ian and Sylvia, James Taylor and Gordon Lightfoot. I passed Bloor Street, where the new Hotel Plaza and Hudson's Bay Centre attested to the development of the area in the past few years.

And then I was walking past Frank Stollery's, where John had bought his work clothes. John. Everything came back to John. Almost 10 years of memories, my buddy since we started high school.

I blinked back tears. I knew I was going to cry at our dinner; Mom always said my tear ducts were too close to my eyes. And back in Grade 8, when our teacher drew a Character House for each person and filled in the lines when we'd mastered a personality trait, I had trouble getting the line indicating 'self-control.'

I'd dressed for success, as the saying goes, wearing a nice dress with a blazer and making sure I'd washed and blow-dried my hair that morning. I'd put on lipstick, which was unusual—I normally didn't bother much with makeup. Gordon, my boss, had commented that I looked nice when I walked into work this morning.

And along with upsetting visions of John, came more upsetting visions of John with her. Her name was Gillian—I knew she was the one even though John hadn't told me. I'd met her at the Christmas party. She worked with John at the office in a job that was the same as his—which of course meant that John had spent way more time with her than he did with me since he was always at the office. It didn't help that she was about his height (read 'short'), with straight, perfectly coiffed blonde hair and a perfect figure. And pretty. If your taste runs towards short blondes, not tall, skinny people with ordinary brown hair like me.

We met there at 5:30. John was looking good, I had to admit, even though the admission felt like a stone in the pit of my stomach. No wonder he was no longer interested in me—his looks had changed dramatically and put him in a whole other category when it came to dating. I personally don't care too much about looks—there are other things, like a sense of humour and kindness, that mean a lot more to me. But I had noticed that good-looking men generally gravitate toward good-looking women.

Sir John's was self-serve, which was probably why their steaks were so reasonably priced. I wasn't sure I liked that—half the fun of a spiffy restaurant is having a waiter or waitress hover over you, waiting to take your order. And the line was awkward. Neither John nor I was great at small talk. I could get information from anybody—it was part of my job description. But I had to have a reason to talk to people; otherwise I clammed up or babbled on and talked way too fast. With John, the things I wanted to talk to him about were too weighty for self-serve line conversation. Normally, we might have bantered back and forth—for many years, John and I had shared an offbeat sense of humour. But that John seemed to be long gone, and anyway, I wasn't in the mood for banter.

We got our steaks—both ordering medium rare, which was one of the things we'd always had in common. We each got a baked potato and something from the salad bar. And wine. I ordered white, and John, who had always shared a bottle of white with me, ordered red. Apparently his taste in wine had evolved, along with his taste in women.

"Cheers," said John, once we were seated at the table.

"Cheers?" I said, even though it felt fake.

My steak looked red, thick and juicy but it tasted like sawdust. I moved things around on my plate and waited for John to start the conversation.

He cut a few pieces of steak and ate them with relish. "Really good," he pronounced.

I didn't deign this with a reply.

He finally took the hint. "So, I guess you're wondering what happened," he said. "Why I moved out."

"Yes," I said, trying hard to control my tears.

"Katie, you'll always be my best friend, but I'm not in love with you. I thought I was, but then I meet someone else, and I realized that you and I weren't really in love."

I stayed silent, waiting for him to fill the space with more of this crap.

"It's a powerful feeling with her. We just clicked. And as we got to know each other, I realized I had to be true to myself. It wasn't fair to keep leading you on when my heart was with someone else."

I raised my eyebrows slightly and took a deep breath.

"Gillian," I said. I hardly recognized my voice when I said this. And I wasn't crying.

"Yes, Gillian. I've gotten to know her very well over the past six months—you know, because we work together. I thought I was happy before, but now I realize what I was missing. We've got so much in common—she's into law like me, and she has been a big help with my work. It started out as strictly a work relationship, but now… now it's something more. She's loving, she's intelligent…

"And I'm not," I said in that same flat, emotionless voice.

"No, Katie," he said, "You are. You've got it all wrong."

He reached his hand across the table to clasp mine, and I quickly moved my hand under the table. He was trying to be friendly, low-key and reasonable. I almost missed the times he had yelled at me about the pub or about my hair or my clunky glasses or my bad clothes. At least he was being honest then—not this faux-empathetic, fake, lawyer.

"I will always value the role you played in my life—and yes, you are every bit as intelligent as Gillian. It's just, it's just... I think of you as my very best friend who stood by me all through my growing up years. But this is different—I love her in a way that I've never felt before. I feel as though I've come into my own with her..."

"It's called lust," I said bitterly, still not crying.

That stopped his stupid monologue about self-discovery and me being his best friend.

"Have you slept with her?" I asked.

"Katie..." he said, looking away, a sure sign that he was indeed sleeping with her.

"I'm really not interested in being friends with you," I said. "Your definition of friendship is certainly not mine."

It was time to leave. I rose, with dignity I thought, and walked out of the restaurant. No drama. I just walked out, slowly and confidently—totally an act of course.

He could have his perfect self-serve steak, and the rest of mine too. And he could pay the bill.

And then, heedless of the looks I got on my way home taking the Carlton streetcar, I started to cry.

24: MACRAMÉ, COOKING & A GREEN THUMB
(Barry, May 1977)

MY LANDLADY WAS not doing well. I knew because there was scummy water left in the kitchen sink, piles of dishes with food still on them, a big bag of cans and bottles that had to have their labels peeled off so that they could be recycled. There were piles of laundry waiting to be put in the washing machine, carried upstairs and then hung out on the line to dry (to save energy of course). Katie was obviously suffering.

But the thing that made it real for me was the plants.

During the winter, a macramé hanger with a plant decorated the east-facing front window in the living room. I knew there were usually a lot more plants in there, but now that the weather was getting warmer, Katie had moved them.

One Saturday, I wandered into the room at the back that she called a sun porch. It was just off the kitchen, and I was waiting to give Katie my rent cheque.

The sunroom was wood-panelled, much like the rest of the house, and not well insulated. It was totally frigid in the winter, but with a couple of woven-plastic lawn chairs, it was fine starting in springtime. Above the panelling were wall-to-wall windows, whose multi-paned frames had the paint peeling off. And since those windows faced west and got the afternoon sun, I guess they were pretty good for growing plants.

But the leaves on these ones were turning brown. I recognized a few of the plants. Wandering Jew had dried up leaves among the good ones. The rubber plant's leaves were turning yellow; a few had dropped. And Phil—at least I think it was a Phil—didn't have many leaves at all. Déjà vu. I remember a time when the plants back at our home in California looked like this—in the months after Tom passed away.

Katie came up behind me as I was looking at the plants.

"So," I said. "I think you're into plants..."

She just looked sad. "I'm afraid I haven't been taking very good care of them," she said.

"What kind are they?" I asked her. "I know this one—it's called Phil."

"Phil? Oh, Philodendron. Yes, you're right. It needs some water..."

"And a good dusting," I added. "When I was little, I couldn't pronounce its name, so I just called it 'Phil'.

"Mom had a lot of plants when we were growing up," I added.

That did it.

Katie started talking, more animated than I'd seen her in a week.

"That's a schefflera—some people call it an umbrella tree. That's Wandering Jew, and that's a spider plant." She paused for effect, "Or *chlorophytum comosum*."

I rolled my eyes, recalling the days when Allan would bore me with the names of plants, chemicals, or whatever list was fascinating him at the time.

She pointed to a plant with long, narrow, striped leaves standing straight up. "Dracaena," she said. "Or mother-in-law's tongue."

I smiled.

"Not that my mother-in-law was all that bad," she reflected. "Better than her son," she added bitterly.

Change the subject! I thought. "What about this one," I

asked.

"That's a fern," she said. "I might plant that one outside soon. They can grow indoors or out…"

By the end of our chat, we had fetched a watering can with a long spout and given all those suffering plants a drink. She had started pulling off the dead leaves, and had found a cloth to dust off Phil. I had offered to help her paint the peeling trim on the sun porch windows. There was a lot of work to do as each window had about eight separate panes. But then again, I'd quite a bit of painting in the job I'd had at the Lakeshore motel years ago.

Sorry, Mom, that I didn't water the plants for you…

- - -

ONCE WE'D BONDED over plants, I graduated to being permanently welcome upstairs for pre-dinner Happy Hour. The concept was totally foreign to me—when my Dad got home from work, he was wiped out from hard, physical labour; he wanted dinner on the table when he arrived. And God forbid we kids were late. My mother was very strict about mealtime— we had to be there at 5 o'clock sharp or go without dinner.

Sure, my parents drank when they had friends over for parties. Cocktails usually—Bloody Marys, Gimlets, Old Fashioneds. Mom liked those kinds of drinks—once she even tried to get one of her friends to make a cocktail that was the first thing the astronauts drank after the 1969 moonwalk. Dad was more traditional—his drink was a whisky sour. Actually, he didn't even care about the sugar and lemon—plain old bourbon or rye was just fine on its own.

Katie explained that the drink-before-dinner routine had been copied from John's parents, who were okay, even if their son was horrible. She added that her parents never had Happy Hour. A cop's schedule—even a senior cop's schedule—didn't allow for regular family before-dinner routines.

The Happy Hour thing hadn't worked out when John was around—he usually got home so late that a bedtime cocoa would have been more appropriate than alcohol. So I think she was pleased that I was willing to come upstairs for the occasion.

Katie and I worked different hours—I'd usually go in early and leave around four. If there was printing to be done, it was generally best to get in early in the morning. Katie would come in around 9:30 and leave sometime after 5:30. After work, I'd watch a bit of TV, or clean the apartment, study for my high school equivalency or fix one of the small appliances I'd found in other people's trash. Then when Katie came home, she'd yell downstairs, and I'd come up.

She served wine—she was really into wine, especially white wine. I grew up in California, which is home to some great vineyards, but I'd always been kind of a beer guy myself. And I was trying to be less-of-a-beer guy these days. There was plenty of beer and plenty of drugs at my last place, though the people in the commune seemed to function okay in terms of jobs and getting through the hangovers. It was nothing like San Francisco in the '60s. But I liked my job at Rosedale, and I didn't want to be seen sneaking beer through the kitchen and down to my apartment. So, I mostly just drank when we went out with the gang from R.P. And during Happy Hour.

Sometimes, it was awkward thinking of things to say. Neither of us was great on small talk. But then Quincy would come in, wag his tail and put his big head on my feet.

"So where did you take Quincy on his walk today?" I asked Katie.

She smiled a bit. "The Ashbridges Bay sewage treatment

plant," she said. "It's actually a good place to take a big dog. This guy is reasonably obedient and he needs to run. He can be off-leash on the grass that covers the sewage treatment plant, and he doesn't bother anybody.

"You should come with me one day."

"Sure," I nodded.

"Did you have pets growing up?" she asked, starting to get into journalist mode.

I didn't answer immediately. I thought about how much of the truth I could tell her without giving anything away. I thought the subject of childhood pets was reasonably safe.

I took a sip of my wine.

"We had a dog," I said. "Her name was Lassie."

"Of course, her name was Lassie!" Katie said. "Do you remember the TV show?"

"Yup. And 'Rin Tin Tin' too," I enthused, lost in memories.

"But our Lassie wasn't a collie," I said. "She was a mix—mostly cocker spaniel, I think."

Oh, the memories of that little dog.

"Was she mostly your dog? Or did you have brothers and sisters?"

"She was mostly my oldest brother's dog," I said without thinking. "Until..."

"Until what?" asked my hard-nosed reporter of a landlady. "I didn't know you had an older brother. What happened to him?"

I hesitated, wondering how to get off this subject. "He left," I said more cautiously. "And Lassie liked me best after my brother left home."

There! Too many questions averted. I hadn't given the name of my older brother; I didn't mention Allan; I hadn't mentioned Dylan and I hadn't mentioned California. But I had better change the subject fast.

Happy hour proved to be a bit of a minefield. I'd have to make sure I didn't drink too much or talk too much about myself or about my past.

But I must admit that even though the wine was kind of bitter and acidic for my taste, Happy Hour was a nice change from sitting in front of the TV or working on my high school correspondence courses.

When the weather was sunny enough, we took our glasses of wine and went into the west-facing sun porch. (Eventually I got used to wine, but I still liked beer better.)

25: OUT WEST
(Barry, 1973-75)

- - - - -

ALLAN'S ARREST IN 1973 was big, big news. I didn't dare watch television upstairs with Dawn and Buffy. In fact, I made a point of leaving the room if the TV news was on. I also read about it in the *Toronto Star*, which I retrieved the next day, after Buffy had put it in the garbage, and read in the privacy of my room. And then I started walking to Bay Bloor Radio in the upscale Manulife Centre. I have long legs and it was a quick walk there, less than 20 minutes. I'd tell everyone I was going out for a walk, and then go stand in front of the bank of TVs they had on display. Even there, I had to hide my emotions.

So, apparently my brother had been living in Toronto all this time, and we'd never run in to one another. Apparently some Toronto cop had stopped some guy for reckless driving and discovered the guy had outstanding warrants. Those warrants added up to a heap of jail time. That guy had made a deal with the cop, whose name was Officer Cooper. He offered to tell the cops where Allan was in return for a reduced sentence.

Apparently, Allan was doing the same as I was, living a quiet life under an assumed name. His landlord was shocked that the quiet, poorly dressed, geeky guy living in the basement was party to what they were now calling the biggest van bombing ever carried out on American soil. His employer said he seemed like a nice guy. "Very bright," he'd said. Of course he was bright, I knew. He had a Master's degree in Organic Chemistry along with his Bachelor's.

There was TV footage of the cops arresting him—he looked

kind of scruffy and really scared. But then he got cleaned up and didn't look so bad. Our parents were happy to be reunited with him, even though the charges against him could land him in jail for a life sentence. They got one of the best lawyers in Toronto to take the case pro bono. Our family was strictly working class—they couldn't afford fancy lawyer fees. I don't know how they could even afford to travel to Toronto. Luckily, Toronto had a few high-end lawyers who believed in civil rights and would take on the case no charge. The focus of the trial was that they wanted him to be tried in Canada, rather than facing extradition to California, where he would be tried for murder, and would probably get the max for what he—what we—had done.

In Canada, he could be tried for the bombing as a political act—and that's what our bombing was according to Canadian authorities. In the States, they were trying to extradite him for murder, since that one man had died.

My parents. Oh, they looked so old. Mom had lost weight and it didn't suit her—instead of "handsome," she just looked skinny. Her face, which was never soft looking, now had so many angles and every bone showed. Her hair, which she had always dyed a deep brown, was now salt and pepper gray, but still short and permed, the way she had always worn it. Dad looked smaller—when he stood by Allan, it was hard to believe that my six-foot-three brother was related to this tiny old man who coughed all the time. It would have been even harder to believe had they seen photos of our family when Tom was alive. Three sons, and we were all much taller than Dad. Even Mom was taller than Dad now.

My parents were here in Toronto and Allan had been here all along, living not far from where I lived with Buffy and Dawn— so close and yet so far away. I longed to reach out and give them all hugs and let them know I was okay and I loved them so much. The newscaster said that Dad had emphysema—not a huge surprise, as he'd always been a pack-a-day smoker. Mom smoked too, but they didn't say anything about her having cancer.

The arrest photos and mug shot showed scruffy, short-haired but badly-dressed Allan, but by the time our parents got involved, he looked more like the short-haired, button-down-collared geek he had been in high school. He didn't do well on television. He either gave one-word replies or arrogant discourses in response to questions just as he had all his life.

Here's how a conversation between Allan and a TV interviewer would go, outside the courthouse.

INTERVIEWER: "So, how did you manage to carry out the biggest vehicle bombing to date on American soil?"

ALLAN: "We built a big bomb."

INTERVIEWER: "How did you do that?"

Allan looked at him as though he was retarded. "We did what we did with the smaller bombs, but we used more materials. It's not that hard—ammonium nitrate plus fuel oil and a detonator. We just did what we'd done with the smaller bombs and built them bigger. We used large drums and we put them all into a big van." He shrugged his shoulders, as though he couldn't get why the interviewer needed the explanation.

"And what motivated you to build the bomb?"

"We did it for Tom." And then Allan's lawyer would hustle him away, leaving no time for an explanation.

He wasn't telegenic but he became a somewhat unlikely cult figure. These days there was sympathy for the bombing from anti-war groups in Canada. People would gather in front of Toronto's new city hall—the one that looked sort of like a spaceship—with placards that read, "Free Allan Bronson," or "End the war in Vietnam NOW," or "Free the War Protesters." Mom and Dad participated in some of those protests, carrying a "Free Allan Bronson" sign between them.

They were interviewed at the protests, and their interviews went a lot better than Allan's. Mom did the talking—who would have thought that a plain ordinary housewife could talk so well. The weather was getting colder, and I could tell they were dressed inadequately in their California clothes, and were shivering in Toronto's damp, chilly weather. It was almost winter here.

INTERVIEWER: "How do you feel about your sons being charged with the biggest bombing on American soil?"

MOM: "I know my sons, and I know they must have had a good reason to do it."

INTERVIEWER: "And what would that be?"

MOM: "I know they both felt strongly about the war in Vietnam."

INTERVIEWER: "Yes, but a bombing? Why would they do that?"

MOM: "I know they participated in a lot of demonstrations. But that didn't end the war."

INTERVIEWER: "A lot of Americans thought that way, but they didn't carry out bombings. Why do you think your sons went to that length to make their point?"

MOM: "I think they did it… for Tom."

INTERVIEWER: "Tom?"

MOM: "Yes, my oldest son, who died because of the war."

But the interviewer didn't pick up on this. "And what words would you have to say to your other son, Scott, who is still at large?"

And then Mom broke my heart. She looked directly at the camera. "Scottie, wherever you are, please turn yourself in."

Why didn't anyone pick up on the "for Tom" thing? I thought it would gain Allan some sympathy from the Canadians who watched TV. But his lawyer was taking another tack—get Allan to talk about the explosion as a politically-motivated crime, not a murder. Good luck. Allan wasn't the person with all the political beliefs—that would be Dylan. He could talk for hours about politics and current affairs and why the Kent State massacre made our bombing inevitable.

One day, I wore a Toronto Maple Leafs cap, pulled low on my forehead, and ventured down to the protest at City Hall. I didn't dare get anywhere near Mom and Dad, and being there just made me feel more uncomfortable than ever.

There was way too much coverage of Allan, plus Dylan and I, who were being named as co-conspirators. There were pictures of the three of us together. I was so happy that I looked nothing like those pictures—my appearance had changed dramatically in the past three years.

But my stomach turned somersaults whenever I saw the three of us on TV. I had to get out of Toronto.

One day, when I was at Bay-Bloor Radio, watching 20 versions of the proceedings on colour televisions large and small, I couldn't control myself.

"So would you say that the LA Research Center bombing was politically motivated?" Allan's lawyer asked, putting words into his mouth, or so I thought.

Allan just nodded. "Mr. Bronson, you can't just nod your head. We need an answer for the court records," the lawyer said.

"Yes, Your Honour," Allan replied, using the polite voice Mom had drilled into us since we were little kids.

"And was this because you had previously participated in demonstrations that didn't achieve the political results you were aiming for?"

"Objection!" the Crown lawyer said, loudly but politely, in true Canadian style. "My friend is leading the witness."

Yes, of course he is, I thought, from my standing position in front of 20 close-up views of Allan's lawyer. Even I knew that. But I also recognized that such a high-profile lawyer would generate great publicity, and that his stature meant he could get away with more than other lawyers could.

"Objection sustained," the judge said, putting an end to this line of questioning, and fuelling my frustration.

"For God's sake, just tell them about Tom," I said to my brother. Even though I didn't shout it, in fact my voice was hardly more than a whisper, I had attracted the attention of the Manulife Centre security guard, stationed just outside Bay-Bloor Radio with its high-end electronics.

He walked over to me and asked why I was coming there so often when I didn't buy anything. I thought about how I must look—a longer-haired guy in ordinary, slightly scruffy clothes, out of place among Manulife's high-class clientele. I hadn't imagined things when I thought that mall security was paying a little too much attention to me whenever I went there.

"No worries," I mumbled. "I'll move along."

I had to leave town. I told Dawn and Buffy that I had another job out west and said I would keep in touch. I was sorry to leave the two of them, and I'd gotten to know some of our housemates quite well too. The problem was that they could link me to California, and with my brother in jail, there was a surge of interest in the case.

Before I left, I went to the Anti-Draft people again, and let them know I needed a new identity. I was much more comfortable when I got the papers saying I was now Richard Matheson, and that I was born and bred in Toronto. Richard. Rick. Ricky. I turned the names over in my head. I stuck my thumb out, headed for Calgary and the oil fields, one of many young Canadians hitting the road and heading west. By the time the first driver picked me up, I had it straight. I was Rick Matheson and I was Canadian.

Chesterfield. Pickerel. Pop not soda. They didn't have Interstates here; they had highways and the big ones were 400-series highways. I had always been a good mimic and I'd had a few years to work on my Canadian accent. I should be okay, I told myself. Rick. Rick Matheson.

And then I did the stupidest thing I have ever done in my life.

HER NAME WAS Helen and she was beautiful. That's my main excuse. She seemed nice; she reminded me of Mary-Anne. And when the two of us ended up in the semitrailer of a transport truck that was deadheading from Winnipeg to Regina, we had lots of hours to kill by talking. Lots of hours in an empty truck trailer with a mickey of vodka. ("Mickey," now there's a good Canadian word—it means 13 ounces or a fifth of alcohol.)

My great Canadian accent didn't count for beans. Because after I'd taken way too many swigs from that mickey, I spilled my guts. I told her about Tom, and how his death had changed me. I told her about my anti-draft and anti-Vietnam beliefs. And then I told her about Allan and Dylan and the bombing. About being on the lam.

She told me she was a peacenik—that she believed conflicts should be solved by discussions and peaceful protests. I told her she had a truly Canadian point of view; that all the peaceful protests across the country had not made a bit of difference in the States. I told her about Dad, and his view that the Germans did not really comprehend what they were doing to Britain until the Allies brought the bombing to German soil; how Dylan, Allan and I were trying to bring the same message to the powers that be that sent young, impressionable Americans to carry out and witness untold horrors in Vietnam. How we did it all for Tom—and the millions of Americans like him, who were traumatized by what they did and saw. I lost my brother to the war, as surely as I would have had he been shot by the Vietcong. No one was listening. But our oversized bomb had got their attention.

All the arguments I had been keeping in check came pouring out thanks to several ounces of vodka.

"But what would Tom think?" she asked me, posing a question that had been lurking somewhere in my subconscious for years. "Aren't you just as guilty as he was. He had to take civilian lives in Vietnam, and to protest, you guys killed someone as well."

I didn't have an answer, and that ended our conversation. I don't know if any of what I had said registered with her, but our discussion was a friendly one—we knew we disagreed, but it didn't matter. I felt so much better, having got things off my chest.

And then she started to sing.

"We shall overcome, we shall overcome, we shall overcome some day-ay-ay-ay…"

It was one of the songs Tom and I used to sing. Helen had a high, clear voice, and my voice was deeper now. I sang the harmony Tom used to sing. It was a magical moment. We sang a couple more songs—"Blowin' in the Wind" and "Turn, Turn, Turn."

It was cold in the truck, so we cuddled together under a canvas tarp. She let me lay my head on her lap as the truck lurched and heaved down the Trans-Canada highway. The vodka had made us sleepy, and we dropped off, leaning against each other for support and warmth until the driver unlatched the doors and the sun flooded in.

"I've got a few things I've got to buy at a grocery store," Helen said to me as we were about to part. She lived in Regina and was heading home. "Wanna meet me for something to eat in an hour. There's a place called Juliana's Pizza that's not too far away." Neither of us had a pen nor paper, so she wrote the address on my hand with her lipstick. It was pale pink lipstick, and it didn't show up too well, but if I angled my hand just the right way in the winter sunshine, I could see it.

"See you soon," I said. "Pizza sounds great!" She smiled and took off.

When I arrived a Juliana's, there were cops. They were plain clothes, but I could tell they were cops. I just knew.

So, I quietly turned around. It wasn't until I was well out of sight of Juliana's that the adrenalin kicked in. I ran towards a gas station, slowing down just before I got there. I stuck my thumb out and got the first ride out of town.

Did I tell her my new name? I couldn't remember. But I did remember that I had told her my old name, and my relationship to Dylan and Allan.

Had I also been stupid enough in my drunken stupor to tell her about the $100,000 reward being offered for my arrest as one of America's 10 Most Wanted?

Either way, as soon as I got to the next city—Calgary I thought—I'd contact the anti-drafters and ditch the Rick Matheson I.D. Too bad. I was getting used to that name.

- - -

THE ANTI-DRAFT PEOPLE were pissed at me for blowing my cover just a week into my Rick Matheson identity. They bawled me out and told me they were getting fed up with me.

My next alias, Douglas Barnard Burns, lasted much longer. I grew a beard and cut my hair, so I wouldn't look like Rick Matheson or my WANTED poster picture. Thank God, I had a baby face in that picture, and I'd grown a couple of inches since the 5 feet, 11 inches listed on the poster. I laid low. I got a job doing maintenance and landscaping for the city. I didn't tell anyone who I was or where I was from. I was lonely, I was depressed, but the police didn't pick me up. I was so tired of running. What kind of future did I have if I had to change identities and have this crazy, nomadic, on-the-run lifestyle?

Helen's question haunted me. "What would Tom think?" Would he have understood our need to use violence to end the war? What would he think of our family, now totally torn apart?

I had lots of time to think—and I thought about my old dream of becoming a tool and die maker. But I needed Grade 12. As Douglas Burns, I signed up for correspondence courses, and began the long and difficult process of getting my high school diploma. I knew, at least, Tom would approve of that.

26: HE'S A REBEL
(Katie, May 1977)

MY PARENTS AND I weren't speaking. We had often had rocky times when I was growing up—it seemed there was nothing I could do to please them. If I got 95 per cent on a test, they'd ask why I'd missed out on the remaining five points, and were only half kidding. They were always giving me a hard time about the way I looked, the way I dressed, my political views and my obsession with pollution control. John's parents were nicer. They were both schoolteachers, and they seemed to understand nerdy kids like John and me better than my parents did.

The one thing my parents approved of was my relationship with John, something that made growing up in that atmosphere of disapproval somewhat more bearable.

John was a smart guy. John was ambitious. John was going to be a lawyer. They didn't understand that I wanted to be a writer—that every ounce of my being knew that. That I'd known I wanted to write since I was six years old. They didn't consider journalism to be a real career, and it had been scholarships rather than parental support that got me through Ryerson. And Mom, a stay-at-home, 1950s-style housewife, didn't really get why a woman needed to go to university at all. After all, a secretarial course or the one-year teaching degree, were enough to get me my M.R.S., the only degree that counted for a woman.

They were delighted when John and I decided to get married two- and a-half years ago. They took charge and Mom planned her dream wedding for me. It was at The Markland Woods Golf and Country Club, which satisfied Mom's need for social status, even though neither she nor Dad were members. John and I were busy with school, so the wedding was really her show, with Dad and John's parents strictly sidelined.

They loved John so much and considered him my saviour. My parents would joke—and I didn't find it funny—that if John and I split up, they would side with John.

Now that was being put to the test. Sure enough, they sided with John, thinking everything was my fault. "You know, Katie, if you'd got your hair cut and started dressing better earlier in the marriage, John might still be around." Or, "I think the problem is that you spend too much time on your career, and not enough time learning how to be a corporate wife."

They didn't seem to get that John had changed. They seemed to think that I had purposefully turned him away, thus ruining the only chance I had for a good, traditional marriage. To a LAWYER. Now, that was a step up in the world in their opinion!

They also didn't like the idea of me living in the house with a male tenant. "It's not proper for you to be living in a house with a man who isn't your husband," my mother would say worriedly.

"It's all strictly platonic," I told my parents, dismissing their fears. "And Barry helps me with house repairs and stuff."

"You really should see if John will come back. I'm sure he'd come back if you promised to change your ways," she wheedled.

Eventually I got tired of hearing all this and quickly hung up when they called. About that time, I spent a couple hundred bucks on one of those fancy new answering machines, which made avoiding their calls even easier.

HAPPY HOURS WERE a welcome break from work, and I was glad I had Barry in the house. He was handy; he painted the frames of all those little windows in the sun porch with surprising attention to detail. Next on my list was getting rid of those horrible fake pink tiles in the bathroom. That turned out to be a much bigger job than we thought it would be. When we yanked at the fake panel of tiles, it came off but took half the wall with it. I just about cried, but Barry didn't seem to be fazed by it. "I've done drywall before," he told me. What hadn't that man done?

So that was one project we did together, and it helped ease the pain of having John leave me. We chose some of those earth-toned tiles that were so much in style—brown with a bit of yellow. These were real tiles, not the fake panelboard ones. I learned about things like grout, and how to fill in those spaces between the tiles and wipe off the excess grout before it dried. I wasn't very good at it—I'd end up doing a rough version and then Barry would quickly correct my errors.

Another project was his school. I'd never really known someone my age who hadn't completed high school—who was a "high school dropout" as my parents would say. My mother didn't have her high-school diploma—but that was the way things were back then. She'd got her typing and shorthand and worked as a secretary until she met Dad.

I made a point of asking Barry about his high-school courses when we got together. Turns out, he'd been doing correspondence courses part time for four years, and he was just finishing the last courses he needed to complete Grade 12. I made a few phone calls for him and found out that he could become a tool-and-die maker apprentice at several different companies—General Electric, Ontario Hydro, or Westinghouse, in either Toronto or Hamilton.

I asked him why he never completed his high school, and he said, "Do I look like a guy who'd do well sitting at a desk." And I had to admit, I'd rarely seen him sitting at a desk. Even at work, he was always walking around, standing up or crouching down to check on something to do with the printer. And down in his room, he lay on the bed, with books and a pad of paper propped against his legs.

He would finish his studies in June, and then he would graduate. I was planning to do something special to mark the occasion.

27: COMMUNAL LOVE & QUINCY
(Barry, 1975-76 & May 1977)

- - - - -

AS DOUGLAS BURNS, my life was so boring. But it enabled me to watch the drama unfold from a distance. I sometimes would buy the Globe and Mail, which called itself "Canada's National Newspaper," and that enabled me to catch up on the trial even though I was on the other side of the country. Allan's lawyer worked hard; he managed to make a very eloquent case for Allan as a politically motivated protester, and he seemed to have some public sympathy, as many Canadians had no love for the Vietnam War. But Allan still ended up being sent to the States to stand trial for first-degree murder. While he ended up pleading to a lesser charge, he was sentence to 25 years of jail time. Some of that could be served concurrently, but he would still be an old man when he got out. Everyone seemed to think that Allan was the ringleader since he had the technical knowledge. But I knew who the real ringleader was.

And then in 1975 they found Dylan. He'd gone to Montreal before he too ended up in Toronto. He'd left Montreal because it was the time of the War Measures Act. Why he headed for Montreal made no sense to me. Everyone there spoke French, and for all their fancy education, neither Allan nor Dylan had ever taken a French course. Dylan might have done okay in Spanish, but as far as I could tell, Spanish was not a major language in Quebec.

There'd been an act of terrorism: the Quebec deputy premier and a British diplomat had been kidnapped, and Pierre Laporte, the politician, was found dead in the trunk of a car.

-193-

All of that meant that there was a huge police presence with powers they didn't usually possess, and they were all looking for terrorists. Which is what they would call Allan, Dylan and I, considering what we had done.

I couldn't believe that we had all ended up in the same city, and I couldn't believe we had never run into one another.

Dylan was fabulous on television. He too had one of the best lawyers in Toronto—but not pro bono, as his filthy-rich parents got involved and pulled a few strings. Like Allan, he cleaned up after he was captured. But unlike Allen, Dylan was made for TV, with movie-star good looks and the money from his parents to buy classy clothes. The parents were very vocal in talking about how Dylan had gotten in with the wrong crowd; how those Bronson brothers had been such a bad influence; how the police should realize that Allan and I were the ones who should be brought to justice.

"Talk about Tom," I pleaded with Dylan's face on the television. I now had my own teeny-weeny second hand black and white television in my Calgary rooming house, and could watch the news without drawing attention to myself. People might identify more with him, if he told them about the deeply personal motivation behind the bombings. Surely it would mean more to the general public if they got a family photo that showed Tom's handsome face before he went off to war, and his ravaged face and body when he came back; if they heard how the war was to blame for taking away the kindest, most caring person in our family.

But Dylan's lawyer, like Allan's, went down the political motivation road, trying to keep Dylan from being extradited. And Dylan revelled in the role of revolutionary. They dug up all the articles he'd written for campus newsletters—both the school-sanctioned ones and the ones distributed illegally as leaflets by volunteers who infiltrated the campus and risked being run off by campus security. And Dylan milked the publicity. If Allan had gained a following in Toronto, then Dylan's was far bigger, even though the tide was turning, and many Canadians saw the war in Vietnam as yesterday's news.

The Bronson brothers did not fare well in Dylan's testimony. To listen to him, Allan and I had concocted the whole plan and he was co-opted by us because the bombings tied in with his political beliefs. The photos shown on television were those of the surfer dude Dylan and the modern-day clean-cut, clean-shaven Dylan, who looked a little bit like David Soul, who played the blonde heartthrob Hutch in that new TV cop series, Starsky and Hutch. He was better than Allan at stressing that no one was supposed to get hurt; that we had chosen our time of night with that in mind, and that we had used a pay phone to warn people to get out of the building. The pictures of the Bronson brothers consisted of out-of-focus Polaroids of me glassy-eyed and stoned, and Allan geeky and scruffy but sober, taken with Dylan's camera at the Haight-Ashbury house. Not exactly our most photogenic moments. They never showed posed, pre-Vietnam photos of the Bronson family, which had then included Tom.

If I experienced frustration while Allan was testifying; then I felt pure hatred as this polished, telegenic version of Dylan distorted our motives and fed his former friends to the wolves. I didn't know if I could be trusted to speak to Dylan without punching him in the face.

Not my normal state of mind, but partly why I view those Calgary years—not the time on the run or my months as a homeless person—as rock bottom in my life.

Once Dylan had been extradited to the States and sentenced to 10 years in jail, a sentence much lighter than Allan's, I felt I could return to Toronto, a city where I knew a few people, and where I felt much more at home. The leniency of Dylan's sentencing compared with Allan's more than rankled—it raised my heart rate and made my head throb. The sentencing showed just what could be done within the Canadian and U.S. judicial systems if you looked good and had unlimited cash.

In early 1976, I went back to Buffy and Dawn's place, figuring the coast was clear now that all the coverage of Dylan's trial had calmed down. I shaved off my beard, so I looked like I did when I'd left. I didn't want to explain too much about my new identity, so I played on the second name in my Douglas Barnard Burns identity. Barney? Barry? They sounded similar. I could keep my high school credits I'd accumulated as Douglas, but to my Toronto friends I would be known as Barry Burns.

WHEN I GOT back to Dawn and Buffy's place, there had been several changes. The biggest one was that it was no longer a commune—instead the two of them were now officially a couple living on the ground floor of the house in Kensington. Eric (and his fantastic sound system) was gone, as were George and some of the others I had met during my stay at their place. I was given the huge room in the attic, where Buffy and Dawn used to sleep, but I had my own door, two-burner stove (with no oven) and a bar fridge. There was a third apartment unit in the crappy old basement, which had its own side entrance. The price of rent had gone up, but I figured I could get a job quite easily. I had quite a good recommendation from the City of Calgary, which said I was very handy and had 'mechanical aptitude.'

I got my job at the printing plant shortly afterwards.

The other thing that had changed was that Dawn started

coming on to me. While I'd always thought she was a very attractive, older and slimmer version of Mary-Anne, I was totally surprised, and not totally receptive at first because I knew she and Buffy had been an item for donkey's years.

"It's okay," Dawn said, coming up to my attic room late one night. I'd been studying—I really did want to get my Grade 12—and she came up behind me. "Buffy's okay if we make out. We have a very open relationship."

"Aren't you gay?" I asked, as she seductively massaged my shoulders.

"I can do both." she said. "I can be with both men and women," she said.

Dawn has always been beautiful, but I considered her to be forbidden fruit—I didn't want to get on Buffy's bad side. But if Buffy was into open relationships, and Dawn was willing…

Bottom line. I'm a red-blooded American male—or one desperately trying to fit in as a Canadian. I hadn't had sex in years. I took her up on her offer—more than once.

And then I found out that there was a reason Dawn had been coming on to me—she and Buffy wanted a child. In mid-November, Dawn announced that she was pregnant. "You can be the favourite uncle," she explained.

But it was all too weird and abnormal and complicated. How could I stand by and watch as Dawn had my kid? Knowing that I had been used as a sperm donor?

By early December, I had found my basement apartment with Katie, near Greenwood and off Gerrard in Little India.

AND NOW IT seemed as though life was layering worse times on times that were already bad for my landlady, Katie. Quincy had not been himself lately. He seemed tired, sad and listless; he wasn't eating, and he had lost weight. The grey in his muzzle was more prominent than ever. For a big dog, a lifespan of 10 years is normal—and he was approaching 11. Katie put off taking him to the vet, but one day, at walk time, he just looked at us and refused to budge.

I helped Katie load him into the back seat of the car—no easy feat as he was still such a heavy dog. Once he was in the car, he curled up, his muzzle pressed against the seat and his big eyes gazing at us sadly.

We took him to the vet in Markland Woods, where he had gone since he was a puppy. They didn't need X-rays or blood tests to tell us what was wrong. Quincy had a huge mass they could feel in his abdomen. Cancer. It was too big of a tumour to treat. They didn't have chemo and radiation for dogs like they did for humans, though some scientists were looking into it. And besides, even if the chemo and radiation were available, would Katie want to put her beloved pet through all that?

I helped her make the decision.

The doctor was kind. He asked if we wanted Quincy's ashes, and Katie said yes. A technician put an I.V. in Quincy's paw, and gave us a few minutes with him to say good-bye. When we were ready, he came in and put the liquid through the I.V. Quincy turned his head toward Katie, almost as though he were asking what was happening. And then he died.

In the car, Katie cried and cried. More than she had for John—big heaving sobs followed by uncontrolled shaking. I put my arms around her, holding her until the shaking stopped and the cries faded to the occasional sniffle. I wasn't crying, but there was sadness all the same. Quincy had been such a lovable, comforting guy.

"Are you okay to drive?" I asked Katie, as she searched for a

Kleenex to dry her eyes. It was 45 minutes through city traffic to get to our place in Little India. "I don't have a license, but I do know how."

"I'm okay," she said, sitting still for a moment before she turned the key in the ignition. I patted her back comfortingly, and made sure I had the box of ashes securely on my lap.

Something changed that day. She wasn't just my landlady or my nice friend any more: Katie was someone I wanted to protect; someone I wanted to stay in my life; someone I cared for very much.

On a cool, sunny day in late May, we scattered Quincy's ashes on his favourite place to run—the grassy mound at the Ashbridges Bay sewage treatment plant.

28: KATIE & HER DAD
(Katie, May 1977)

DURING THE MONTHS after John left, things went from bad to worse. He wanted his money out of the house, suggesting I should sell it and give him half our equity. That should be plenty of money to get me a one-bedroom rental apartment downtown, he said. My parents had been saying something similar before I cut them off. Sell the house, they'd said. It's not right for you to be living in a house with a single man who is not your husband.

They could all go to aitch-ee-double-hockey sticks [HELL]!

After I hadn't answered the phone for a month, my parents changed their tactics. I had no way of seeing who was at my door when somebody knocked (there was no peephole, and the bell didn't work). So, I was caught unaware one Saturday when Dad knocked on the door in civilian clothes, carrying a bag of take-out Swiss Chalet chicken. My favourite.

I was torn. I was angry with my parents, and I wasn't looking forward to a big lecture on all the things that were wrong in my life. I had lots of reasons to keep them at bay. But Dad had come all the way across the city by himself. I wasn't working; he clearly had nothing better to do. I was their only child, however flawed. And the kicker—he did come bearing Swiss Chalet.

He didn't bother with the usual hellos. "Quarter chicken dinners?" he said. "Dark meat for you and white meat for me. With fries and extra sauce?"

I opened the door wider and invited him inside.

WE SAT AT the round dinette set that John and I had bought with the money from our wedding. The acrylic chairs were padded with brightly coloured cushions that matched in a weird way with the dated, but very colourful, wallpaper with its trellis of fruits. (That wallpaper had to go!) I'd brought out real plates and cutlery rather than the Styrofoam containers and plastic cutlery the restaurant had supplied. Swiss Chalet always tasted better when it was laid out on real plates, and all that cheap Styrofoam and plastic they supplied was an environmental abomination. I put the coffee pot on, and got two cups plus cream and sugar to put in mine.

"Where's the dog," Dad asked, prompting my eyes to well with tears. It had only been a week, and my emotions were still raw.

"He's gone," I told Dad.

"Oh, Katie, I'm so sorry," he said. He looked as though he wanted to approach me, but wasn't sure how I'd respond.

"Katie," Dad said in a voice I hadn't heard before. "I think your mother and I may have been a little hard on you."

Really? I thought, not convinced his chastened tones were sincere.

"Yes," I said, slightly defensive. "I have thought that too." I concentrated on dipping my fries in the Chalet sauce. They tasted very good.

Then I let my eyes wander to the kitchen window, which looked out on our revived plants in the sun porch, and then the long, narrow backyard that was so typical in this neighbourhood.

"Your mother and I are actually very proud of you," he said after a bit of a pause, while he dipped some of his chicken in the sauce. "We really, really are," he added.

"Uh, thank you," was all I could think to say.

"You've got more education than either of us—girls didn't go to college when your Mom was young, and I went straight from high school to the police academy."

"… And rose through the ranks and became a Superintendent. That's no slouch," I said, wanting to take the focus off me and concentrate it on him.

I was mellowing a bit—maybe there was something in that sauce…

"Katie, we're very proud of you getting a job in your field. You knew what you wanted and went after it."

There was another pause as he digested some chicken. "And we are pleased to see what a lovely young lady you have blossomed into over the past year."

New haircut, new clothes, new contact lenses, new me! I thought with a trace of bitterness, but I was glad they recognized and liked the changes.

"Thank you," I said again.

"We don't want to lose you. You're our only child," he said.

"Thank you, Dad," I said. "That's really nice to know."

We ate in silence for a few minutes, cutting off pieces of chicken and dipping them into the sauce. I buttered my dinner roll and dipped that into the sauce too. I got up and poured our coffee—black with no cream, sugar or even sweetener for him; both cream and sugar for me.

Then Dad started asking me questions—he was in what John had once called 'interrogation mode' back in the days when John and I got along.

"So, Katie," he said, toying with his fork. "Do you think John will be coming back?"

I was totally annoyed by this question. "No, Dad. There's another woman involved and he's living with her. I don't think I'd have him back, even if he wanted to come.

"Which he doesn't," I added.

"Okay," said Dad. "So that's not an option."

I nodded my head emphatically in agreement.

"So, what's involved if you two separate and ultimately divorce?" asked Dad, using the D word I had been avoiding since John left.

"He wants me to sell the house," I said. "He wants his money out so he can live with 'the other woman'."

"And you don't want to sell?" Dad asked, knowing the answer.

"No. You were the ones who told me to buy real estate. Ever since I was a little girl. Look at you. You saved up to buy that first little bungalow we lived in. Then we moved to Markland to a much bigger house, and now you've totally paid off your mortgage. And your house is worth a bundle—what? More than a hundred thousand?"

Dad nodded. Apparently my guess was in the ballpark.

"What about the car?" Dad asked.

"He doesn't want it,'" I said. "He says it's more rust than car," I added, quoting John, and realistically describing the state of our 1970 Maverick.

"Okay," said Dad, more thoughtfully and carefully than usual. "So, you'd like to keep the house and the car."

"Yes," I said, thinking we had made some progress if he was willing to talk about this.

"How's that going to work out financially?" Dad asked.

I hesitated. Barry's rent helped with a few bills, but without John's income, things were going to be very, very tight.

"I need to make a bit more money," I admitted. "Barry downstairs is paying his rent regularly, but I was thinking of having another person—a woman—rent the second bedroom upstairs."

"Why not get two women, and get rid of that man downstairs?" Dad said, sounding a bit more like his usual self. My hackles rose.

"You've never liked Barry, but he pays the rent on time and he's been a big help around the house. He's helping me fix up the bathroom, he painted all those window frames in the sun porch—I don't think I could have survived these past couple of months without him."

"Okay, okay," said Dad, backing down more quickly than usual. "I can just tell that man's lying; he's keeping something from you. And I pretty sure he sounds like he's from the States."

I rolled my eyes.

"He's obviously never lived in Vancouver. In fact, his accent sounds more American to me."

"So what?" I said. "Maybe he's a draft dodger or something, but that's not a bad thing." That had been my latest suspicion about why Barry was so secretive sometimes. "But he didn't have all the opportunities that I had, growing up in Markland Woods. He didn't even get a chance to finish high school…"

"A dropout," Dad muttered.

"… But he's taking correspondence courses and he's going to graduate soon."

"Okay, okay," said Dad, throwing his hands up in mock despair. "I get it. You want him to stay. Just be safe, okay. This neighbourhood's not the best when it comes to crime, and I'm still not sure that man isn't a criminal of some sort."

I shook my head sadly, knowing we were still worlds apart on this particular issue.

Dad had finished his chicken and fries and stood up to leave, taking a final swig of his coffee.

Before he left, to my surprise, he pulled out a chequebook, tore out a cheque and wrote out $500. And he gave me a business card for someone at an Etobicoke law firm.

"No matter what happens," he said, reaching for me to give me the hug that he hadn't dared give me when he arrived, "you're going to need a good lawyer."

ARE YOU AMERICAN?" I asked Barry later that evening. "Moira seemed to think you were American when she hired you, and Dad doesn't think you're from Canada either."

Barry hesitated a bit before he answered. He seemed to be weighing things in his mind.

"Yes," he said. "I'm American. And I'm a draft dodger."

That explained a lot.

HAPPY HOURS HAD become a little more relaxed than the formal occasions I remembered from John's parents' place. For one thing, Barry bought a case of beer, Molson Canadian, and we'd been drinking that. I still preferred wine, but was starting to develop a taste for beer. We didn't always sit on the furniture either. Sometimes, like now, we sat on the floor, our backs against the dark blue corduroy couch, mesmerized by the flames of our fake fireplace.

"So, why did you become a draft dodger," I asked him, my eyes firmly on the flames flickering in front of me.

He hesitated, and then he said, "it was because of my brother, uh, William. He went to Vietnam, and he came back totally damaged. He was my favourite brother, and he was never the same again. He said he had to shoot women and little kids… And eventually, he died."

"How did he die?" I asked.

"Suicide," was his answer.

Well, that was a conversation stopper, I thought, giving him a couple minutes to recover from what must have been a very difficult thing to say. I patted his leg reassuringly. "I'm sorry to hear that," I said. "That sounds to me like a good reason for becoming a draft dodger."

I gave him another minute as we sipped our beer in silence.

"So, did you ever live in Vancouver?" I asked Barry, changing the subject.

"Naw," he said. "I did live in Calgary for a while."

"Did you like Calgary?'

He paused and said thoughtfully, "I don't think I ever gave it a chance. I lived on my own, went to work, studied, and didn't really make friends there. It wasn't a great time in my life."

I could tell he wanted to tell the story of his years as a draft dodger, and something was holding him back.

But the journalist in me kept asking more questions.

"So why do you tell everyone you're from Vancouver," I asked.

He smiled ruefully. "Usually I don't," he said. "People just assume that I'm from Vancouver when I say I'm from out west. It's the hippie hair that does it."

I stared down into my beer—I didn't drink it from the bottle the way Barry did. I preferred to use one of the beer glasses John and I had received as a wedding present.

"So have you ever even been to Vancouver?" I asked.

He shook his head. "No."

"Would you like to go there sometime?"

His face lit up again. "I'd love to go there. I hear it's a lot like San Fran…" and then he hesitated a bit. Had he lived in San Francisco? Is that where he was from?

"I've heard it's a lot like San Francisco too," I said. "It's got mountains and water and a coastal climate. And major parks: Golden Gate Park in San Francisco; Stanley Park in Vancouver; Golden Gate Bridge and Lion's Gate Bridge. And beaches. My best friend Allison lives in Vancouver now, and she says the beaches are great for swimming in the summer, and nice for walking during the other seasons. Their climate is much milder than ours—they get lots of rain but hardly get any snow and the crocuses come up in February. Not late April like Toronto."

He kept nodding, more relaxed now that I was doing all the talking.

"Allison lives in Kitsilano—so if Dad ever asks you, that is a much better neighbourhood than the East Side, and it's one that would sound right for a 'hippie' like you. Come to think of it, Allison is a bit of a hippie too…"

And then I couldn't help it. I had to start on one of my eco-rants.

"Vancouver and the whole of British Columbia are really far ahead of Toronto when it comes to the environment too. A couple of years ago they had a United Nations conference called Habitat, which said that adequate shelter and services were a basic human right. Services like potable drinking water in all parts of the world. I wish I'd been able to attend that conference. Allison was there. It was held right at Jericho Beach—really close to where she lives.

"Vancouver is where Greenpeace was founded—I don't agree with everything they stand for, but I do think it's important to stand up and protect old growth forests. It's important to protect the seals and the whales. And David Suzuki comes from there too."

His eyes were glazing over, and he was looking just a little too relaxed. I could just see the words forming in his head. Crazy landlady. Environmental rant. Again. If he was from the

States, he might not even know who David Suzuki is…

I changed the subject again, and immediately got his attention.

"We should go there," I said. "Vancouver. We could stay with Allison. I think she lives in some hippie commune set up…"

He smiled at me. "We could hitchhike," he said.

"Or we could take the car," I said.

He rolled his eyes. I guess there was some doubt as to whether my old rust bucket could make it all the way to Vancouver.

We sipped our beer and looked at the fire. It was something nice to think about—a positive plan for what had recently seemed a very negative future.

29: GRADUATION & BAD NEWS
(Barry, June 1977)

IT WAS JUNE, and I'd now been at Katie's place for seven months. I'd been totally pissed off with Dawn and Buffy for most of those months, feeling as though they'd used and abused me; that I was simply handy as a sperm donor. But as the months wore on, I remembered some of the good times, when they'd taken me into their minibus for that trip across the U.S., and later into their home. I probably wouldn't have survived my first few years on the run without them. And I had mixed feelings about Dawn's pregnancy. She was having a baby, and that child, who would grow up with two mommies, was part me.

So, in May, I borrowed Katie's home phone and called them. They had one of those new answering machines, and I knew immediately that I'd reached the right place. "You've reached the dykes on Baldwin Street," the message said. "Please leave a message."

I did, and within a day they had called me back on Katie's phone. Katie came and got me downstairs, and putzed around the kitchen as Dawn and Buffy took turns talking on the phone, asking how I was and saying how much they'd missed me. Yes, Dawn was still working. (She was a secretary somewhere.) And Buffy was still driving the truck delivering flowers. At one point, she'd thought about long haul trucking, since it paid more and there were longer stretches of time off. But now she'd decided to deliver flowers, and maybe get another part-time job delivering newspapers or flyers once Dawn was staying home…. because of the baby.

The baby was due in late July—not too long now. Dawn was due for an ultrasound soon, and hopefully they could tell the sex of the baby. One of the bedrooms on the second floor had been converted into a nursery—decorated in yellows and greens since they didn't know which sex the child was, and of course they wouldn't want to stereotype their child with pink or blue décor. Dawn had already been in touch with the La Leche League because they both believed strongly in natural childbirth and breastfeeding—possibly even into the toddler years, as the League recommended.

"And Barry, we're so, so glad you called," said Dawn. "We miss you. You're our favourite American, and you're the baby's daddy. We do want you to be a part of his-her-um—its—life…"

We arranged for me to come to their home the following week.

When I got off the phone, Katie couldn't contain her curiosity.

"Who was that?" she asked.

"A friend of mine, from the commune. She's having a baby," I stated breezily.

Katie looked crestfallen.

"She's so lucky," she said and then her eyes filled with tears. "John and I were going to have kids. We teased each other about what they would look like. Curly headed little monsters with hair like John's. Tall like me…"

I rubbed her back gently and cursed John, who was such an ass.

- - -

BY LATE JUNE, I had my final correspondence course mark back—I'd finished that course with marks in the high seventies and was now officially a high school graduate.

Katie insisted that this called for a celebration, that she'd take me out for dinner.

"Nothing too high-end," I said. "I don't have any fancy clothes."

"No, no, no. I have something totally different in mind," she said.

- - -

ON A SATURDAY in June, we took the streetcar and the subway downtown to Adelaide Street, near the city's big bank towers, where there was a restaurant called Mr. Greenjeans. When we entered, I felt like I was back in California. There were plants galore, and all-white tables and chairs that looked like high-end lawn furniture. Sleek looking metal lamps hung from the ceiling.

I teased Katie by showing off my new-found knowledge of plant names. "That's a Phil-o-den-dron, much bigger than ours. And those are Areca palms. And that's a Schefflera…"

"Shut up," she said in a loud whisper. "Just because you're a graduate, it doesn't mean you get to show off."

"… And that's ivy and that's a Tradescantia Zebrina."

"Shut up," she said a little louder, giving me a playful nudge.

"Table for two for dinner," she said to the hostess. "By the window if possible."

We sat down among a forest of palms, and eyed the menus, which were enormous.

I looked around at the clientele. For the most part, people were dressing up a bit—after all, we were right in the middle of in Toronto's business district even though the weather was starting to warm up and it was a Saturday. The men, for the most part, were wearing casual tweed jackets with patches on the elbows. Some of the women, like Katie, were in work clothes like business suits or skirts and blouses. A few wore pantsuits. I was becoming a little more interested in fashion, thanks to Katie's earlier struggles to please John, but my only concession to the occasion was to wear pants that weren't my regular blue jeans.

Katie was fussing with the paper placemat. "I don't know why they bother with these things," she said. "Think of all the trees you could save if all restaurants stopped using placemats like these. Cloth ones would be better. And the serviettes are paper too."

"At least the cutlery is the real thing," I said, "not plastic."

"Don't get me started on that," my eco-conscious landlady said, rolling her eyes.

But when the waiter came, she changed her tune.

"We're celebrating a special occasion," Katie told the server in her best take-charge reporter voice. She pointed at me. "It's graduation day."

"Is it you or your brother who's celebrating?" the waiter asked, as Katie worked hard to control a giggle.

He looked at me dubiously. As the worst dressed person in the place, I was way too old to be graduating from high school, but, though the age was right, I wasn't dressed like a college guy celebrating his graduation either. Katie probably seemed a more likely graduate.

"We're celebrating my doctorate," I said, confidently, prompting a little grin from Katie.

"Oh, what subject," the waiter asked, just because he was Canadian and nice.

I decided to riff on the plant discussion we had earlier. "Plant Science," told him. "I have a doctorate in Plant Science."

He still looked a bit dubious.

"From U. of T.," I said. And just because I too was becoming a bit more Canadian and a bit nicer, I added. "The plants in here are beautiful."

"Mr. Greenjeans started as a plant store," the guy informed us, setting two glasses of water on the table.

"We don't need the straws," Katie said as he was walking away. He returned and took the straws, looking baffled. As he left, she muttered, "Serving water when we didn't ask for it isn't good either. Think of all the water we could save if…"

I smiled at her. I was used to her eco-rants by then.

"Your brother?" I said, changing the subject, knowing it would get her attention.

She giggled. "Well, I suppose we do look a bit alike. We're both tall and skinny and we both have straight, mouse-brown hair."

"Speak for yourself," I said, flipping my longish mane. "You might have mouse-brown hair, but mine is dark blonde!"

She laughed. "Point taken!" she said. "Either way, it's exactly the same colour as mine!"

"What should we eat?" I asked, changing the subject again.

"You have to order a burger," Katie said. "They are ginormous and very good. And you have to have Buffalo Chips."

I looked askance as our waiter returned to the table.

"They're sort of like a cross between a French fry and a potato chip and they're really big."

"They're our most popular item," the waiter chimed in.

"Yeah," I said, sounding a bit dopey, not at all like a Ph.D. grad. "I'll have a burger and some of those chips. How about you, Sis?"

Katie winked at me and ordered the same thing.

"Drinks?" our waiter asked.

"I'll have a beer," I said. "Molsons."

"And I'll have some white wine," said Katie. "Chardonnay, if you have it."

He closed his notepad and walked away, with a smile for Katie and raised eyebrows for me.

"You twit!" said Katie. "You really played that guy."

"Just having a bit of fun with him," I said. "...And you!"

And I was having fun, I realized. Between work at Rosedale and the pub nights, and Happy Hours with my landlady, I was finally enjoying my life. And I felt useful. I knew Katie was having a tough time financially with the house and the separation from John, and while I couldn't afford to pay her more money for rent, I could be handy around the place. The bathroom was almost finished—we called it Operation DePinkify—and soon it would be brown and yellow-tiled, with yellow paint and a restored claw-foot tub. Some of my jobs were less fun—I'd also helped her get rid of the mice that infested the pantry off the kitchen.

I'd even picked up the old guitar John had left behind and started to play a few tunes.

I had loved Quincy and treasured our walks. I think I missed him almost as much as Katie did.

Sometimes I could go for a week and not think about being on the run, and the burden I carried from that fateful night seven years ago.

"They have s'mores for dessert," Katie said, and I laughed.

"That's a good American dessert," I said. "I remember sitting around a fire at Scout Camp, eating s'mores."

I then regaled her with stories about camping up in the mountains, and some of the hijinks we had got up to while we were there—stories I hadn't shared since the days before Vietnam, when Tom, Dylan, Allan and I were a team.

I'd decided a while ago that I would tell her about Tom,

Allan and Dylan—I used their middle names, which weren't too hard to remember. Whenever Mom was mad, she would call us by our full names including the middle ones. "Thomas William Bronson," she would yell. Or "Allan George Bronson." So, Tom became Bill and Allan became George. The confusing part was that Dylan became Thomas, or Tom. He was named after some dead Welsh poet, he'd told us. I didn't use my middle name, which was Douglas—ironically my first name under my latest alias.

But at least I could talk about my past, and the draft dodger thing was on the table too. That sort of opened up the conversation. As Bob Dylan would say, "the times, they are a'changin'." The 20-year Vietnam War finally ended in 1975, and in January of this year, '77, President Jimmy Carter had officially pardoned the draft dodgers. So technically, the draft dodger thing was no longer a crime, and if that had been my only offense, I could have returned to the States.

The s'mores weren't quite the way I remembered them, sitting around the campfire when I was young. For one thing, they were served with ice cream on the side, something that wouldn't have worked on a camping trip, where we carried everything in a backpack and roasted things over the fire pit. But they were good.

Katie produced a birthday candle and a pack of matches, stuck the candle in the ice cream and lit it.

The waiter hustled over. "We have cake," he said. "And candles to celebrate… your graduation."

"We're okay," said Katie.

"Would you like us to sing?" he asked.

No, no, no, I gestured, but Katie seemed to like the idea. Five of the servers, including some very nice-looking girls, gathered around me and sang.

"Happy Graduation to you!
Happy Graduation to you!
Happy Graduation, Happy Graduation,
Happy Graduation to you!"

The words didn't quite fit, but everyone was having a good time and there were some good singers in the bunch.

Katie raised her wine glass when they had left.

"Happy Graduation to my brother, Dr. Douglas Barnard Burns," she said.

It was after 11:00 p.m. when we got home. We walked together up Yonge Street to see the lights, my arm wrapped companionably around Katie's shoulder. We ran into a homeless guy and gave him all our spare change. "I've been there," I told Katie, whose look begged for more information.

At the streetcar stop in front of College Park, we kissed—a kiss that was anything but brotherly and went on for a long time. A kiss that promised the start of something more.

"Get a room," some drunk guy yelled at us. And we broke apart, laughing, arms still entwined. Then we took the Carlton streetcar home.

- - -

WHEN I GOT home, the light on the answering machine was flashing. Dawn had left a message, saying it was urgent and I should call her right away, no matter how late.

I had other ideas about how the evening should proceed, but Dawn had insisted that I should call, so I did.

Dawn got right to the point. "Barry, I don't know what the hell you've done, but the cops were here today. They're looking for you."

"Thanks for letting me know," I said.

"Barry—we've had our ups and downs, but we really care about you. That's why we chose you to be our baby's daddy. We didn't tell the cops a thing."

"Want a nightcap," Katie asked me, mouthing the words and pointing to the wine bottle so she didn't disturb my call.

"Good luck, Barry," Dawn said softly.

It was all I could do to keep my face neutral, say thanks again and hang up the phone.

Katie wasn't taken in. "Bad news? Want to talk about it?"

I shook my head and avoided her eyes, prompting more scrutiny.

"I think I'll just turn in," I said. "Thanks for the wonderful dinner.

She reached forward to give me an awkward hug. I hugged her back, thinking how unfair it was. She would have to deal with two men leaving her in the space of just a few months. And, in my case at least, it wasn't her fault.

Downstairs, I packed my backpack with shirts, pants, a jacket, the knife that I had pilfered from Dawn and Buffy's kitchen years ago, and the ratty old blanket from my homeless days. I wrote Katie a note on the lined paper I had used for my courses.

"Dear Katie," I said. "I did some things I now regret before I left the States and they are now catching up with me. That's why I am leaving. Thank you for your friendship, for the job at RP, and for welcoming me into your home."

I attached a cheque for the coming month's rent, which would be due shortly.

I thought about the signature and decided that "love" was too mushy, and "yours truly" was too formal. In the end I just signed my name, Barry.

I waited until well after the lights were off on the ground floor to leave.

I took the Carlton streetcar to the subway, and the subway all the way out to Islington Station. The Mimico Creek ravine was there—and since it was out in the 'burbs, the cops probably wouldn't look for me there.

As I took one last look at that house in Little India, I realized how far I'd fallen in just a few hours—from being the celebrated 'Dr. Douglas Barnard Burns' to life on the lam. It was futile to think that my life could ever be anything other than that of a criminal and a fugitive.

30: ON THE RUN AGAIN
(Barry, June 1977)

I KNEW EXACTLY where I wanted to go, but it wasn't easy to find it in the dark, so I spent an uncomfortable night in a grove among some trees on the same blanket I'd used as a homeless person back in 1970.

I was looking for Katie's favourite place—she'd spent hours and days there as a kid when her family had lived a few blocks away from that ravine, before her Dad rose in the ranks of the police and they could live in the more upscale neighbourhood of Markland Woods. She and her friend Allison would pretend they were explorers and would name all the landmarks. Sometimes, Allison's little brothers would come with them, and they would have a ball sailing toy boats or even just sticks down the rushing stream. And they'd found a cave—just a place where the land had eroded away under a tree that was still standing, exposing the roots. That's where I was headed once the dawn came, and I could see where I was going.

The part of Mimico Creek just north of Bloor Street was too open for my taste—there was a high school to the east and subway station and the busy intersection of Bloor and Islington to the west. But as I walked north and crossed Dundas Street, there was more tree cover. I had to walk along suburban streets for a bit since there was no obvious path in places, but by the time I reached the stretch just south of Rathburn Road, the ravine was quite wild.

The cave was still there—one day the erosion will be too much and that tree will fall, but it would work as a hideout for me right now. I tried not to think of anything other than the task at hand, disguising the cave with branches I found lying on the ground. I used some live branches with leaves, which I hacked from trees with the kitchen knife I hadn't carried since I was on the run to Alberta. I thought about Tom, Allan and Dylan, and those wonderful days we spent as Cubs and Scouts, and how things had changed so much for all of us. Tom gone; Allan and Dylan in prison; and me here, on the run and hiding once more.

It was a Sunday, and it was so quiet here. No one showed up—and believe me, I was listening intently, using the skills we had learned in Scout Camp. I finished building my shelter around noon, eyes peeled and alert at all times, and spent the rest of the day indoors, arranging my meagre belongings, bored out of my mind. Who would have believed back in the late '60s and 1970, when we were planning the bombing, that its consequences would include long stretches of boredom? I thought about my own situation right now; with nothing to do. I couldn't even show my face without risking a takedown. I thought about Dylan and Allan sitting in jail cells—Allan for more than the foreseeable future, and Dylan for the foreseeable future because money bought him better justice. I thought about Tom—not for the first time—and what he would think about all this. I realized—and this was a thought planted by Helen that had been growing for some time—that in a way, we were no better off than he was. We too had killed—not the Vietnamese children who had haunted Tom's dreams—but an innocent researcher who wasn't even studying weapons of war.

I just wanted a normal life, I thought. I'd been happy lately—with friends who cared about me, my buddies from Rosedale at the pub, Dawn and Buffy, Katie who was so much more than a landlady. It was so nice to walk into work and hear everyone say hello and ask how I was. I was looking forward to starting a tool and die apprenticeship in a Toronto-area factory in the fall—it was a half-hour commute, short by California standards, and Katie had said I could use the car if I helped her with the repairs and insurance. I liked living in Little India—there were more nationalities in the neighbourhood than I could count, Greek and Italian as well as Indian, and for the most part, everyone responded well to a smile and a quick hello. I would like to see Mom, Dad and Allan again, and Mary-Anne too, though she had probably moved on to another boyfriend by now. But that part wasn't possible. I had never felt it more keenly—the uncertainty and lack of a real future for a guy constantly on the move, one step ahead of the law.

I thought about Katie, waking up and finding out that yet another man had fled from her home—and not knowing why. I wished I could redo last night and leave her a better note that would let her know exactly why I was running. But then that didn't make sense—maybe it was good that she didn't know everything.

By three o'clock in the afternoon, constructing my shelter, boredom and the events of the previous night had made me very tired, and I lay down on my homeless blanket to sleep. But I couldn't get comfortable—there was something under the blanket that poked into my back. A tree root, probably, I thought. I couldn't sleep at all, so I decided to investigate. It was a doll—a baby doll, the kind little girls carried around all the time. For a moment, I thought back to the stories Katie had told me about her and Allison in the cave. Maybe it was their doll from way back—and I had to do some math to figure this out—about 15 years ago. And then I realized that maybe the cave wasn't as good a place as I thought to hide out. Because the doll was muddy, but it certainly hadn't been decaying in a cave for 15 years. Maybe Katie and Allison weren't the only ones who loved this cave and considered it their own—maybe there were more recent child explorers involved.

I decided I would give the cave one night only, and then move on.

And then, an hour later, I heard the voices. Kids' voices. I didn't know much about little kids and less about girl children, but I figured these were little girl voices and that the girls were probably somewhere between six and ten years old. I had no place to hide; I huddled in the cave, staying as motionless as possible, hoping against hope that these weren't the kids who knew about the cave.

But of course they were.

"Oh look, someone has added a front to the Secret Hideout," the higher of the two voices piped out.

"What do you think? Isn't that kind of scary?" the second, lower voiced, kid asked. "What if that person is still around?"

The first girl was clearly the leader, and much braver than the second one. "Why would anyone be in there? We've been coming to the Secret Hideout for ages, and we've never seen anyone in there."

"I'm still a bit scared," said low voice. "Remember what Mom said about watching out for strangers down by the creek."

"Mom's a bit of a scaredy cat," said higher voice. "She just doesn't like us playing at the creek, that's all."

"But there are branches in front now; and someone has added them. How can it be a secret if someone is changing our hideout?"

"I'm going to take a look," said higher voice.

I decided I had to show my face and convince them I was as friendly as possible. I stuck my head out the opening. "Is this your fort?" I asked them. "Sorry, if I scared you. I'm just using it for one night, and then I'll give it back. It will be all yours again."

I saw two girls who looked like sisters—one a head taller than the other. As I say, I didn't know any kids to compare them with, but they were both older than really small kids and younger than teenagers. Strangely, high voice, the bolder one, was also the smaller and younger of the two. Both stood, speechless, mouths in perfect 'o's, looking at the strange, dirty, sweaty man, who had invaded their secret place.

"Are you a homeless person," high voice asked.

"No, no, no," I said, perhaps a little too vehemently. "Um, I'm just doing a one-night camping trip, you know, like you do in Cubs or Scouts." I wasn't even sure they had Cubs and Scouts in Canada, but the two little girls seemed to know what I was talking about.

"We're in Brownies," the high-voiced one said. "We get to go to Brownie Camp. It's sort of like camping out."

"Well, I studied wilderness camping in Cubs and Scouts, and I wanted to give it a try," I said. Where was all this chatter coming from? I wondered. Over the years, I must have become really adept in telling lies and half-truths.

The younger, bolder one with the higher voice seemed to buy into this, but the older girl looked skeptical.

I decided to change the focus and play what might be my trump card. "I found this," I said, reaching for the doll and pulling it outside of the shelter.

"Mary!" the older one gasped. "You found Mary! We've been looking all over for her. She's my sister's favourite doll."

"Well, she seems to be in pretty good shape—just a little muddy, that's all."

I seemed to win them over once I had produced Mary and handed her to the little one. I noticed they were both carrying brown paper bags.

"What's in the bags?" I asked, just to make conversation.

"Candy," said the younger girl. "There's a candy store at Martin Grove Road and Burnhamthorpe. Mom sometimes gives us the plastic milk bottles to return to the store. Today we got two bottles to return. We got 50 cents and Mom said we could use the money to buy candy."

"Fifty cents! That must mean a lot of candy," I said, basing that observation on the size of the younger girl's candy bag rather than my in-depth knowledge of penny sweets.

"Yup," said the younger girl. "Jennifer here likes to spend all her money on one thing, the whole 25 cents! I like getting a whole bunch of little things—gumballs, Lik-M-Aid, Kraft caramels, you know, that kind of thing."

I nodded, but after that the conversation lagged for a bit.

Finally, the younger girl asked me, "So, what do you eat out here?"

That was a tough question, and I hoped my answer would seem realistic. "Oh, I like to eat water lily bulbs and frog legs," I told them, thinking back to survival camping trips and hoping like hell that they had those things in Ontario, Canada.

"Ugh," said both girls, wrinkling their noses in disgust. "That sounds horrible."

The older girl, who hadn't said much since I showed my face, handed me her candy bag.

"I think you'll like this better," she said.

And then they turned away, saying good-bye as they left.

"Shhhh," I said. "Don't tell anyone I'm here. It's our secret."

"Okay," said the younger girl.

"Thanks for the candy," I added.

"Thanks for finding Mary," the older one said.

I opened my bag. As her sister said, Jennifer had bought just one thing with her milk bottle money.

It was an O'Henry bar.

THEN THE RAIN came down, and I decided to stay put for the night—the ravine would be treacherous in the storm and in the dark. I was thankful it wasn't too cold out, and that there wasn't snow like there was for the first ever Toronto Blue Jays game several weeks ago. I pulled my homeless blanket around my shoulders and over my legs. It was an inadequate covering, and I was uncomfortably damp and chilled.

As I waited, I thought about how I could possibly explain myself to Katie. Of course, I thought about Katie—this was her special place, still cherished a decade and a half after she and Allison last played here. And I felt so badly about my sudden departure. To pass the time, I thought of her journalism voice quizzing me, asking why I had done what I'd done.

Why did I ever think this would be a good place to hide? I thought, as I heard footsteps approaching over the sound of the rain that was pouring down all around me. How could the anyone find me so quickly—had those little girls told someone about the strange man in the ravine? They'd been so cute, but little girls aren't known for keeping secrets.

And then there was a dog barking right outside the cave. And I heard a megaphone, saying: "Scott Douglas Bronson, you are under arrest for the bombing of the LA Research Center and for the murder of Edward Sung. Come out with your hands in the air."

A seriously frightening German Shepherd dog—nothing like Quincy—stood guard as I eased myself through the wet and muddy entrance to my shelter and put my hands up.

THE BOMBER IN THE BASEMENT

I stood there, face to face with two cops, one I didn't recognize and one who was Katie's Dad.

31: AMERICA'S MOST WANTED
(Katie, June-August 1977)

- - - - -

I COULDN'T FIGURE out why Barry had left, but I thought it had something to do with the mysterious call he received last night. One minute, we were having fun fooling the waiter into thinking Barry was my brother and a doctor, joking around, walking north on Yonge Street, and taking the Carlton streetcar home after that amazing kiss. And then, after that phone call, he was totally freaked out and headed downstairs with no explanation.

He wasn't around on Sunday, and when I got to work on Monday, he wasn't there either. There were at least two newsletters due to be printed, and I couldn't imagine him staying away on such a busy day. But the printer sat motionless, and both Linda and Jenny popped their heads into my office, worriedly asking if I knew where Barry could be.

Then the cops showed up at the office. My Dad showed up with another guy. Every eye in the office followed them as Linda led them back through the maze of cubicles to the private offices where Hugh and Gordon worked. Then the two of them were closeted in our tiny boardroom with Dad and the other guy, whom I'd seen once before on a rare visit to Dad's station. Then they dismissed Hugh, and Gordon called Moira into the boardroom. My heart sank lower and lower, certain that this all had something to do with Barry's disappearance.

And then they wanted to talk to me.

I don't think I've ever been as scared in my life as when I entered that boardroom. Especially since one of the cops was Dad.

"Hello, Katie," he said acknowledging our relationship. "I think you may have met Officer Joe Rennit before." I shook hands with Officer Rennit and sat down in the chair they offered. My Dad had on his cop face—it was hard to read—but what they said was both authoritative and serious.

"Toronto police have arrested Scott Douglas Bronson, one of three men on America's Most Wanted list, who are wanted for the 1970 bombing of the Los Angeles Research Center in Los Angeles, California, the largest vehicle bombing ever carried out on American soil. We understand that Mr. Bronson was living at your home and working here at Rosedale Publications."

To say I was in shock would be underestimating things. And why was Dad breaking this news to me? What did he have to do with Barry's arrest?

And then the impact of it all began to register. Barry wasn't just a renter—over the past months, he'd become more than a friend. He'd helped me survive the most awful months of my life; and we'd even confided in each other—to a point. There was nothing about Barry to suggest he was a dangerous bomber. He was quiet; he had a sense of humour; he'd been kind; and he was working so hard to build a better life for himself.

"We arrested Mr. Bronson late last night in the Mimico Creek ravine, on a tip from people in the neighbourhood reporting a strange man down there," Officer Rennit said.

That explained things a bit. We used to live in that neighbourhood up until 10 years ago, and everyone in that neighbourhood knew Superintendent Thompson was a top cop. It made sense that a neighbour would ask for him when reporting the sighting.

And then I knew... I knew with certainty exactly where Barry had been hiding.

Officer Rennit explained that the two other perpetrators,

Allan George Bronson and Dylan Thomas Hearst, had been caught and brought to justice, but the younger Bronson brother had been evading police since the bombing was carried out in 1970.

The newscaster then showed a picture of Scott Bronson seven years ago and an age-enhanced drawing showing what Scott Bronson could look like now. My jaw dropped. It didn't look exactly like Barry, but it could be him. They then released a mug shot showing a man who was unmistakeably my renter.

They asked a lot of questions about Barry, or Scott. I answered as truthfully as I could. Yes, he had lived at my home since November 1976. He was a quiet renter—very helpful with home repairs. Yes, he always paid his rent on time. Yes, I had worked with him at Rosedale since January. Yes, he seemed to be doing a good job here.

"And he just graduated from Grade 12," I added, hoping it would help Barry's cause. "He took correspondence courses."

The two of them interviewed the other Rosedale employees, one by one, and left around noon. Gordon told us we could take the rest of the day off, and some employees did, but not me. I worked on the newsletter departments—People, Coming Events, News Briefs and New Products—typing mechanically, trying to concentrate as my thoughts swirled in another direction entirely.

- - -

ON THE CARLTON streetcar on the way home, I thought back to our conversations. There must have been some truth in what he told me. He'd said he was a draft dodger, so I assumed he had to be from the States. He'd talked about the reason he evaded the draft as well—his brother was permanently damaged from his experiences in Vietnam and had committed suicide. Did that have something to do with why they set off the bomb?

At home, I couldn't stop watching TV news. They talked about the other bombers and showed their pictures. The news broadcast talked about how Allan was serving a prison sentence of 25 years, and how Dylan had a much lighter sentence of 10 years. How Barry was considered armed and dangerous, but they had arrested him "without incident."

I thought back to the newscasts and newspaper articles from my late high school years. I didn't remember much about Allan's trial, but I did remember Dylan's. My friend Allison had thought Dylan was DDG—our code for Drop Dead Gorgeous—even though neither of us understood why he had been involved in the bombing. Who knew then that one day, another of the bombers would be living in my basement?

The newscaster had interviewed Gordon, who looked devastated and told them that Barry had been a good employee with great mechanical skills. He said he had a hard time believing that he could be a Vietnam era terrorist on America's Most Wanted list.

As the newscast carried on, giving the full names of the bombers, I realized something. Barry had talked about his brothers, William and George, and their friend Thomas. How William had died because of Vietnam. George was his geeky brother and Thomas was the name of the guy who was their friend—not a very good friend at times. Barry had opened up a bit, but he'd still had secrets. And then I realized that he must have been using their middle names. The newscaster hadn't said anything about the brother who died, but his other brother was Allan George and the third bomber was their friend Dylan Thomas.

What if he had surrendered to the police? What if he had

turned himself in voluntarily? That would have helped. He'd committed the bombing such a long time ago, when he was still a teenager. I bristled at the commentator's words, "Armed and dangerous." And knew I had a battle ahead of me, defying my father and helping Barry any way I could.

THE NEXT THREE months were a bit of a blur, although so much happened in such a short time. I was surprised that Dad didn't give me more of a hassle about harbouring a fugitive. I think he believed me when I said that I really didn't know about Barry's background. And I was his only child—he didn't want to lose me. I think that counted for something.

Besides, I was doing what he'd suggested. I put an ad in the paper for two female renters, confident I'd get some nibbles closer to September, when students went back to school. And I called a lawyer, to get the divorce with John going. After making sure there was no conflict of interest, the lawyer I called was Alex Johnson, the guy I had talked to at John's Christmas party. Certainly, he knew his stuff. To my surprise, Alex told me that he couldn't personally handle my case, but would refer me to someone who could. I'd trusted his recommendation. Of course, John has free legal advice since he works at a law firm. But I think I will be up to the coming battle.

I talked to Gordon at work, outlining my concerns about working with Margaret. I talked calmly. I didn't cry. I wrote out my questions in advance and stuck to the script. He said he'd think about things and get back to me. Apparently, I wasn't the only person who'd complained about her. And then, a few weeks later, he took me off ECO and assigned me some booklets RP was preparing for the federal government on "Energy

Conservation in Industrial Buildings." It was an interesting project, consisting of ten different booklets on subjects ranging from ride sharing to more energy efficient process design. My job would include compilation of many, many case studies about companies that were implementing energy conservation measures and saving money. I liked my new job, and I no longer had to deal with Margaret!

But I went through the summer months in a daze, trying to come to terms with the fact that my good friend had committed crimes—maybe even murder they said.

I cleaned out Barry's basement apartment, thinking it would look quite good for the girl who would rent it. He'd improved the place a lot with his "found" furniture and ability to fix things.

I found the letter he left, and it told part of the story from Barry's point of view. And he'd already told me a lot, using pseudonyms and disguising the information.

Against Dad's advice, I visited him a couple times in prison. It was hard for him to talk to me, since he had to bend down to speak through the hole in the bulletproof glass panel between us, and everything he said was monitored. In whispers, he tried to explain more about why he had participated in the bombing. How they had done it 'for Tom.'

I decided to concentrate on the recent past, not Barry's—no Scott's—past before I ever met him. I decided I would attend his trial whenever I could.

32: FOR TOM
(Barry, June-September 1977)

THEY TOOK ME to the Don Jail, the same place they'd taken Allan and Dylan. They'd recently closed the original jail, so I was in the East Wing, the only part that was still open. I had no idea where Allan and Dylan had been held.

When I entered the jail, I found it creepy, with all kinds of weird metal sculptures hovering over my head as we walked through the catwalks to my cell, where I would be held while I was awaiting trial. More than what I saw upon entering the jail, it was the noise and the smell that registered. The noise was a mass of overlapping voices, many of which sounded angry or just plain mean. The smell was easily recognizable—urine on concrete. Despite my chequered past, I had never been inside a jail before. My initial impressions of this one were far from reassuring.

My overwhelming feeling was a sense of boredom, tinged with a touch of fear. The Don was a holding place, where people awaited sentencing. There was a routine—wake up, dress, eat, exercise outdoors for half an hour, eat, free time with nothing to do, eat, undress, sleep repeat. Lots of roll calls. My roommate seemed okay, though he talked even less than I did. I felt lucky—there were some real hard cases on my block.

They assigned a lawyer to me—the same one Allan had when he ended up being sentenced to 25 years of jail time. I wasn't thrilled about that, but I had no choice. Like I said before, the Bronsons had no money to hire Dylan's high-priced attorney. I could only hope for three things. First, that public perception of the Vietnam protests had mellowed over the years. Second, that stressing the idea, however misguided, that Allan and I did it for Tom, would help my case. And third, I hoped that my age at the time of the bombing would have some effect on my sentencing—in 1970, at 19, I wasn't technically a youth here in Canada, but I was still younger than Allan or Dylan had been at the time.

There were some good things that happened. Katie came to visit. She'd found the letter I'd written the night I left, and she was surprisingly supportive. That must have been tough for her—especially since her father was involved in my arrest.

And I could finally see Mom again. Yes, she was coming up from California to visit me. It was too late for Dad—he had full-blown lung cancer by now, and was practically bedridden, I learned. He certainly couldn't travel. I'd had no idea he was so sick—another regret to add to the big pile of them I'd accumulated over the years. I thought about our shared mechanical ability; how he'd helped me strip and then fix up the Econoline van, not knowing what an instrument of death and destruction it would become.

The prison visitation setup was less than ideal—I had a phone on my side, and had to lean down so that Mom could hear me better through the little hole in the glass.

Mom looked a lot better than she had when she came up for Allan's trial. She'd put on a bit of weight, and she had a new hairstyle—still gray, but more of an upswept style with fewer tight curls than she'd had the last time I saw her on TV. I was surprised at how different her accent was from the Canadian ones I'd encountered every day for the past seven years.

"I get to see Allan sometimes," she told me, fishing in her purse for a photo to show me. "His prison is a short drive from home—I see him every couple of weeks. He's got a long haul ahead of him, but I think his sentence might get shortened for good behaviour." The photo of Allan was a mug shot, clipped from the newspaper, and it was not flattering. He looked older, heavier, defeated, unsmiling for the camera.

Was that what I would look like in a few years? The prospect was not encouraging.

"How's Dad?" I asked, although I'd heard he wasn't good.

"He's got lung cancer, Scottie. He doesn't have long now—maybe six months, possibly a year. You should come home, like Allan did," she added. "At least you'd be close by, and Dad and I would be able to see you."

The extradition to the States had not gone well for Allan—he'd been tried for murder there, one of the reasons he had a 25-year sentence.

"I have a new hairdresser," Mom said, when I commented on her new hairstyle. "Your old girlfriend. Remember? Mary-Anne Gillespie?"

"How's she doing," I asked, trying not to convey my interest in hearing what she had to say on this particular subject.

"Oh, she's doing well. She's got her own salon now, very close to our place. She took over from Frank—remember I went to him for years? And she's not Gillespie any more—she got married. Here," Mom said, fishing around in her purse for a photo. "She gave me this when I said I was going to see you. She's got two girls now—aren't they cute?"

I looked at the photo with interest. Mary-Anne's face had slimmed down, she looked a bit older, but she still looked beautiful to me. Her husband looked ordinary, tall with dark hair, and I didn't recognize him as one of the kids we'd gone to high school with. The girls were cute, though. The older one must have been at that awkward age where kids' teeth start falling out—there was a big gap between the top centre ones and the bottom ones seemed a bit jumbled. Her hair was lighter than Mary-Anne's. The younger girl was still a toddler, with darker hair, who looked like a teeny-tiny version of her mother.

I gave the picture back to Mom, after memorizing it to help fill the boring hours I faced in the coming weeks. In those boring weeks, I would analyze my feelings. Mary-Anne was still very attractive, but I no longer compared every woman I met to her. I was more open to other types of women—slimmer, taller, lighter haired.

"You know, Scottie, I had great hopes for you two when you dated in high school. She's a lovely girl."

I had to change the subject. "Speaking of high school," I said. "You know, I completed my Grade 12," I told her. "I did correspondence courses and I graduated this year."

"Is that a fact," Mom said, clearly pleased with this development.

"I hope to study to become a tool-and-die maker while I'm in prison," I added, based on some rumours I'd heard about some prisons offering courses, and hoping like hell that I'd get to go to a prison like that.

"Good for you, honey," Mom said, gently lifting her hand up to the glass, in one of the only ways to show sentimentality during our prison visits. I reached up to the glass and covered it with mine. "I'll be here for a few weeks," she added. "I'll be there when the trial starts."

MY LAWYER WAS allowed to meet with me in a small box of a room, where I was shackled to a chair and the furniture was bolted to the floor. I didn't expect to like him—I thought I'd been saddled with someone who hadn't done my brother any favours. But he was known as one of the best defense lawyers in Toronto, and he assured me that my case was very different from Allan's. I had been younger, I was not the ringleader, but most importantly, public opinion had changed in the five or so years since Allan had been caught. The Vietnam War was over; Carter had pardoned the draft dodgers; America was not as polarized as it had been in the late '60s and early '70s. There was Dylan's trial to consider too—the fact that his sentence was so much lighter than Allan's.

"You'd probably do okay in the States, particularly if you went voluntarily and if you pled guilty. There's really no point in doing otherwise—the evidence against you guys was well established in Allan's and Dylan's trials."

"You'll be a free man by the time you're 35," he said.

Thirty-five still struck me as old, but Dad was in California. I really wanted to see Dad before he passed away.

- - -

MY IMMIGRATION HEARING was open to the public. I was stressed and emotional when they led me from the holding cell into the courtroom downtown at 361 University Avenue—a building that was implementing some great energy conservation measures, according to Katie. My hands were shackled, and I felt uncomfortable appearing in public in the baggy orange prison jumpsuit. The opening arguments passed in a blur until I gave my answers.

Guilty.

And yes, I would consent to being extradited to the States.

Once I'd given those two responses, I could relax and look around a bit. I was astonished to see so many people in the courtroom. Some of the RPites—Moira, Mark, Shazma and

Katie—Gordon must have given them permission to be there. Good for him, and good for them. I managed a little smile for all of them, particularly Katie—it's hard to wave when you're shackled.

Mom was there. She met my eyes and smiled—she was happy I was coming back to California. Happy I could see Dad while he was still alive.

Down the row from her was—I couldn't believe it—Tony from the Lakeshore Motel. My God, it had been half a decade since I'd seen him. He must have read about my trial in the paper. And recognized me. I was surprised and delighted that he still remembered.

Then I saw Dawn, who gave me a little wave. And Buffy, who was holding a tiny baby. I'm not sure if it was a boy or a girl since the baby was dressed in unisex yellow. My heart gave a little leap, as I knew that baby was part me.

EPILOGUE
(Katie, October 1982)

I'VE BEEN ON planes before, but never on business and never to the U.S. After more than five hours of farms, cloud cover, barely visible snow-capped mountains, and bleak desert punctuated by the odd perfect blue lake, the plane banked steeply and headed south, overflying the San Francisco Airport and then heading back north. As we headed south, I could see the coast—perfect beaches at the bottom of what looked like steep cliffs. And then when we turned, we were over San Francisco Bay looking at ponds in various shades of magenta, blue and green. Salt ponds, I'd been told. Getting salt from the sea. The bay was huge, with a couple of miles-long bridges reaching from shore to shore, and the faint outline of San Francisco in the distance. I could see the famous Oakland Bridge as the plane banked and headed north. I didn't see the Golden Gate Bridge, though. My window seat was on the wrong side of the airplane.

Alex Johnson had driven me to the airport. During the summer of '77, I'd called him to see if he would handle my divorce. To my surprise, he said no, that he would recommend a friend of his at another firm. The friend turned out to be a good divorce lawyer, and since that summer, Alex has become more involved in my life. The occasional dinner, with great conversation, has turned into a weekly ritual. We've gone shopping together, to movies together and to restaurants frequently. Do I love him? I'm not sure. Do I enjoy his company? Always.

To say I was nervous as the plane descended into San Francisco airport, would be putting it mildly. My stomach was lurching, and I had a low-grade headache. It had taken a few years, but Margaret was gone, and I was finally editor of ECO. I was registered for a three-day environmental control conference starting two days from now here in San Francisco. I was anxious about that, as I had never been to an international conference before. But in some ways, I was more anxious about the couple of days I would be spending with Barry—no, Scott—before the conference.

He was living in a place called Alameda, an island on the Oakland side of San Francisco Bay. We'd written each other letters over the five years since I'd seen him in the University Avenue Courtroom for his hearing. His letters started out being quite brief, having lots of spelling and grammar mistakes, but got better as time went on. Scott ended up being in jail just four years, and he'd been in one of the more progressive institutions where they encouraged inmates to better their education. He was there long enough to get his Bachelor of Science degree, not his first choice, but they didn't offer tool and die making. He even won some sort of prize because he got a 4.0 grade point average—which in Canada we would call an A with marks in the 90s or a Bachelor of Science with first class honours. Our joke about Dr. Douglas Barnard Burns wasn't quite as far-fetched as it used to be!

He didn't say much else about prison in his letters—it can't have been pleasant, but he used his time wisely and was let out early due to good behaviour, Dylan's shorter sentence and the fact that Vietnam era crimes were no longer as important in the eyes of the public. Dylan was out on parole too, and even Allan, whose sentence was originally 25 years, was out after serving just a third of that time.

Barry—Scott—was doing maintenance for an Oakland area hotel. Apparently, this was something he'd done while he was in

Toronto, and some guy he worked for years ago had provided a reference. He was meeting me at the airport, and he'd booked me a room at the hotel in Oakland. He was going to feed me dinner at his place, and we planned to get together tomorrow as well.

I rummaged in my purse, found a comb and some lipstick, and prepared to disembark from the plane.

- - -

HE LOOKED OLDER, with faint lines etched in his skin. He'd filled out a bit and his hair was shorter than I remembered, but I would have recognized him anywhere. The smile was the tell—crossed teeth on the bottom and a gap between the ones on top. A smile that was contagious. A smile I had missed.

"Hey," he said.

"Hey," I said back, and after a moment's hesitation, gave him a hug.

"So, what should I call you," I asked.

"Just call me Scott," he said.

Neither of us were good at small talk. That had not changed.

His car was old, "vintage," he said, and it was a Mustang convertible. It was a colour you'd never see on a modern car—kind of a pale turquoise. There was some rust, and the windshield wipers didn't work—there was a string mechanism attached. I wondered how often it rained in California. Wasn't San Francisco known for rain and fog? Thank goodness it was a warm, sunny day, and we didn't have to worry about using the string thing.

Scott seemed amused by my reaction to the car. "She needs work," he said, "but she's my pride and joy. I learned to drive on a Mustang like this one. 1965. Only that one was red and souped up a lot more than this one.

"She runs fine," he added. "My landlady lets me use her garage, and I'm working on the body—and the wipers."

He turned south, away from San Francisco, and we crossed the bay on the San Mateo Bridge. Wind whipped my hair and face—my friends didn't have convertibles and there wasn't that much great weather to drive them in Toronto. And there weren't many 1965 cars on the road in Toronto—too much salt and sand; old cars rusted out quickly in our part of Canada. I felt so free—I loved the feeling!

We turned north along the double-decker Nimitz Freeway, and soon saw the towers of Oakland rise in the distance.

The hotel, The Oakland Motel, was not the Hilton—just a two-storey motel with outside corridors. It was cheerful though—the whole place was painted bright red. We pulled up under the carport and Scott escorted me into the office. There was a well-tended rubber plant in the corner, and Coke and ice machines along the wall. At the desk was an older woman who looked careworn, but welcoming.

"Is this your former landlady?" she asked Scott. "I'm Marsha, by the way," she added, smoothing her flyaway hair, and reaching to shake my hand.

"Yep. She's the one," said Scott.

"Oh, weren't you lucky living with this one," Marsha quipped. "I have that honour now. He's renting the upstairs."

"Shall we give her the penthouse?" Marsha asked Scott, with a gleam in her eye.

"Of course! The one with heart shaped jacuzzi and mirrors on the ceiling?" quipped Scott.

"The very one," said Marsha.

"It's on the house," she added as I took out my wallet to pay. "I heard you were very good to our Scott."

There was no jacuzzi, heart shaped or otherwise, and in a two-storey place, anything above the ground floor was a penthouse. But the TV worked, and the bed was clean and neatly made.

"Take a look at this," Scott said, leading me into the bathroom, and lifting the top off the back of the toilet. Inside was a brick.

"Water conservation," he told me. "It displaces some of the water. It saves about a quart every time someone flushes. Makes sense here in California, where we're in the middle of yet another drought.

"There is a swimming pool too," Scott said. "Did you bring your suit?"

I did bring my suit—wasn't California all about swimming?

"You can see the pool from here," Scott added, opening the heavy curtains—red, like the exterior. "I keep telling Marsha we should use solar heating—I'm looking into a government grant so we can get that going."

All the windows were carefully caulked to keep in heat or cold depending on the season. And Scott was trying to talk his boss into using a heat pump, which would probably make sense for both heating and cooling in California's mild climate.

AS MARSHA HAD mentioned, she and I had something in common—she was his new landlady. As a widow, she was renting out the top floor of her home on the island of Alameda, just 15 minutes from the hotel.

Scott showed me around the island, driving through the Webster Street Tube to the centre of the island, and taking a detour to show me the Naval Station that took up most of the west end. His home was east of the tunnel. Alameda was pretty—a few streets reminded me of the older parts of some of our Southern Ontario cities. The trees were so old and tall that they formed a canopy over the road. And, this being October, the leaves were turning yellow, just like they did in Canada. The houses were different though. Scott's street had an eclectic mix of houses, old and new, big and small, Spanish style, some with crenelated roofs like a castle, some the size and shape of older Toronto homes, but clothed in stucco. His place was a well-kept two-storey covered with ivy and stucco, built in the 1920s or '30s, a California version of my place in Little India.

"Marsha likes to say we live on a tropical island off the coast of San Francisco," Scott said, pointing to a row of palm trees lining a main street not far from his home. There was only one house with a scraggly tree, and Scott told me that house was owned by a prostitute. "Local lore," he added. "Marsha grew up here."

"You've come up in the world," I joked, as he led me to his second-floor apartment. "But of course, you started in the basement."

His four rooms were much nicer than his basement apartment had been. His apartment was cosy, with an eclectic mix of styles. A '50s vintage table and chairs. A shag rug from the '60s. And some real antiques as well—I wondered which items he had found on the street or in second-hand stores, and thought that maybe some of the antiques had belonged to Marsha.

On the bookshelf in the living room was a photo of a short, attractive woman with long brown hair, and two young girls. I picked up the photo and looked back at Scott.

"Your niece?" I asked, pointing to the oldest girl. She looked so much like him.

"My daughter," he said. "That's Krystal. She's 11. And her

sister is Anna."

And that's when I learned about Mary-Anne, Scott's high school flame. How she had helped him flee California. How he didn't know that she'd been pregnant when he left California. She'd separated from the guy she'd married after Scott left, and they were back in touch. Long distance, since she had a hair salon in the Los Angeles area.

"I have a son too," he said, holding up another picture. This one showed two women with their arms entwined around a five-year-old boy with a gap between his two top teeth. The two women looked to be around 40 and very much in love. I'd made a point of meeting Dawn and Buffy at Barry's—no, Scott's—hearing. We'd chatted a bit about the fact that we'd all lived with Barry, but I hadn't realized the baby was his.

"His name is Matt," Scott said. "I haven't met him yet, but he knows about me. And I send him cards and presents on his birthday. He's really into dinosaurs. I'm hoping they will come to California for a visit one day."

I heard about his road trip as he fled across the U.S. in the company of Dawn and Buffy—how he'd lived with them on and off before he came to my place.

Clearly, there was a lot I didn't know about my former tenant, but somehow that didn't matter. I felt comfortable in his new home, and thankful we didn't have to navigate a minefield of lies when we talked about his past. In many ways, it was as though we simply picked up where we had left off five years ago. Marsha joined us for drinks before dinner—beer, not wine, but the Happy Hour tradition was still in place. Then she puttered off downstairs, leaving the two of us to talk.

"So, how's everyone at Rosedale?" Scott asked.

"Pretty much the same," I told him. "But Margaret's gone."

He gave a little clapping gesture. "Hooray," he said. "And

you finally have ECO all to yourself."

"I do," I acknowledged and told him a bit about my conference.

"I've got something to show you tomorrow—something you'll really like," he said.

Scott wasn't much of a cook, but we made pizza from a kit, and shared a store-bought jellyroll for dessert. After dinner, I asked him about his parents.

"Mom still lives in Hermosa Beach, but Dad has passed away," Scott said, adding that he is so glad he came to California to serve his sentence, as he did get to see his father a few times before he died.

I found out that Allan was working as a lab technician. His chemistry degrees were underutilized, but he was gainfully employed. Scott said his Mom got a lot of pushback from certain people who were upset that both of her criminal sons were gainfully employed while much of America was suffering from unemployment during the recession.

Dylan was working for his father. Not sure what he was doing there as he wasn't a lawyer. And no, he and Scott didn't stay in touch.

The night breeze was cool as he drove me back to The Oakland Motel, where I collapsed in bed after a day that had begun in Toronto at 2 a.m. California time.

THE NEXT DAY dawned, bright and clear with a light wind. Scott picked me up in the Mustang and took me on a tour of the area, heading east toward Tracy and Manteca. As we rounded yet another dry, golden grass hill, he looked straight at me.

"There it is," he said. "The Altamont Pass."

And my eyes widened. There were dozens and dozens of windmills lining the secondary roads, spinning steadily on this hill and as far as the eye could see.

Scott pulled the car over to the side of the road and we stood at the edge of the field in the warm October sun. I could hear birds and I could hear the wind blowing through the grass, and maybe, just maybe, another sound that was the wind generators themselves.

"They're quiet," I said, gazing at the structures that dotted the hills, looking for all the world like a flock of seagulls from our vantage point near the highway.

"Remember the wind buggies?" he asked, putting his arm around me.

"We don't have wind buggies in every driveway, here in California," he said, "But I think this is a pretty impressive start.

- - -

SO, HOW ABOUT that swim?" he asked when we headed back around 3 p.m.

We drove back to The Oakland Motel and went for a swim. Scott had a key to the pool, and we had it to ourselves. The afternoon was warm for October, Scott said, as we relaxed under a clear sky. Most Californians wouldn't use the pool at this time of year. Just crazy Canadians.

He'd thought of everything. Wine by the pool in plastic glasses. "California has great wines," he told me, something I already knew.

After that, he took me for dinner at the China House restaurant on Santa Clara Ave. in downtown Alameda—something of an institution in the town I was told. We sat at a table for two by the window, overlooking the older buildings that made up downtown. The food was delicious.

Memories of Mr. Greenjeans—it had been a long time since Scott and I had been in a restaurant together.

At The Oakland Motel, I hugged him. The hug lasted a long time, and I remembered our embrace waiting for the Carlton streetcar so long ago. So much had happened in the five years since then, and yet, so much felt exactly as it had back then.

"Get a room," I whispered in my best imitation of the drunk who had yelled at us as we waited for the streetcar.

"We have one," he whispered back, holding up the key.

ACKNOWLEDGMENTS

MANY PEOPLE HAD a hand in creating *The Bomber in the Basement*. First and foremost is my father, Thomas McCavour, who passed away in July 2022. Dad was also an author, publishing 17 books between the ages of 80 and 92. As *Bomber* was being written, we had competitions to see who could write the most words on any given day. His critiques and encouragement are sorely missed.

Thanks go to my readers, Laurie Cooke, Frances Gravel, Anne Huhn, Steven Isherwood, Thomas McCavour, Shirley McCavour, Marie Poliquin and Erin Sanko. Fellow authors Jerry Amernic, Bruce Gravel, David Eisenstadt and Dr. Yvonne Kason gave me valuable advice on the world of book publishing. Thanks also to Kathy Olenski of Acacia House Publishing Services for believing in my book.

Bill and Sherry Westernoff gave me a tour of Alameda, CA, providing background for the epilogue.

Thanks to Adrian Gibson, for his incredible skill in taking my book from manuscript to publication.

And the biggest thanks of all go to the love of my life, my husband Steve, for his constant strength and support.

ABOUT THE AUTHOR

COLLEEN ISHERWOOD WORKED as a business writer and editor for 40 years, producing newsletters and magazines on subjects ranging from environmental control to hospitality. Now retired, she is writing books, and *The Bomber in the Basement* is her debut novel. Colleen lives in Toronto with her husband Steve. She has three adult children and six grandchildren.

IMAGE ATTRIBUTION & COPYRIGHT

FRONT/BACK COVER/TITLE PAGE:

- Luis Quintero - Pexels - https://www.pexels.com/photo/silhouette-of-a-person-1799904/

(**NOTE**: ORIGINAL MATERIAL HAS BEEN MODIFIED)

- fredfredfred - CC Attribution-Share Alike 3.0 Unported License - Wikimedia Commons - https://commons.wikimedia.org/wiki/File:Running_Fuel_Fire_-_panoramio.jpg

(**NOTE**: ORIGINAL MATERIAL HAS BEEN MODIFIED)